I0699048

CAT CITY

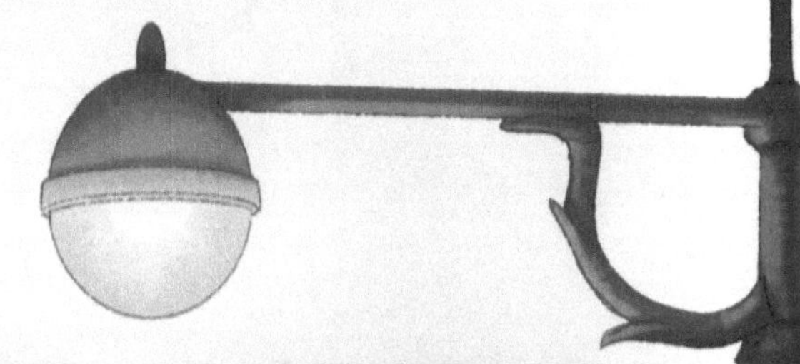

WHISKERS IN THE DARK

CAT CITY

NICK SMITH

Cat City
Copyright © 2025 Nick Smith. All rights reserved.

4 Horsemen
Publications, Inc.

Published By: 4 Horsemen Publications, Inc.

4 Horsemen Publications, Inc.
PO Box 417
Sylva, NC 28779
4horsemenpublications.com
info@4horsemenpublications.com

Cover Illustration by Oxford
Cover Typography and Typesetting by Autumn Skye
Edited by Kris Cotter

All rights to the work within are reserved to the author and publisher. No part of this publication may be reproduced, stored in a retrieval system, or transmitted in any form or by any means, electronic, mechanical, photocopying, recording, scanning, or otherwise, except as permitted under Section 107 or 108 of the 1976 International Copyright Act, without prior written permission except in brief quotations embodied in critical articles and reviews. Please contact either the Publisher or Author to gain permission.

All characters, organizations, and events portrayed in this novel are either products of the author's imagination or are used fictitiously. No generative artificial intelligence was used in the creation of this book or its cover.

All brands, quotes, and cited work respectfully belongs to the original rights holders and bear no affiliation to the authors or publisher.

Library of Congress Control Number: 2024948097

Paperback ISBN-13: 979-8-8232-0716-4
Hardcover ISBN-13: 979-8-8232-0717-1
Audiobook ISBN-13: 979-8-8232-0719-5
Ebook ISBN-13: 979-8-8232-0718-8

Table of Contents

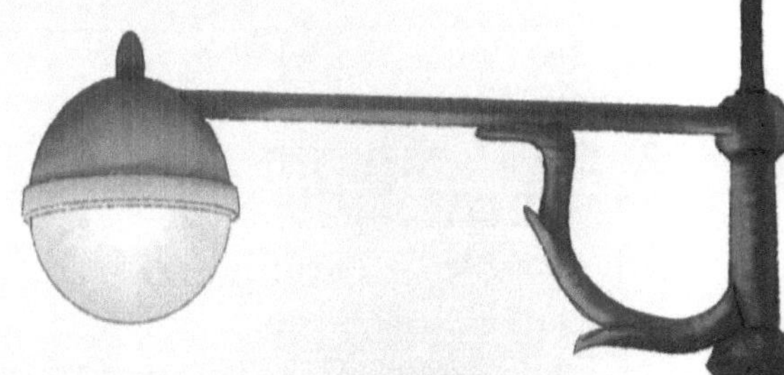

Part One: Bast

Part Two: Carabas

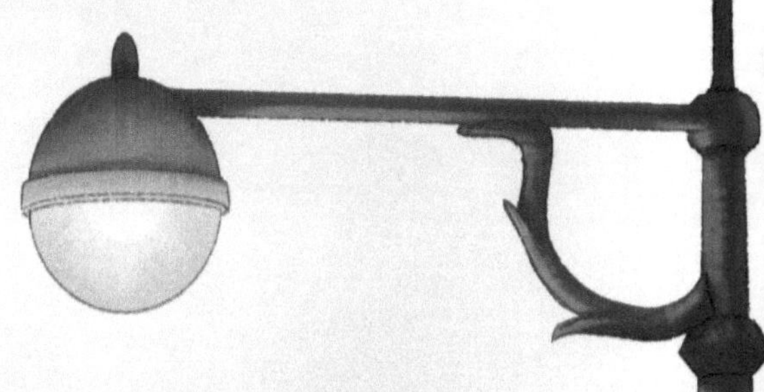

Part One:
Bast

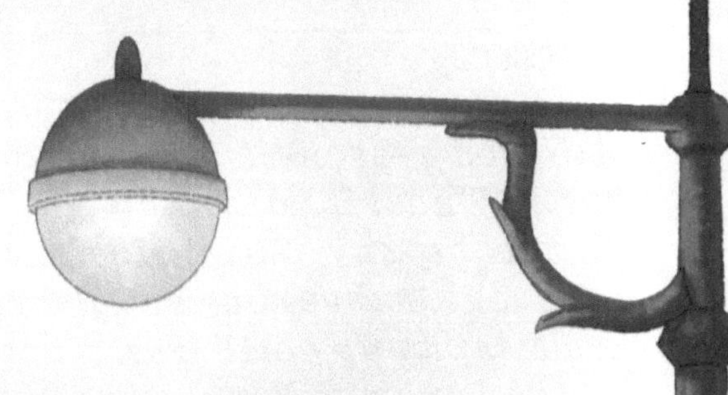

Intro

This is DJ Scratch, smoothest voice on the air-waves with the story so far. We're rocking the city of Bast, a teeming sprawl of skyscrapers and moneymakers. It has all the things you'd expect from a bright-lit big city: a bustling service sector, heavy-duty docks, a big-mouthed mayor, and churches with more moolah than their gods could possibly need.

But this ain't no ordinary city. Oh no, my good listeners. Bast is exxtra special with an extra "X" for extra effect. This city is run by cats, and it has been since the dawn of understanding. In this burg, the food scurries across restaurant tables until the diners catch it. Newspapers aren't black and white and read all over—they're sniffed for their scented messages instead. That mayor's big mouth is a lion's hungry maw. The currency of choice is a fresh mouse or pigeon, and the life expectancy of the average citizen is thirteen years—times nine, of course.

All good reasons for me to love the burg of my birth. Whoa! Hold up, though. Life ain't all pretty in this big city. Voted most civilized place in the land for a decade constant, Bast lost out last year to a sister city up north. See, today's the anniversary of the Longhair Riots, when this place almost fell to pieces. Not cool. Bast has seen better days, and though the pieces are getting picked up, there's still a lot of unhappy cats out there.

So here's what I want you to do: Give me a call and let me know what you'd do if you were in charge, king of the beasts for a day. How would you heal a wounded city? And how would you keep a million cats full of urban attitude happy? The number is 555-COOL. You heard me right. 555-2665 to talk to Scratch with plans to hatch.

Enough negative talk. Here's a platter that matters to cheer you right up: Mimi Mimu singing her number one hit, "I Got My Fun on a String." Enjoy.

1

The Milky Way

Dawn approached. The dairy was silent, ready for the sun to rise and reveal it like an unwrapped gift. As amber twilight caught the building's chrome corners, a group of small figures approached. They trotted up to the dairy gates, hundreds of fuzzy silhouettes gathering expectantly. There was time, still, for them to greet each other, but pleasantries were kept to a minimum.

The gates rose high above them, fat metal panels on massive hinges. The visitors licked their lips as they dreamed of what lay within.

Eva Rote was awakened by the sound of crying. She was used to this; it had become part of her routine since she'd reopened her dairy, and she barely emitted a sigh as she got off her cushion, washed, and mentally prepared herself for another day's hard work.

After a hasty breakfast of biscuits and gravy, Eva slunk from her home behind the dairy across a neatly swept, tiled courtyard. With a bat of her paw, she operated the lever that opened the iron gates, letting in a flood of mewing, preening male cats.

The toms circled Eva, blinking their hellos at her, flashing their briskets, and sniffing the air. She pretended not to notice their attention.

The sun was high enough to strike the yard by now. Some of the visitors closed their eyes, enjoying the early morning warmth. They didn't stop for long—they had some serious begging to do—though Eva wouldn't choose any of them.

One of the cats rubbed himself against a delivery cart, full to the brim with packs of butter. "Paws off," said Eva, moving toward the miscreant and setting off a ripple in her pool of followers. "You know there's only a place for one of you today. Now, which is it to be?"

The larger, stronger toms had already muscled close to Eva, pushing their weaker competition back toward the gates. But the dairy queen needed more than brawn. She looked the back cats in the eye, searching for an extra spark of intelligence and stamina.

She found it in an unlikely candidate, a scrawny, old tabby with silver-gray fur, deep green eyes, and a wrinkled nose. She selected him with a nod and the other cats, respecting her decision, trickled out of the courtyard; they knew they'd get another chance the next day.

"I hate to disappoint them," Eva said, partly to the tabby, mostly to herself. "But they know how scarce work is at the moment. I give jobs to as many as I can, and if you work hard today, I might be able to find a place for you here when things pick up."

"I'll do whatever I can," said the tabby. "My name's Julius. Julius Kyle."

"Eva Rote. Everyone around here calls me Lady Boss, you included. Follow me; there's a lot to be done." She turned, sticking her tail straight in the air, and Julius followed it close.

The tail led him to a white building with a convex roof. Inside, Eva showed him the place of his dreams—a warehouse with vats of cream, churning tubs of butter, and hundreds of canisters of milk.

"Where do I start?" Julius asked, eyes wide.

"That trough in the corner." Eva indicated a pair of young cats standing in a long aluminum tray full of cream. They were lifting their paws up and down, whisking the liquid with their claws.

"I've got to get in there?" Julius frowned.

"It's better than waiting in line outside the gates. Besides, you get to lick your fur clean afterward." That sold the idea to Julius. He padded over to the trough, blinked a greeting at the two whiskers, and wedged his way in between them. Yellow clumps formed as the butterfat particles stuck together. As the cream thickened, Julius began to tread harder, resisting the urge to purr.

Satisfied that her newest recruit would behave himself, Eva returned to the courtyard, where she found another employee. This one wasn't so industrious; he was curled up in a sun patch, taking a morning nap.

"Brian! Have you even started your chores?" Eva spat, making her son jump.

"I was taking a quick break," Brian replied, sullen.

"I know you and your naps. Clean the tubs out first." Brian, a skinny runt with his fur in clumps, licked his nose and slowly walked into the warehouse, stretching his hind legs and looking forward to a siesta in the noonday sun.

Julius helped his colleagues tilt the trough so that the cream oozed into a huge wooden barrel. The container was suspended from the ceiling with ropes, which, through a system of pulleys, left their ends dangling just above the treaders' heads. As the cats jumped up to snatch at the ropes, the barrel shook from side to side. One cat stayed in reserve, ready to take over when the others grew tired.

After a while, the yellow clumps thickened in a shoogling pool of white buttermilk. Julius removed the clumps and dowsed them in cold water, allowing them to harden into butter. He licked his lips as he eyed the leftover sweet buttermilk dripping into a separate wooden box. Brian watched the whole process, bored and unhelpful. He kept his ears cocked in case his mother was coming, but he knew she'd be busy with paperwork all morning.

"Make sure you scrub those barrels clean," Brian mewed. "All the tubs too."

"We could do it a lot quicker if you helped us out," Julius scowled, introducing himself to the young scallywag.

Brian arched his back. "You're new here; you don't know how things go. You've got one chance to listen and learn. I've been doing my job, supervising you all day. To make sure you freeloaders don't snaffle up half the day's profits. I oversee, and I delegate."

"We'll see what Eva has to say." Julius tried to push his way past Brian, but the young cat stopped him, claws popping from his forepaws. With a sigh of resignation, Julius mirrored the action. The other two cats sank onto their haunches, watching the show.

Brian scratched at Julius, nicking the tabby's chin. Julius parried the next swipe, baring his teeth in annoyance. He moved fast for an old tom, relying on muscle memory to defend himself.

"You're too slow; you got to go," Brian chanted, his furry tummy jiggling with mirth. "You're too slow; you got to go!"

Julius took him by surprise, pouncing on the exposed belly and knocking the runt against an open milk churn. Coated with milk, the cats rolled across the floor, scrabbling for a dominant position.

The noise summoned Eva, who halted the squabble with one low growl.

The scrappers didn't look at each other. They washed themselves, enjoying the milk on their fur despite their predicament.

"Get out of here," Eva hissed. Julius didn't budge. "I mean you. The new guy. You've had your chance."

"What about my pay?" Julius asked as he padded past her. "I worked hard today."

She placed a paw on his shoulder, wiped a drop from his shoulder, and flicked it in his eye. "You got your wages all over yourself. Get going."

2

The Lioness in Winter

"**W**here is my breakfast?" Bridget Canders's voice could be heard clear across the cruise ship Leo, startling stewards and sending them scurrying about their business. Bridget had been known to sate her frustrated appetite by sinking her teeth into her attendants instead of her food. "I require sustenance, and I am not accustomed to waiting for it!"

She was right there, and the proof was in her pudding of a tummy. No lithe lioness was she; middle age and an endless succession of power lunches had taken their toll on her figure. Unfortunately for the stewards, that meant she had a larger space to fill with grub.

"Here it is, madam, as you requested." Pollet, Bridget's unlucky server, hurriedly placed a tray in her cabin, which was decked out like the most fabulous throne room: all gold gilt, velvet cushions, and custom-carved wooden struts scarred from the big cat's multiple scratchings. Keeping his paws well out of biting distance, Pollet left the tray to be scrutinized by his employer and backed off without waiting for a tip.

"Indolent wretch!" Bridget roared after him through a mouthful of meaty gristle. "What is this garbage?"

Pollet poked his head back into the cabin. "From the ship's stores, madam." After months at sea, Bridget had eaten a major portion of the food in the galley, but the steward didn't dare to tell her that.

Bridget spat the meat at the little cat, her tongue jutting between her teeth. "Bring me a gazelle this instant." While other members of her species would have preferred to personally procure their eats, she took pleasure from getting other, lesser creatures like Pollet to pander to her. It was one of the few things that made her feel good—that and a biannual cruise along the coast. "And none of that salty rubbish you served me yesterday."

Pollet went to collect the tray, head hunched down in obeisance, mumbling apologies as he moved. "I'll have it replaced immediately, ma'am," he said, trying to take the dish from Bridget. As a strong liver smell filled his nostrils, making his stomach churn, he found that she wouldn't let go of it, clutching it tight in her heavy paws.

"Leave this with me." She continued eating. "Bring me that gazelle. Less salty this time, mind."

Pollet let go of the tray, his battle lost. "Very well, ma'am." Better that the meat got chewed on than him. Making his apologies, he left the cabin for a second time, leaving Bridget to devour her food. As usual, her greed had outweighed her fussiness.

Bridget didn't blame herself for mistreating her servants; in fact, the thought never crossed her mind. As the ex-mayor of Bast and a big cat out of her favorite urban environment, she was entitled to grouse and boss them about. There was little else to do on the liner apart from eat, nap, and shred the upholstery.

Once the tray was licked clean, she dropped it and let out a low, well-practiced belch. She had left Bast to avoid the riot and various political complications that had made her life difficult. It had pained her to leave her son Otto in charge of the city, but he was almost as stubborn as she was. If her plans went smoothly, Otto would wear himself out picking up the pieces after the riot and rebuilding Bast. Once the citizens had lost faith in him, she'd make a triumphant return and become mayor again. Blood ties meant nothing to Bridget when such power was within her grasp, and Otto was getting too cocky for his own good.

He'd accompanied her on cruises long ago, when he was her favorite heir. She'd taught him not to pick his teeth with his razor-sharp claws while the ship was in rough seas; she'd taught him that the best way to stay trim while on a long voyage was to chase the stewards around the deck. Above everything, she'd taught him to stand up for himself, take charge, and act like the liege she'd always wanted to be.

Bridget had done her job too well. Now Otto refused to listen to her advice, stubbornly opposing her plans and blocking her power plays. For her, he was the perfect son and a royal pain in the mane.

Drowsy, she closed her eyes and scratched her belly lazily. Things would be different when her ship came in. Even if it took every ounce of her influence, she'd shift the balance of control back in her favor. She'd be mayoress again, and Bast would regain the calm it had once taken for granted—the calm of her what-I-say-goes rule.

The ocean slicked against the hull of the ship, distant, reassuring. It had always been there, since cats could count and probably before that too. Like the ocean, Bridget was a stalwart force. She would survive and sweep away anything—or any son—that got in her way.

3

In the Doghouse

Julius didn't even know if he was doing the right thing. For a long time, he'd tried to keep his head down, not causing any trouble, venturing out of the house only to look for a new job. He was no hero; he was a bona fide fraidy cat.

There were too many uncertainties out there, crimes waiting to be committed, accidents waiting to happen. At home in his own environment, Julius felt safe. His career as a reporter had proved to him how spiteful cats could be, how merciless the Fates were, and how fragile he was in the big, bad city. Any attempts to stick his neck out and make life better had only made things worse. He'd learned his lesson now; he would risk nothing and ask for as little as possible from Moira.

She was a sleek, elegant Siamese with porcelain white fur, a lithe body, and an attractive wedge-shaped face. Her eyes were as blue and deep as a sun-soaked ocean, and she had the small paws of a dancer. Her regal look belied her unruly nature; few cats dared to pick a fight with her.

Julius loved Moira and took every opportunity to display his affection toward her, mewing plaintively when she left for work—especially if she forgot to fill his breakfast dish—and rubbing his flanks against her legs when she returned. He'd circle her, looking at her wide-eyed. Yet he never put his feelings into words. That kind of commitment was the stuff best left to heroes.

Moira tolerated him and gave him plenty of the attention that he craved. She knew that some questions were best left unanswered—ask Julius to analyze his feelings for her, and he'd likely come up with a trite reply that she didn't want to hear. She preferred to wait for him to realize the truth, tell it straight, and go from there.

Moira always seemed to know what to do, partly because her work kept her busy and tired and left her with scant time to dither, let alone reflect. Julius wished he could predict the future, plan the right course of action that would lead to some perfect happy ending. He needed a guru. Trouble was, he was old enough to be someone else's.

A little voice prowled around his head, telling him to take the next job that came along and stick with it, save some moolah for his fast-approaching dotage. But he felt that he was better than that. He was a special cat, above average, not destined for servitude in some milk bar or bookstore. How ironic that would be! A writer stuck in a store surrounded by books, not one of them his!

When opportunity knocked on his flap again, he'd be ready. He'd grasp that chance, hold it tight, and stop dwelling in the past. Until then, he spent most of his time at home.

Julius lived in the Doghouse, a seedy, no-hope quarter of Bast. The feline had fallen on hard times since quitting his job at the local paper, *The Scratching Post*. Despite his lack of fortune, he was happy. He lived with Moira, a Siamese who even tolerated his hoarding habits. He'd kept boxes of old newspaper clippings from his days at the *Post*, keepsakes from breakthrough stories, childhood baubles, and souvenirs from far-off war zones. She'd thrown a few jibes his way—"Why don't you ever throw anything away? What are you doing, holding on to all those old balls of string?"—but they were good-natured ones.

Moira found room for Julius's junk in a storage shed, secured with a chain and a heavy padlock. She'd been raised in the poor neighborhood and defended Julius when he fell afoul of the local ne'er-do-wells. He had a knack for upsetting the neighbors with a snooty look or misread comment. But he had no intention of leaving her, and he never stopped looking for work in the recession-struck city.

"How did you get on?" Moira gave her mate a friendly nudge with her nose. Her house was damp and draughty, but she kept it clean, with Julius chipping in the occasional chore.

"I'm not the cat that got the cream, if that's what you're asking," Julius scowled. "I'll try someplace else tomorrow."

"You're running out of places to try." Moira led Julius into the kitchen. He jumped onto the counter surface, walking to and fro across the Formica.

"Anything to eat around here?"

Moira shook her head. "Not yet. I was going to prepare some..." Telling a cat to wait for food is tantamount to torture. Julius descended from the counter, landing on all fours, then pawed at the fridge.

"Don't open it," said Moira. "Remember, you're on a diet."

"Diets are for models and health freaks. I'm not self-obsessed." Moira didn't reply. "I demand the right to eat when I'm hungry," Julius mewed.

With a sigh, Moira opened the fridge. A mouse scampered out, darting this way and that, eyes wide with fright. Julius pounced on the morsel, holding it tight between his forepaws, watching it as if he'd never seen a snack before. The mouse felt cold. He let it go, and it scurried for cover under the cooker. Julius was too swift, clamping down on it with claws outspread.

"Will you please stop playing with your food?" Moira stacked her Tupperware in a wall cupboard. "I thought you were hungry."

"No harm building up my appetite a little," Julius opened his jaws wide, "more." He sank his teeth into the shivering morsel.

"Great. I just squeegeed in here. Can't you use a dish?"

While Julius spent his days job-hunting, Moira brought home the bacon. She'd found employment as an interpreter at City Hall, translating messages from far-off lands. Her background had made her resourceful and diligent, and over the past year, she'd become a great asset to the mayor.

Julius had applied for work with the council with no success; he had been offered his old job back at *The Scratching Post,* but his pride was too strong. He knew he wouldn't get on with Swampy McMahon, the editor and publisher. McMahon had everything he could possibly want—good looks, fame, money, and muscles. Julius envied him.

Julius always did things the hard way. It built character. It was more satisfying on the rare occasions when he won through; it seemed fairer that way. Choices that didn't require him to be bitter or stubborn seemed cowardly to him. But he had a burning wish to shower Moira with riches and dead birds.

"Satisfied your cravings?" asked Moira demurely.

"It was only one mouse," Julius grumbled, his mouth full. "You working tomorrow?"

"Of course. Someone's gotta pay the rent."

Sometimes Julius thought it would make more sense to stay in bed. He felt like he'd applied for every job in the city of Bast, from insurance sales (with nine lives to cover) to real estate agent (tough when most cats were content with a cardboard box). He was expending energy needlessly, which he abhorred. With a mate covering the rent and bills, he wasn't hungry enough to find work and keep it.

Instead, he spent most of his time writing fiction. He'd take long walks at night, plotting a grand novel in his head. His last book hadn't done so well—he blamed his publisher for that—but this one would be different.

"I'm away to my nook," he told Moira, trotting out of the kitchen to the laundry closet where he could curl up on a shelf and bang out some lines on his typewriter. Half the time he went there to sulk, or avoid a difficult question from Moira.

"Don't be too long in there! The reception's tonight, remember?"

Reception? Julius thought, relaxing in his closet, tail coiled around his fetal form. *What reception?*

4

The Lion's Dentist

In which an otherwise sane individual is paid to stick his head in a lion's mouth.

Cal Futum rushed through the extraction, the bridgework, and the denture fitting. He didn't take the time to offer young cubs a pilchard lollipop or a sticker after their check-ups. He didn't even flirt with Daisy, the dental nurse, which had been part of the daily routine since she'd joined his practice. Everything was done at double pace: no milk breaks and no chance to worry about his Very Important Patient. The morning rushed by and at noon, the waiting room was cleared. Cal's dental clinic was secured, and he prepared himself for the mayor's arrival.

"What's he doing?" Cal asked Daisy as he nervously licked his paws clean.

"Pacing," said Daisy. "Up and down, around the room."

"Is that good? I mean, lions do that a lot, don't they?" Big cats always made Cal nervous, especially the ones in politics.

"I don't know." Daisy adjusted the large cushion that formed the focal point of the operating room.

"For goodness sake, just keep everything neat," Cal snapped. "He hates mess." Daisy stared at him, too polite to give her boss any sass. "Well, don't just stand there." Cal thrust out a paw. "Give me his file, quick!"

Daisy picked up the mayor's file and as the dentist snatched it from her, the file fell and the records scattered all over the floor. A roar resounded from the waiting area.

"Send him in," said Cal. It would never do to keep Otto waiting.

Cal scrabbled to pick up the records and shove them back into their folder. His paws felt like blocks of wood, heavy and useless. The files were in the wrong order, and he could hear Otto's heavy pads echo down the hallway. Giving up on the folder, Cal crammed it onto a shelf, sandwiched awkwardly between *Conquering Kitten Breath* and *Root Canal Work for Dumb Aminals*. He turned to block his slip-up from the mayor's sight.

"Mr. Mayor," said Cal cheerfully. "How lovely to meet you again!"

"I have a dozen pressing items to attend to, judgments to pass, an empty belly, and a raging toothache, thanks to some incompetent servant or other."

"I hope he was suitably chastised, Your Honor."

"Oh, I can think of more than one way to skin the ingrate."

"Of course, sir. Would you kindly be seated?" Cal managed a winsome smile. Daisy led Otto to the cushion, looking like a game show hostess showing off a fabulous prize.

"The mayor of Bast does not sit while others stand," Otto declared.

"Absolutely." Cal got down on his haunches, exposing his brisket in deference to the lion. Daisy sat on a small swivel stool and trundled around the room as required. Otto finally sat himself down.

"The lights offend my eyes!" Otto bellowed.

"All taken care of, Your Honor." While Cal picked up a utensil, Daisy put a pair of dark sunglasses on the lion's face. Otto gave her a stern look that made her wary—did he think she was trying to mock the highest authority in the city?—but the big cat suffered the indignity.

"Presto, no more bright lights!" Cal felt foolish as soon as the sentence had left his lips, but his patient had made a career of making his subjects feel small and insignificant, which was one of the major reasons why he retained his power. "If you don't mind, sir," Cal swallowed hard, "I'm going to need you to, er, open wide."

Otto reluctantly obliged, displaying rows of razor-sharp teeth in his massive maw. Cal checked each tooth as quickly as he could. Some were capped, a few were crowned, and a couple were solid gold. The mayor enjoyed the best medical, dental, and spiritual care in the city, as was his privilege, with all the relevant clinics situated within a couple of blocks of City Hall. So it hadn't been that long since his last appointment at Cal's clinic. None of the teeth were rotting, and the gums didn't appear to be inflamed. There was, however, a fetid stench of old meat coming from the lion's mouth. Cal tried not to gag as he gave Daisy a series of coded numbers.

"A-Three, Four, and Five all good," he told his assistant. "Where exactly is the ache coming from, Your Rulingness?"

Otto clamped his mouth shut, and the dentist swiped his delicate paws away just in time. "My teeth." The mayor suffered fools badly. "It's coming from my teeth."

"Yes, sir." Cal obviously wasn't going to get any help there. With his paw back in Otto's mouth, he started to push at the incisors to find out if any of them wobbled.

"Not there," Otto mumbled. "The back teeth!"

"Of course. How stupid of me." Cal tapped on a couple of molars with his explorer, the utensil he used to check each fang. His patient couldn't feel a thing. Cal considered telling him that he was unable to get to the root of the problem, then thought better of it. Slowly, with great care, he moved his paw away from the mighty mouth.

"I'm going to place a mask over your nose and mouth," Cal stammered.

"Will it match the sunglasses?" Otto asked tartly.

"I'm not sure." Daisy strapped the mask over Otto's face. "That looks fine," Cal continued. "Now breathe deeply ... this anesthetic gas will numb your teeth while I extract the bad molar."

"Yes, yes, I know what the gas does," the mayor slurred. "You always give me the gas. You always pull a tooth. I'll have no teeth left if this carries on."

"An extraction will prevent the rot spreading into your gums and other teeth." The dentist stepped back so as not to inhale any of the isoflurane gas. "Suck it up, please."

Otto closed his eyes and began to snore. "It's done," Cal announced, and two thick-set tomcats entered the room.

"Security?" Cal asked them.

"Dealt with. Don't worry; we didn't hurt 'em. Much. Let's bundle Leo here out of your way." This was easier considered than done. Though the toms were hefty, they still had trouble lifting the supine lion off his cushion. The mane got in their faces, the tail snagged on the spitbowl, and the broad paws hung down like ballast. They half-swung, half-dragged the big cat out of the building, covering him with a tarpaulin and wheeling him away, along with his equally senseless security guards.

Cal felt better after that. Once he'd tidied up his files and Daisy had removed all the tufts of hair and other evidence, the dentist allowed himself to relax a little. He sat on the floor, his belly sagging on his lap, his tail lying listless. He felt tired and ashamed. He had no beef against the mayor, but he wanted to keep his own teeth, and the toms had threatened to extract them if he didn't help them. He'd got the impression that they wouldn't be using any painkillers.

All his life, he'd been scared of the mayor and his pride. The lions were bigger, stronger, and louder than him, and they knew it. Now he'd traded one fear for another. *So might is right,* he decided, *and us plain, weak folk can either lump it or fight it and lose our chompers.*

"Your next patient's waiting, Doctor. Scheduled for 12.30."

"Send him in," sighed Cal. "I'll put him to rights."

5

City Hall

Sal Finney had no idea what was going on, but that wasn't unusual. Like many other youths, he'd been displaced by the riot that had shattered Bast. He'd also sought work in the lowest of places. Unlike Julius, he'd found a job that lasted more than a day, joining the City Hall waiting staff.

If food motivated the citizens, then gluttony ran its council, with Mayor Otto and his family receiving the lion's share of gourmet delights that were brought upriver to their lair. Hundreds of daily delights required a legion of servers, with Sal the snowshoe an obscure furry face in the crowd. His tapered tail, wedge-shaped face, and brown markings were hardly remarkable. Only his blue eyes, as round as saucers, and the white feet that gave his breed its name distinguished him. He did what he was told, kept his ears clean, and tried not to scoff the leftovers. Still, his obedience was matched by his ignorance.

Since the commencement of his training, he'd spilled soup on a sphynx, passed port to starboard, and, worst of all, smashed a saucer and left a fragment in Otto's *hors d'oeuvres*. That chance chip had threatened to wreck the reception.

This function celebrated a new peace agreement between the civilized cats of Bast and the dogs that lived north of the mountains. The political atmosphere had been tense since the riot, for which the dogs had been unfairly blamed. Thanks to go-betweens like Moira, those tensions had recently been eased, and the military forces of both powers had backed down.

Woodrow Cormer held sway at a podium set on a raised dais. He was a pompous sealpoint, with a fur bouffant between his ears. "His Honor, the mayor, has been detained," Woodrow announced to a throng of guests, massing before the dais in a brightly lit, gilded atrium. "An orthodontic emergency. Be assured, his blessings are with you all tonight."

Sal, who knew who Woodrow was, counted his own blessings that the reverse wasn't true. He held a silver tray high, his pointy tail weaving as he balanced his load. His athletic, muscular body seemed out of place amongst the elegant elite, almost bumping into Moira and Julius—late arrivals.

Moira wore her slinky black dress, bought specifically for city occasions. Julius was disheveled in a cheap pinstripe suit, looking as if he'd been woken abruptly from a deep sleep. Which, of course, he had. He was alert enough to catch the silver tray as it dropped from Sal's paw.

This wasn't the right place to clown around. Bast's best all attended the function, looking refined. It wasn't just that this was the place to be seen; no one wanted to disappoint the mayor. Cats who dared to do that tended to disappear too often for comfort.

The reception was a melting pot of different cat breeds. Ragdolls lapped at prawn cocktails. Korats snorted at unfunny jokes. A rex flicked lint from his tux with manicured claws. The servers offered crab wontons, tiny tuna melt sandwiches, and chicken *vol au ventes* in dishes decorated with cute fishbone patterns. Julius stopped Sal, who returned with a full dish in his paws. Julius dipped his face into a dish and scarfed a scallop, licking his lips as he came up for air.

"Got any more?" Julius asked as the food slid down his gullet. Sal shook his head, and Julius frowned at him. The server looked faintly familiar; Sal vaguely recognized Julius, too.

"Hey! You're the nibsucker!" Sal declared, retrieving his tray. "Careful, Mr. Kyle. If you keep juggling with the silverware, they'll think you work here."

Julius's eyes narrowed at the "W" word. "You look pretty good for a corpse. I thought you drowned."

"Got lucky. Washed up in the pluff mud. Glass of sour milk?"

"Got milk." Julius could still taste the dairy on his tongue. "Stay good," he told the server as Moira dragged her partner away.

"If you hadn't fallen asleep, you wouldn't be embarrassing me like this," Moira hissed. "I'm trying to make a good impression here."

"Do they know that's the only formal dress in your wardrobe?"

"No, and you're not going to tell them."

"It's not the smartest purchase you've ever made, darling. It'll show up all your white hairs."

"Quiet, or you'll be showing off a black eye." Moira clamped her mouth shut as Woodrow looked directly at her. Julius felt guilty for getting her into trouble until his attention was distracted by a fish stick spread. Julius spotted Bishop Kafel, church leader of the city; Prowler Chief Feargal Cutter, head of Bast's police force; and Eva and Brian, very serious, steadfastly refusing to enjoy themselves, there for networking purposes only. It was such an unlikely place for the dairy owners to find Julius that they didn't recognize him at first. He ambled past them a couple of times until he was sure that they saw him.

"They'll let anyone into these parties," he told them with practiced disdain. They were too shocked to reply.

Woodrow's speech droned on. "I'd be stating the obvious if I were to say that cats and dogs don't get on well together. Now I've said it. We've always feuded, since the first tiger cut its sabered teeth. It's hard for us to forgive some of the messes the dogs have made around here. Despite their indiscretions, we've come to an agreement. There will be no more conflict between us. The civilized advances of our societies, though disparate, have conquered any primal urge that threatens our existence. The leading proponent of peaceful coexistence is here with us tonight. Please join me in welcoming Tarquin Quintroche."

A well-coiffed Abyssinian stepped onto the dais, raising his paws in greeting to the guests. He looked around the room as if gauging their intelligence. Once he'd decided the right level to pitch at, he addressed them all.

"I was raised to lead by example," said Tarquin, his waistcoat buttons gleaming in the spotlight. "And that's what Carabas is all about. I faced intolerance when I was young; I was picked on just because of my breed. I hoped that one day there would be a city where longhairs, shorthairs, yes, even dogs, could pass in the street without turning on each other. Now, thanks to the hard work of myself and my visionary staff, my dreams have come true."

"Someone else is joining us from Carabas." Woodrow smiled. "Mr. Quintroche's carefully selected ambassador, Fido Frenkel."

The guests gasped as a Staffordshire terrier joined Tarquin and Woodrow on the dais. While Frenkel restrained himself from woofing or snarling at them, the cats couldn't stop their fur from standing on end.

"I am here not to bark, but to listen. Not to raise my voice, but to raise awareness for the issues we face in our humble neighboring city." Frenkel looked around at the cats, their hackles raised, tails flicking with unease. His expression was serious and attentive. The cats were ready to run—whether at him or away from him, he wasn't sure. "It is easy to imagine a stranger as dangerous," Frenkel continued. "Menacing. Goodness knows I get riled up if a visitor comes unannounced to my door. Even if they turn up at the same time every morning. I do not expect you to like me at first blush. I do not expect you to believe me when I tell you that where I come from, cats and dogs exist in harmony. Our resources are scant, yet we do not fight each other over our scraps. I appeal to your feline nature—."

A cat in the audience hissed at Frenkel. Woodrow gave the cat an admonishing look.

"There it is!" Frenkel went on, desperate to break the ice. "Feline nature at its truest." Some of the cats chuckled. "I stand before you as a common-or-garden hound. As you can see, I am no threat to you. I am simply a neighbor, asking you to consider a better future where cats are kind and dogs are harmless. Our little staging post sets a shining example for all, and my experiences there have encouraged me to make the further, bold step of visiting you."

Frenkel glanced at Woodrow. The ambassador wasn't getting through; the cats were still on the defensive, some of them letting out low whimpers of their discontent. Woodrow gave Frenkel a nod of encouragement.

"I'm not asking for détente here," Frenkel sighed. "I'm just asking you to throw me a bone. A wag in the right direction for the sake of both our futures. If you allow me, I can be your best friend."

"I've never heard anything so ridiculous in all my lives," said the hisser. "A cat's best friend is himself." The cats around him nodded and yowled in agreement. Woodrow looked around at the hostile audience and placed a paw on Frenkel's shoulder.

"Perhaps they're not quite ready for you to mingle with them," Woodrow told Frenkel quietly. The dog was ushered out of view as discreetly as possible.

"If you have any questions about the flourishing cosmopolitan city of Carabas," Woodrow told the crowd, "I'm sure Mr. Quintroche would be more than happy to answer them. As for the positive ramifications of his social experiment, you need look no further than our trade..."

Sal had made his way across the atrium to Woodrow's dais. "Sorry about the mayor," the server whispered, interrupting the speech. Woodrow tried to ignore the wide-eyed waif of a snowshoe, who said, "I hope he's better in time to sign the green mint."

"Agreement," Woodrow whispered back, losing his cool. "It's an agreement between Bast and the Isle of Dogs. You're not supposed to talk to me."

"You're right." Sal stopped whispering. "There can't be any conflict if no one talks to each other."

The audience stood, frozen, waiting for Woodrow to explode. Instead, he left the podium with a cursory, "Enjoy your evening." Sal decided that this was directed at him and his tail relaxed in an attitude of pure contentment.

"Can I get you anything?" he asked Julius, who sauntered up to pat him on the back; there was sympathy in the writer's eyes.

"Woodrow will destroy you if you're not careful," said Julius.

"You mean the guy who's always making fancy speeches about nothing much?" Sal handed Moira a saucer of cream.

"The peace treaty's something. Moira and I know how reasonable dogs can be."

Moira agreed. "Things will be different from now on."

"I agree." Tarquin had sidled up beside them. Moira had worked with him for several weeks before his move to Carabas; there, he'd taken a dead-end post and turned it into a fiefdom.

"Moira," he smarmed. "You know you're one of the main reasons why I asked to return to Bast—to refresh my memories of you."

"Really?" Moira turned to face him. "Didn't know you cared. And to think, you'd be hiding on a high shelf if Otto were here."

"We don't see eye to eye on everything, true. But he's let me fix Carabas without interference."

"Maybe he forgot about you," Moira suggested.

"My work is important," Tarquin sniffed.

"Doesn't mean you are," countered Julius. "Excuse us, if you will." As Julius led Moira away from Tarquin, a string quartet struck up a gentle serenata. Julius and Moira faced each other, lining up with other cats for a dance.

Julius inclined his head slightly, and Moira curtsied in response. They moved in a clockwise direction, never losing eye contact with each other. Then they moved gracefully in the other direction. Moira smiled. Sometimes Julius could be surprisingly suave. She curtsied again before they both took a step in opposite directions, bending low and turning. They began to spin as the music got faster. Throughout the dance, Moira never lost her grin.

By the time the tune was done, Julius and Moira were the central attraction, thanks to their passionate dancing. The applause made Julius feel abnormally bashful.

"Want some fresh air?" he asked his lover quietly. But before they could step away, the lights dimmed. A female Abyssinian in a slinky vermillion dress stepped up to the podium. Mimi Mimu was a phenomenally popular songstress and one of Julius's personal faves. This appearance was a surprise for the guests and a delight for the writer.

Unlike most cats, Abyssinians were gifted with singing voices as fine as nightingales. Unfortunately, singing was not regarded as a reputable profession, and members of Mimi's breed were nicknamed "sinners." Mimi was an exception, transcending her origins with her talent and her earning power. Sal and Julius moved as close as they could to the podium, leaving Moira to mingle with her colleagues.

Mimi began to sing a sensual ballad that made Sal's whiskers twitch.

"You make my ears perk up
"Like cream in my favorite cup.
"You make my heart sing
"Like a dancing, dangling string."

Stepping down into the audience, Mimi swayed through the throng, giving Woodrow a slow blink and brushing her paw delicately across the sealpoint's cheek. As the singer approached Julius, he tried to stay calm.

"You set my soul on fire
"Like all the things that I desire.
"Only you can douse the flame,
"'Cause you're to blame."

Mimi spun around Julius and swayed slowly out of the room. Julius became aware that Moira was staring at him, and he came to his senses. He turned, feeling thirsty. With the main attraction gone, some of the guests were leaving already while others made a beeline for the salmon spread. Moira disappeared into the crowd.

Moira stopped at the foot of the stairway, her face like fizz. Males were all the same. So fickle. So unreliable. She'd been working hard to support Julius, and there was always a chance that he'd drop her at the first sign of a fluffy young female. Well, she'd made her choice with Julius, and she was willing to work at him some more. Fight for him if need be.

"I wondered where you'd got to," said Tarquin, pushing his way past well-wishers to join Moira.

"Mimi's a friend of mine, you know. If you like, I could arrange for her to sing to us on our first date."

"Are you crazy?" She hardly knew him.

"I was always too timid to approach you before. Now, with my new job and the power that it's brought me ... I feel like I'm worthy of you."

"Sorry, Tarquin," said Moira. "You'll never be worthy of me."

"And Julius is?" Tarquin asked, petulant.

"He tries." She turned her back on him, dismissively twitching her tail in his face.

"Let me try." Tarquin watched Moira ascend the stairs. "Moira! Let me try!"

She didn't answer or even turn back to look at him. Whiskers drooping, he returned to the party, enviously watching the merry cats around him.

At the top of the stairs, Moira heard a strange whimper coming from one of the judicial chambers. She traced the sound to a small, dusty room that one of the city judges used as his private office. In the middle of a cream-white rug lay the source of the whimper— the canine ambassador from Carabas. Over him stood a quivering, hairless, desperate-looking cat who didn't seem to have had a decent meal in weeks. As he glowered at Moira, she noticed a distinguishing mark on his forehead—a red V-shaped scar just above his gleaming green eyes.

Before she could move, the cat delivered a killing slash to Fido's throat; the whimpering stopped. The killer stared at Moira again, as if deliberating whether to silence her as well. Instead, he leaped upward, disappearing through an open transom.

Downstairs in the atrium, Julius was starting to fret. "I take my eyes off my missus for one second," he grumbled to Sal, "and she's being chatted up by some swaggering tom."

"Who?"

"Moira, my mate." Julius began to sniff around, trying to catch a familiar whiff amidst all the strange scents of the guests.

"I meant the tom."

"Oh, males ain't fussy," said Julius. "Any tom that swags along. Are you sure you can't see her anywhere?"

"I haven't looked. Hang on a minute." Sal stepped onto the podium and hollered, "Has anyone seen this pen pusher's missus?"

According to the response Sal received, no one had any helpful information for him. In fact, none of the remaining guests had a good word to say to Sal.

"You're fired," said Woodrow, ordering his staff to yank the snowshoe out of the room.

"Look what the cats dragged out." Sal sounded happy. "Hey! I've got the sack! We're like two peas in a pod," he told Julius, who had been pretending not to know him.

"I know this cat." Eva Rote poked a paw in Julius's direction. "It's Julius Kyle." The name attracted dozens of stares. "He's nothing but trouble."

Protesting, trying to explain that his mate was missing, Julius was ejected from the party by two cats in stuffed shirts. Sal trotted out after him. As they passed a large, opulent staircase, they heard a cry for help above the joyful din of the reception.

"That's Moira!" Julius exclaimed, scratching at his chaperones until they let him go. Racing up the stairs, he found Moira in shock, staring at the dead ambassador.

"He was murdered," she said sadly, looking to Julius for a word of comfort. He could think of none; instead, he crouched down beside the body and examined the hound's bloody wounds.

"Claw marks. Too small to be a dog's. Did you see...?"

"It was a cat," said Moira. "A cat killed him. Cold and vicious. I was too late to do anything."

"Don't look at me," Sal said. "I was downstairs making a fool of myself."

"Judging by the fresh scrapes on the rug, Fido was dragged in here against his will." Julius's nose for news was twitching.

"At least he put up some kind of fight."

The stuffed shirts had summoned Woodrow, who let out a deep sigh when he saw the dead dog. "Has anyone else seen this?" he asked his minions. They shook their heads. "Nobody will. Remove the body."

As the shirts carried out their order, Moira scowled at her superior. "We have to sound the alarm," she told him. "The other guests might be in danger."

"This isn't one of your neighborhood street corners," Woodrow retorted. "If this gets out—a dog dying in this manner right in the middle of City Hall—why, there'd be turmoil. The last thing we need is another riot." The last point was addressed to Julius. "What are you still doing here?"

"I was about to report on a crime scene," Julius replied without an ounce of respect for Woodrow's authority. Moira gave him an admonishing glance but secretly felt proud of her mate.

"Moira," Woodrow's voice became silky smooth. "I trust you won't be following Mr. Kyle's lead?"

"I'll be doing some reporting myself, as soon as His Honor, the mayor, turns up."

Woodrow gave Moira a close look, sizing up her intentions. "Don't bother clearing out your desk," he said at last.

Within minutes, Moira, Julius, and Sal had been thrown out of City Hall. "I never liked those toffs anyway," said the snowshoe, "all stuck up and no place to grow. The well-to-do have never done anything well for me. They aren't proper folk." He washed his paws with his long pink tongue. "They should try living real life for a while. That would shatter their delusions."

"Did you mean what you said in there?" Moira asked Julius. "Are you really going to report on this?"

"In my own way," Julius told her, choosing his words carefully. "Woodrow was right about one thing— we don't need another riot. I'll investigate the murder quietly. I'm going freelance."

6

The Alley

Although Moira had been too sur-prised (and smart) to ask Woodrow if she could give the city prowlers a statement about the murder, she had no qualms about describing the killer to Julius on the way home: short, squat, bald, rangy with that distinctive reddish V-scar on his forehead.

"I've seen folks hurt and killed in my time," she told Julius. "You know that. Those were hot-blooded crimes, though. This assassin... The look on his face was so cold, like he was performing an everyday task ... I'll never forget that cut, wrinkled face of his."

After a nap and a bite to eat back home, Moira urged her partner to seek out the murderer. "Do it with caution," she told him. "No heroics."

"Hey, this is me, remember?" Julius smiled, donning the old trench coat that made him feel like a character from one of his mystery novels. The smile drooped as Moira gave him a long-suffering nod.

To get some answers, Julius visited the mangiest section of the city—The Alley, a garbage-strewn dystopian strip of land that ran parallel to the river. Even the streetwise Moira was wary of visiting the area, infamous for its underground connections. Julius had been there before on assignments for the *Post,* but he still took Sal with him for moral support.

Though cats are fastidiously clean creatures, they still need somewhere to dump their trash. All the garbage dumps in Bast were long since full of waste and every few years, the city ran out of ratholes in which to dump its detritus. Eco-aware priestly protesters complained when new landfills were dug in the tundra just north of the city, so the overflow often brimmed into The Alley. That suited its denizens; the garbage attracted vermin, which equaled dinner with a side order of squeak.

When Julius found Chuffy, a plump cat with twisted whiskers, he was chowing down on a brunch-time rodent.

"I ain't sharing," Chuffy belched.

"You look like you could spare a rat's leg or two." Julius snatched the rat from the alley cat, who raised his hackles, then thought better of it, backing down and lowering his gaze.

"Been busy, Chuffy?" Julius asked between chews, tossing a grisly rat's paw to Sal.

"Trying to keep my nose clean. Which is tough in a place like this." Chuffy's chuckle was forced.

Sal jumped on top of an old, discarded wheelie bin, making fast work of his scrap. Julius asked another question. "Haven't seen a sad-looking hairless cat with a red V-shaped scar on his forehead, have you?"

"Can't say that I have."

"C'mon, Chuffy," Julius coaxed. "You know everyone that passes through this alley and everything that happens. Sure you don't know any cat that fits that description?"

Chuffy lost his patience. "You've already ruined my meal, Julius. Trying to ruin my life, too?"

"What you scared of, Chuffy?" Julius asked.

Sal had been teetering on top of the wheelie bin. It tipped over, and he fell in a disheveled four-pawed heap. "Are you Julius's informant?" he asked Chuffy. The question caught the alley cat by surprise and he nodded. "Then give him the information already."

"Ask Melamo. That's all I'm gonna say."

Julius squinted at Chuffy; that was all he needed. Melamo was the Boss Cat, a big yellow-gray wheeler-dealer of a tom who'd kill strangers on a whim. The scofflaw controlled the area and took a cut of any profits made by the cats who strip-mined the alley trash.

"Thanks for your help," said Julius sarcastically.

Moira couldn't go to the cops to find out more about Fido Frenkel, and she couldn't question her colleagues. But she did know how to slip into City Hall with the minimum of fuss. That night, when the office workers had gone home and the guards were at their least alert, she snuck through a back entrance and headed for the mayor's office. She didn't need any lights—her *tapetum lucidum* soaked up the twilight, allowing her to scan file names without the aid of a desk lamp.

Otto's secretary—commandeered by Woodrow in the lion's absence—was a neatness freak. Every paper clip and file folder was placed just so. Moira slid open a filing cabinet, cringing as its metal sides squeaked against the runners. In the first drawer, she searched for "Frenkel"; there was no such file. All the same, Moira felt sure that the meticulous secretary would have kept notes on the canine visitor—for security's sake, at least.

Security; that was it. The guards had probably lifted Frenkel's details. She would have to visit the security office.

They knew her well, and she decided to look on that as a plus. She would sweet talk them, focusing on a tom called Joey Hondo—he was a jovial, easy-mannered cat who'd always been kind to her.

She padded down the stairs, trying not to leave her scent on anything that she passed. Moira desperately wanted to rub her jowls against the banister, but she controlled her urge. A cat's scent was more prominent than a paw print—any discerning nose could easily identify it.

Moira moved quickly through the atrium, now cleared of balloons and cake crumbs from the event. The dais was still there, ready for Woodrow's next speech. That was one good thing about getting the pink slip—she wouldn't have to listen to that blowhard rehearsing his patter anymore. While Mayor Otto had made plenty of speeches in his time, he preferred roaring to talking. Woodrow loved giving speeches and never missed an excuse to deliver one. He was a natural-born orator, although he still needed help from his team of speechwriters—chief amongst whom was Moira. She couldn't wait to see how he got on without her, or hear what he came up with without her there to conjure up new material.

Beyond the atrium was a small room where the security personnel had set up their surveillance equipment. There were no guards in view, but a bank of monitors emitted a glow, adding warmth to that part of City Hall. Moira stepped inside the room, then cursed as an alarm rang. She looked over her shoulder and noticed a skinny fiber running across the entrance to the room, jutting from one side at ankle level—she'd tripped a security whisker. Security was on its way.

Hurriedly, she looked around and saw a few files gathered on a desk. One was marked "Ambassador Frenkel." She grabbed it quick, stuffing it inside her jacket. The sounds of meowling and running guards were getting closer. She was about to leave when she saw another folder—this one with her own name on it.

Moira couldn't take this one. It would single her out as the intruder straight away. Without time to think things through, she picked up the whole pile of folders and ran back the way she'd come, ducking under the stairs as the guards ran past. Within moments, she was back outside and heading for home, already regretting the theft yet curious about her file. She was regarded as a security risk? Fine, but why had her information been lumped in with the murder victim's?

Moira couldn't go home. If the prowlers came and searched her house, they'd find the files for sure. Instead, she went to the only safe place she could think of.

Julius and Sal followed a trail of fishbones and rat carcasses that took them farther into the moonlit alley. They passed old and infirm cats who'd given up hope of ever recovering their dignity, slumped in the clutter of their own hairballs. The alley seemed a lot busier now than the last time Julius had visited, researching a hard-luck story about a litter of abandoned kittens. Just a few blocks away, city cats dined on the finest food in popular restaurants like The Grand Canary and *Le Chat Amoureux*. How could these gourmets stuff themselves while the alley cats starved? "Survival of the fattest," he said to himself sadly as he skirted a skeletal tortoiseshell.

The alleyway led to a large pile of bones, Melamo's pickings. Two cats were curled up beside the heap, playing cards on an upturned trashcan lid. As soon as they saw the interlopers, they puffed themselves up and began to hiss.

"We're here to see Melamo," Julius told them in his most commanding tone. The two alley cats approached, their hisses drawing others out of the shadows.

"Didn't mean to interrupt your game," said Sal lightly.

"Mind if we sit in?" Julius didn't wait for an answer.

"What've you got for the pot?"

"Him." Julius pointed a forepaw at Sal. "I'll bet my friend here."

A deep chuckle came from within the pile of bones. A hollow had been dug into its side: from that hollow stepped Melamo, his fur a mottled yellow, his clothes faded purple, his jowls sagging with age and overindulgence. Of all the cats in the barrio, Melamo always made sure he got fed.

"I'll play against you, little tabby," he boomed, squatting down beside the trashcan lid. "But no cheatin'. I can't abide cheaters."

"Yeah, leopards aren't much fun either," Sal joked nervously.

Melamo's henchcats laughed at this until their boss silenced them with, "Shuddup. Pots don't talk."

Sal was about to agree, but he closed his mouth tight when he saw the serious expression on Julius's face. Their only chance of leaving The Alley rested on a game of straight Fishbait.

In this game, the cards had four suits: cats, dogs, worms, and fish. The players aimed to collect as many fish as possible and lose all their dogs. The worm cards could be used to collect fish. The game was particularly popular with blue-collar workers; Julius had played it often in his youth. Moira abhorred the game as yet another indication of deep-seated anti-canine sentiment.

Sal watched the game unfold, with Julius explaining why they'd come to see Melamo. Although Sal trusted his friend to keep him safe, he couldn't wait to leave The Alley. Even the cat gangs he'd once hung out with refused to touch this turf.

Melamo dealt Julius a card. It was a worm, and Julius used it to hook two fish. The first round was his. "You're doing well, little tabby," said Melamo. "At this rate, it looks like you're going to win."

"In that case, why don't you just tell me what I need to know?" Julius picked up a cat card. "That's the only reason I'm here."

"Where would the sport be in that? You're here saving your friend's neck, mind. If you win, I'll let him go. And if you win big, I might help you out with your inquiry."

"Reassuring." Julius allowed himself to smile. "Good job I'm going to win big then, isn't it?"

The game continued, Sal breathing hard through his nose. The cats were running even with unexceptional flushes and pairs. Julius rallied with a straight. Melamo put down more cards. The other cats giggled amongst themselves. Melamo had a full house—three fish and two cats. Game over.

"You're all washed up, city slicker."

Julius threw his remaining cards down on the trashcan lid, his mouth open in surprise. "How did you...?" he asked.

"Talent," Melamo replied. "Hand over the kitty."

"Julius?" Sal looked at his friend for reassurance. "I don't want to be handed over."

"Sorry, rules are rules." Julius nudged the snowshoe toward the alley cats. "I guess the odds were against us." As he looked down at Melamo's cards, the Boss Cat tried to cover them with his paw. "Mind if I take a look at those?" Julius asked good-naturedly. "Loser's privilege."

He took them and examined the cards carefully. "I thought you just needed a manicure," he said. "But you clawed the edges of these fish cards on purpose, didn't you? Marking them. I win the game after all."

Melamo glared at Julius, but the reporter didn't back off. The bullying Boss Cat was taken unawares by Julius's defiant stance.

"You're too good," Melamo said at last. "In more ways than one."

"We're free to go?" asked Sal.

"You'll help us?" Julius added, insistent. "Why, if your chicanery was common knowledge, then your standing as an honorable thief might be jeopardized."

"I dunno." Melamo scratched his chin thoughtfully. "This is the land of liars and swindlers. They might respect me more if this did get out."

Sal held his breath, letting out a small, "Eep."

Melamo made his decision. "Tell ya what. You swear to keep my petty *faux pas* to yourselves and I'll aim you in the right direction to find this mystery cat of yours."

"Done," said Julius. "We'll keep your cheating off the record."

Melamo controlled his temper. "There's a nasty runt by the name of Carmine who bears the mark you mentioned."

"And you know him how?"

"His associates work for me from time to time. Extract some garbage from The Alley. They're called the paladins."

Julius had heard of them; the kind of trash that they took out was feline and finished. They were ruthless hitcats who killed for the highest bidder; apparently, someone had hired Carmine to off the doggie delegate.

At the far end of Miro Street, two blocks down from Moira's house, lived a gracefully maturing cat who was known to all local residents. Like Moira, her fur was white and amazingly soft; like Moira, she could handle herself in the poverty-stricken Doghouse. But although both of the cats were Siamese, they weren't related. The older cat still treated Moira like a daughter; however, she was the unnamed matriarch of Miro Street, the one the neighbors turned to if they needed comfort or advice. This Siamese guru had no name. She was simply known as She, the cats' mother.

Moira burst into She's house all perturbed. This was unusual; Moira was calm and collected most of the time, not high-strung like this, dashing about and dumping a slew of files in She's front room.

"Calm down, child," She said gently. Moira caught her breath, catching sight of She's calming eyes. "You're safe here."

"I know. Sorry." As Moira tidied up the files, She stretched herself out, lying on her side. This was obviously her favorite place to lounge because white hairs lay in a huge, downy patch all around her.

"Tell me what you've been up to," coaxed the mother cat. "When you're ready."

Moira felt her pulse slow, and she instinctively flexed her claws in She's direction, purring and pawing at her tummy.

"What you doing, making biscuits?" the mother cat asked.

Moira purred an affirmative.

"Would you mind making them with a little less gusto? My hide may be tough but I still have some feeling in my sides. It's okay; I didn't mean to interrupt. If you feel the need to knead, I can understand that."

"I didn't even realize I was..."

"Don't dither, child. Doesn't become you. You go right along making those biscuits."

Moira went ahead, but she felt self-conscious now. So she soon put a stop to her milk treading and paced over to the files, opening Fido Frenkel's folder with one delicate claw. She watched her through drowsy, half-closed eyes, marveling at Moira's youthful energy.

"The things I could do with your vavoom!" she exclaimed, then gagged as a musky smell wafted toward her. "Phew! What's that smell? Don't be stinking up my house with that! Close it quick."

Moira shut the file with a grimace. "You recognize it?"

"Throw 'em all out, honey. They'll all be infected with his stench. Guys like that, they just wanna spray everywhere."

"You got issues, She?"

The mother cat couched her words carefully. "Only with that particular cat. He's no good. Mean. Likes to inflict pain on other cats."

"Dogs too?"

"I don't see any dogs around here no more, do you?" She slumped back into her heap of hair. "Make me a promise, Moira. Stay away from the beast."

Moira wanted to know why She was so wary of the evil-smelling cat. The other names on the files meant little to her—except for one: Cal Futum.

"You know everyone who so much as breezes through the Doghouse," said Moira. "Does Cal Futum ring a bell?"

"No bells." She could tell that Moira wasn't going to stop snooping or give her any peace until she gave an answer. "Only teeth. Isn't it time you got yours checked?"

"You may find this hard to believe," Sal told Julius as they left The Alley. "But I get scared of the dark. And also of almost becoming supper for a cannibal cardsharp."

"I understand." Julius gave him a friendly nudge. "Go back to Moira's house, Sal. I'll do this alone."

Although he was able to move faster without the snowshoe, it still took Julius a while to find O'Malley's, a drinking establishment on the main road leading from The Alley to the docks. The bar was dark-walled and barely marked in contrast to its neon-lit night-time neighbors. The place was shut up tight, but he could hear the sounds of laughter and music coming from within. Tugging his coat tight around him, he scratched at the entrance to get some attention.

Surprisingly, Julius wasn't challenged by the hefty bouncer who let him in. His money was as good as anyone else's, he supposed. He jumped onto a bar stool, circled around on it a couple of times to get himself comfy, then ordered a pint of milk from the barkeep.

Keeping his head down, Julius scanned the room. It was so dark that it took his eyes a moment to adjust to the seediness. He'd wiled away many happy hours in dives like these, many of them with his late friend Mick. But since O'Malley's was notorious for its bar fights and bad cats, Julius did not feel safe.

A mural behind the bar depicted two large green eyes staring back at him. Although they resembled Mimi Mimu's, Julius couldn't be sure if hers or his obsession was kicking in. The bar was stocked with every kind of milk imaginable, on the turn to lumpy, with some other, unlabeled bottles of hooch in between. Flies occupied a far corner of the establishment, which was reserved for the nastiest, most heavily laden litter tray Julius had ever seen. It smelled so bad that all the cats around him were drinking to forget what their noses noticed.

Two cats caroused together at the top of their lungs. Another lay sprawled on his back after one pint too many. Even the barkeep looked exhausted from too many heavy nights. Julius ordered a two-for-one sour milk special and settled on his circular perch; it was going to be a long night.

Justin Fleaber played on the jukebox. This young punk was as middle-of-the-road as they came, with his beachy ballads and rock-pop ephemera. It made sense, Julius supposed; everyone liked his music. Putting him on was sure to please a crowd and keep the peace, at least for the time it took for him to spout his silly lyrics.

"Let me in
"You got food I wanna eat.
"Then let me out
"I got lady cats to meet.

"I changed my mind
"I'll stay inside after all.
"If you need me,
"I'll be pukin' down the hall."

Bopping to the beat, sipping on his milk, Julius spotted a group of tough-looking customers in a back booth. They were alert, ears pricked and swiveling, eyes wide as if they were looking out for trouble.

Do I constitute trouble? Julius wondered as he hunched down on his stool, lifting the collar of his coat up with a flip of his paw. As he lapped at his milk, he saw a tatty cat pad over to the jukebox. The music lover had no hair on his body.

Julius left the stool and walked over to hand a coin to the disheveled cat. "Put one on for me, will you?" he asked, keeping his voice as deep as he could. "Suspicious Package. Any of their hits will do. Got to be better than this Fleaber trash."

Julius could feel the toughs in the back booth watching him. If these were paladins, he was mixing with some of the meanest creatures in Bast. He considered leaving the bar and going home, lying to Moira that he'd found nothing. Then he remembered the ambassador's dead body, the dog's blood staining the carpet at City Hall. He was close to finding out why that had happened. What would a couple of broken bones matter if he managed to satisfy his curiosity?

"Keep your change, stranger," said Carmine. "I was going to put 'em on, anyway." He selected "Suspicious Package: The Ultimate Package," and the rap group's growling sounds pounded out of the jukebox.

"Pull my tail, I don't care
"I will kill you with one stare.
"I can scratch you, make you bleed.
"On your kidneys I will feed.

"Sneak up, I'll move so fast you won't
"See me comin' it's summin' if I don't
"Take the fur from your body and make me a coat.
"I'm a two-layer player say a prayer for your throat.

"Don't apologize, it's wise to retreat
"To the hole you were born on a street called defeat.
"Down in the dark, you'll be known as my mark.
"Not so brave in your grave, my victory's complete."

Julius returned to his stool but was soon ushered over to the booth.

"Carmine here sez you share our taste in music." The head of the paladins was a scarred, battle-hardened Havana Brown named Franco.

"I think most perspicacious cats appreciate Suspicious Package," said Julius. Uh oh. Big word alert. The toughs looked at him as if he'd just insulted their mother—not that they knew who their mothers were. "I mean, whisht, I guess I dig that crap. If you're pressing me to an opinion."

Franco squinted at Carmine. "Take this effete morsel out back and waste 'im."

"I don't do freebies, *Patron*." Carmine's tone was light, but Franco wasn't amused.

"Then take his goods off his dead body. I don't care. Jus' get him outta my fur."

With a faint whir, the jukebox switched to another Suspicious Package hit. The rappers were performing a number one hit that was the closest they'd ever come to a tender love song, "I'd Eat Your Hairballs, Baby."

"That meeting could've gone better," said Julius as Carmine shoved him outside. "You're not really going to 'waste' me, are you? That was your leader's sore attempt at wit, right?"

"What you doin' here?" asked Carmine, flinging Julius against a dumpster. "You don't belong around here."

"State the obvious much? I'm here because you killed the ambassador for Carabas."

"You can't prove zilch," said Carmine. "You never saw me do nothing."

"Never heard of guilt by association?"

"You better get outta spittin' range before I do some damage."

"I'm not here to arrest you or anything like that," said Julius. "I'm a reporter. I observe and record. I try not to get involved."

"I wondered how a ponce like you'd survived in this city," Carmine snarled. "You're a coward."

"There doesn't seem too much room for heroes around here anymore."

"That an observation or an opinion?"

Julius looked down the alley, hoping to see an escape route. There was too much trash lying around for that.

"A personal bit of both," said Julius. "Tell me why you killed the dog at City Hall, and I'll be on my way."

"Life ain't so simple, my skinny friend. Here's how it works: I scratch your throat and you try'n scratch mine."

Julius swallowed hard. "I don't want to fight."

"Like I said. A coward." Carmine came closer. Threatening, invading Julius's personal space. "How'd a lily-liver like you find me, anyway?"

"An acquaintance gave me a hint: Melamo. I think he hired you for a hit or two."

"But not this one." Julius could tell that Carmine was impressed. "You got out of The Alley alive, huh?" the paladin asked. "Shame no one can be that lucky twice in the same day."

"I don't know. I think it's about time some good luck came my way."

"Why dontcha just hand me your worldly possessions now?" Carmine sighed, popping his claws out and bringing them close to Julius's eyes.

"Excuse me?"

"I hate rummaging through a dead cat's pockets. Somethin' gross about it. Pass me watcha got now."

"I suppose so, if it will save you some effort." Julius handed his wallet to Carmine, who flipped it open with one paw and was taken aback when he saw Julius's ID.

"Julius Kyle. You the super-selling writer."

"Used to be. The last mystery novel didn't do so good, hence my crack about heroes..."

"Dude, I've read all your books," said Carmine. "Bought all the merchandise: the scratch pads, the cradle. The officially licensed ball of yarn. Listened to the new radio show."

"Radio show?" Julius leaned forward, even though Carmine still had his threatening claws exposed.

"Yeah, it's the best thing I've ever heard. Wonder Cat cracks me up; he's so goofy. Always tryin' to save the day, but whatever he does just makes things worse. His teammates end up having to mop up after him. Where do you find all your ideas?"

"Did you say radio show?"

Carmine handed back the wallet, then pursed his lips. "Are you sure you're Julius Kyle?"

Julius hadn't heard of any radio show—he hadn't listened to the wireless since he'd used the city's largest station to broadcast his warning message on a massive scale. But at present, he had other concerns, like the claws Carmine held close to his face. Julius's eyes shone with an idea.

"Want a cameo in my next book?"

"How much would it cost?" Carmine squinted.

"You don't *pay* for something like that. It's a mark of deference."

Carmine gave him a blank look.

"A favor," Julius gasped.

That was something Carmine understood. "Awright, I was hired to put that dog to sleep. But I would've done it for free."

"Why?"

"I don't like dogs." The more Carmine opened his mouth, the less agreeable he became.

"Who hired you?" Julius pressed.

Carmine clammed up.

"You know, I have to dedicate the book to somebody," Julius continued. "It's a writer's tradition, especially if I owe someone a big favor."

"I was hired by someone in City Hall. Don't know his name—it's safer that way."

"Do you know why he wanted the doggy dead?"

"All he said was 'Snuff the mutt.' I know he's ruthless, though. He'll do anything to get to the top."

Julius didn't know whether to believe Carmine or not. But the paladin was already breaking the code of the brotherhood by telling him this much.

"I'll check it out." Julius relaxed as Carmine retracted his claws.

"And you will mention my name?"

"Only in my next novel." Julius started back toward the main road. There was no way he was going to cut back through O'Malley's.

"What's it gonna be called?"

Julius glanced over his shoulder to give his answer. "Er, *Carmine's Way*. That's only a working title, mind. Might change."

"Better not, or I'll rip out your heart. Just kidding!" Carmine called after him. He didn't stay jolly for long. "Write it quick, now."

7

Bad Cat

"I get nervous," Sal told Daisy. He sat in Cal Futum's dental clinic, hunched up tight on a convex chair that seemed designed more for torture than for dentistry. Not that Sal could think of any difference between the two. The light from a bright lamp bounced off the sterile white walls and into Sal's face, making him squint and squirm.

Julius and Moira sat nearby, watching Daisy closely. Like Cal, she was under suspicion.

"Oh dear," said Cal as soon as he entered the room. "Oh dear, oh dear."

"I haven't even opened my mouth yet," Sal moaned.

While Daisy left to resume her duties at the front desk, Cal gently touched Sal's cheek. It made the snow-shoe flinch. "Open wide please," the dentist requested.

"Ashup?" mumbled Sal.

"Cavities. Tartar. Poor nutrition. Bad breath."

"He had fermented herring for breakfast," said Moira.

"Okay, forget the bad breath."

"Believe me, we try," said Julius.

"Nevertheless," Cal said to Sal, "if I don't fix you up now, you're going to get an abscess. May I proceed?" Cal delivered this more as a statement than a question. Sal started to shake his head, but saw Moira's and Julius's urgent nods.

"He'll do it," said Moira.

"Okay, just a moment."

Sal watched Cal step into the back room, then jumped off his chair and complained to his friends in a forced whisper. "Are you nuts? I can't do this. That guy's got drills back there. Files. Sharp, pointy metal things."

"We understand," Moira soothed. "No cat likes getting his teeth fixed. But if Futum has something to do with the ambassador's death, we need to find out."

"This is the best way to do it," Julius added. "With discretion."

The sound of a drill buzzed from the back room. "There won't be no discretion when I start screaming," frowned Sal. "Can't we just ask him?"

"Not yet. Here's the plan: We'll overpay him for the work. It'll seem accidental but..."

"You want to bribe him. You think he's crooked as my teeth."

"We don't know yet," Moira shrugged.

"What if he gets upset?" asked Sal. "Pointy sharp things, remember? I'm out of here."

"He says you need fillings," said Julius.

"I can live without them." Sal flattened his ears. "I'd rather have an abscess next week than agonizing pain right now. He's not coming back, anyway."

Futum had been gone for a long time. Julius and Moira got up and peered cautiously into the back room.

It was a small office area with mirrors, charts, and tools. One of them was in Cal's head. While they sat right next door, he'd been murdered.

"Now we know what made the drilling sound." Julius pressed a button on Cal's drill, then wished he hadn't as the instrument flung pieces of the dentist's brain onto his fur. Sal sneaked a quick look around the room and clapped a paw over his mouth.

"You smell something?" asked Moira.

"Other than the odious smell of antiseptic?" Julius replied.

"Something more odious." It was the same musk scent she'd smelled in her file. She ran out the back exit.

"What are you waiting for?" said Julius to Sal, who stood staring at Cal's head.

"That could've been my mouth," the snow-shoe mumbled.

"Quit lagging behind. You don't want to stay in here, do you?"

Sal got the message and followed Julius outside to look for Moira. "Did you hear a terrible noise?" he asked his friend.

"Only you." Julius shushed Sal and crept down the street, sniffing the air.

"Over there. It's Moira!" She was being pulled down the alleyway that ran behind the dentist's. She made as much noise as possible: hissing, scratching, grabbing at rusty old drainpipes, knocking over trashcans. Julius couldn't see her captor clearly—he was some kind of cat, a great hulking shape, too strong for Moira to elude. But she could slow him down, allowing Julius to catch up. Before he could consider his own safety, he sprang through the air, a fierce yowl in his throat, teeth bared. The catnapper released Moira and hoisted himself upward, digging thick claws into a telegraph pole. Making sure Moira was okay, Julius left her with Sal and climbed after her assailant. The tabby's claws looked tiny in the pockmarks left in the wood by the larger animal. Still, Julius didn't look down. He had no idea when he reached the top.

Moments later, he was jumping from the pole onto the domed roof of City Hall. His nose twitched slightly; a vent from the kitchens leaked smells that confused his senses. There were too many shadowy hiding places on the roof—the creature could be lurking, ready for an ambush, or long gone.

Julius moved slowly along the roof's edge, trying to find the neighboring rooftops that were within leaping distance. Away from the vents, he detected subtler smells, including the distinct ammonia tang of the large male cat.

It was an ambush after all. The big male landed heavily on Julius's back, digging a set of ragged claws into his shoulders. Teetering on the edge, Julius tried to twist his body and move away from the steep drop. *Is this cat crazy? Does he want to kill us both?*

Julius used the tom's weight to pull them backward, the terrible claws still deep in his skin. Landing with a thump, the two cats struggled to regain their breath. Julius was lucky enough to find his first, using the moment to break free from the claws in his hide and back away from their owner.

Julius didn't consider himself an active cat; his idea of exercise was eating fast. So he surprised himself as he hurtled toward his prey, teeth bared.

Hurtling was easy. The stopping part was hard, especially on a flimsy, loose-tiled roof. Julius tried to put on the brakes as he caught his first good look at his enemy, a puma with cold blue eyes and a mouth full of fangs. The puma moved aside and Julius overshot, grabbing a skinny chimney to prevent a nasty fall.

"Out with your claws," Julius challenged, short of breath. A shiv-sharp row of cuticles popped from the puma's pads as the animals sized each other up in the moon's eerie glow. The puma's claws looked massive, but Julius managed to parry an attack with a tinny clatter. Then it was the black cat's turn to lunge, crashing into the chimney and knocking a few bricks loose.

Julius havered, surprised by this display of power. A moment of hesitation was all the puma needed, dipping low, then moving in, sinking his teeth into Julius's side. Before the tabby could let out a yowl, he was knocked onto his back with a hefty swipe, his belly exposed.

Claws full out, Julius lifted his paws to protect his exposed belly, then flipped over, landing in a crouch. Twitching his tail to maintain balance, Julius glanced from side to side. He needed to take full advantage of his opponent's size.

The puma stretched a paw toward Julius, batting him with a casual blow. Julius went spinning, seeing stars, then collapsing in a crumpled heap. Before he could collect himself, he was bitten again, this time in his back. He could feel a dark wetness at the base of his spine, a spittle-clogged seepage of blood that made the black cat gag. Julius shrugged him off and found himself on the rooftop ledge, a step drop right behind him. Woozy, he sneered at his opponent, daring him to strike again.

"Bite me," he said, spreading the sneer as wide as it would go.

As the puma pounced again, mad now, Julius took a step backward and allowed himself to fall. He landed on a narrow ledge, hugging the wall with his left shoulder. The black cat joined him, then realized that this was a mistake—his paws were wider than his perch. With claws at the ready, Julius used the puma's bulk to push himself back, moving with assured balletic steps. His opponent tried to follow him but couldn't; there didn't seem to be enough room. Teetering, the puma gave his foe a puzzled look. Then Julius hissed, making the black cat flinch and lose his balance, plummeting from the ledge into the trash-strewn alley below.

Julius scrabbled down a drainpipe, anxious not to lose his quarry. His tail snagged on a rusted bracket, slowing him down and giving the puma time to lope away.

"Who was that masked cat?" Sal wondered, sitting on a trashcan, holding his aching side.

"He wasn't wearing a mask," Julius informed him. The tabby held Moira tight, as if he'd lose her if he relaxed his grip. "It was a stripe of dark fur across his eyes. You didn't get a good look at him then?"

"Not a, uh, good look. A bad one maybe. That's the trouble with dark alleys—no light."

"How about you?" Julius asked Moira, his voice softening. "Does this mean anything to you?"

Moira said nothing. She stood up, faltering slightly, regaining her bearings.

"The Doghouse is this way," Julius groused, nursing his nose.

Moira could have followed the stench. The cheap side of Bast smelled of blocked drains, fish bones, and unemptied litter trays. No trams stopped there, and prowlers patrolled the area in pairs. Still, it was home to thousands of cats. Moira had lived there all her life, and she wouldn't contemplate moving to a wealthier neighborhood, despite her accelerated career. Better to wait for the city council to gentrify the area.

Julius didn't think it would ever happen, not while shabby animals like Sal were around. But he never talked about the future to Moira. They lived day to day, relaxed with one another, leaving many things unsaid.

As soon as they reached Moira's house, Julius slunk into the kitchen, dipping his head and licking his chest self-consciously. He checked his war-torn nose in a mirror. For a cat, home wasn't home without a reflective surface in every room. "Lost my looks," he sighed.

"What looks?" Moira joked, looking over his shoulder at his grizzled image. Licking the back of her paw, she smoothed down a stray hair on her soft white cheek. Though she lived on the wrong side of the tram tracks, she was still a Siamese through and through.

"You must've stuck with me for some reason," Julius wheedled. "Don't you find me ... cuddly?"

"In a vulnerable kind of way. You make mistakes. You're not too cocky. I like that in a tom."

"I can do cocky!" Julius strutted around the kitchen, chin tilted upward. "I'll have you know I was the captain of cockiness at school, the prefect of posers. No one could out-cocky me."

"Where did all that bravura go?"

"It's in there, somewhere."

Sal stayed quiet, nabbed some leftover casserole from the fridge, and wolfed it down, his head buried in the dish.

"Maybe you shouldn't go to work tomorrow."

Moira's eyes widened at Julius's comment. "There's enough layabouts around here already," she told him, looking directly at Sal. "Does he have to be here?" She was unsure of how to feel about a strange cat on her territory.

"Haven't you ever been followed home by a stray before?" Julius replied. Sal lapped at his casserole, oblivious to Moira's disapproval.

Leading Moira into the living room, Julius got serious, curling up close to her on the sofa. "Listen to me for a minute, please. That puma's still out there."

"I am—was—a city employee. I don't expect to be liked." Moira seemed too calm, considering what she'd been through. Julius chalked it down to her tough upbringing. Her foster dad had been a dog, and her brothers and sisters were all dead. There were elements of her life that he didn't know about, didn't care to know. For all he knew, she might have enjoyed the adventure, a sweet contrast to her humdrum admin work. Either that or she was doing the typical cat thing, playing it cool, pretending to be unfazed while a tangle of nerve endings buzzed beneath her fur. "The mayor's due back tomorrow. I'm going to try to meet with him in the afternoon."

"Spit in his eye for me, won't you?" Julius asked.

"I sure will."

Julius and Moira shared their loathing for Otto. He was lord of the concrete jungle, and as his subjects, they had to abide by his laws. Law Number One: Come running when the mayor roars.

"What're we going to do with this bozo?" Moira asked, flicking a paw at Sal. He had licked the casserole dish clean, leaving not so much as a crumb for his hosts. Now he was curled up on a living room easy chair, tail draped over his paws, fast asleep.

"Can we keep him?" Julius asked. "He needs to find work, just like me. We could go job- hunting together."

"He's a liability. He's spent years hanging with the wrong crowd and using catnip. Ditch him."

"But he looks so cute when he's sleeping like that." Strands of kitten drool hung from Sal's lips.

"He's dangerous."

"The city's full of danger, honey. I'm the one who should be worried about you, not the other way around."

"Fine," Moira huffed. "Take him with you tomorrow. Watch your back, though. That's all I'm saying." Julius shook his head, considering the fact that his practical partner was invariably right.

8

Fighting Talk

To look at him entering the McMahon Scratching Arena, it appeared that the puma's wounded pride had healed completely. His attitude was deceptive. He'd never lost a scrap before, and to lose to a scrawny, old tabby cat deepened his desire for a rematch. Next time, he wouldn't hold back. If he got the chance, he'd tear Julius to shreds; all he needed was his client's permission.

The client waited in the third row of the auditorium, a choice spot where spectators were close enough to feel the sweat spraying from the ring. He was avidly watching a scratch match, eyes flicking from one combatant to the other as he sucked on a large cigar. The puma pushed through a huddle of fluffy bodies, hundreds of pairs of green eyes averting their gaze from him in deference to his imposing size. Reaching the third row, he barged past a hawker, interrupting cries of, "Pilchards! Ice-cold milk!"

"You're just in time for the main event, Toxic," said the client. "I usually take a ringside seat, y'know, but this is more discreet."

"Yes, sir." Toxic the puma clawed at his seat a little, then settled down, ears cocked at a slight angle toward his employer.

The main event was a much-hyped match between two famed fighters, Reptile Rex and Lizard Kid. Rex was a veteran of downtown bouts, a six-time champion with the belt to prove it. The Kid was a fresh, young cat whose pep was matched by his arrogance. He was a protégé of Swampy McMahon, who had enjoyed a phenomenally successful career in scratching and wrestling before branching into publishing. As McMahon often joked, he didn't see much difference between the cutthroat pursuits.

"My money's on Rex," said the client through a wreath of smoke. "The Kid's no match for him." Toxic nodded, wondering how much the rich spectator had splurged on his gamble.

Reptile Rex entered the ring, relaxed, sharp teeth glinting in a bright spotlight. "I'm gonna take my claws," he yelled to the adoring crowd, "and scratch that mousy Lizard Kid in two. Then I'm gonna scratch those pieces into two more and so on 'til there's nothing left of him but his puny HAIRBALLS!" The last word was a drawn-out victory cry, and the audience began to chant at his behest:

"Hairballs. Hairballs. Hairballs!"

Lizard Kid, wearing a scaly green mask and matching trunks, arrived at the opposite corner. He said nothing but raised his forepaws high in response to the crowd's cheering meowls, his fur raised to make himself look as large as possible. To Toxic, he seemed slight; underneath the bravado and the thick pads molded to look like bristled fur was a frightened kitten ready to bolt.

The two fighters faced each other, moving slowly, shoulders hunched, light on their paws despite the bulky padding. Their tails twitched like busy, synched-up metronomes, and they didn't take their eyes off each other.

Rex lunged first, ramming Lizard Kid with a sideways thrust. The Kid lifted his paws, landing them hard on Rex's back, trying to push him onto his belly. Rex was having none of it. He stepped backward out of the Kid's grasp, ears flattened, teeth gritted for a serpentine hiss.

"You should be long gone by now," the client growled at the puma.

"Yeah, well," Toxic replied, refusing to apologize, "I had to change tack."

"Why? What happened?"

"Her boyfriend happened. Made an easy job not so easy."

"You shoulda killed him, Toxic."

Lizard Kid managed to get in one good nick to Rex's left wrist, causing the older wrestler to hiss even louder. The Kid had succeeded in angering him. In a blind rage, Rex lashed out, bringing a paw to each side of the Kid's head and dragging all ten claws down his face. The crowd went wild.

Wincing, squinting, the Kid's flight response kicked in. He scarpered to his corner, followed closely by his opponent, who loomed over him. The noise from the crowd stopped as everyone held their breath—the Kid had to be mincemeat.

Rex was already coiled and ready to spring when the bell rang. He trotted back to his own corner, acting casual, then squatted down. Round One was over. His trainer gave him a quick groom, licking his back and injured wrist, while another trainer shoved a dish of water under his nose.

"Tap or bottled?" Rex rumbled.

"This is tap water."

Rex sent the dish flying, swatting his trainer away at the same time. "You know I can't stand the smell of fresh tap water. Get outta my face."

Toxic took advantage of the lull in the action to respond to his client. "Sure, I could have killed him. Except you said no killing. Said it would draw too much attention."

"You always do everything I tell you?"

"Yeah, when you're talking sense." *Hardly ever*, Toxic thought. "So, what are you trying to tell me now?"

"We need Moira Marti. If her mate gets in the way..."

"He wasn't alone."

"If *anyone* gets in your way, that's tough on them. Dead tough."

The bell rang again, signaling the start of Round Two. Rex charged to the center of the ring, determined to finish the fight in a jot; the Kid had other ideas. He sprang, twisting his body in the air, aiming a kamikaze strike straight at Rex's tail. He gave it several furious scratches, sending fur flying into the air and leaving the referee's mouth agape. It was a dirty move, sure, but the Kid was declared the winner by a nose—or a tail.

Unmoved by the action in the ring, the client finished issuing instructions. "Stay at the rendezvous point until I come for you, then you'll get the rest of your payment. Do not stray, understood? We're talking low-key here. Lay low."

"Understood," Toxic replied, thinking that he wouldn't even give this bossy cat the time of day if he didn't have such power and wealth.

"That Kid was pretty good," said the client as they left the auditorium.

"Not a patch on Swampy McMahon," Toxic replied. "Give me wrestling over a scratch match any day. This is all faked, you know. In his prime, that Swampy was—."

"Enough. Get the job done. Report back to me. I've wasted enough time on this, and I'm getting impatient." Something in his client's eyes told Toxic that his impatience would not be a virtue. Without another word, the puma left in search of Moira.

9

Kitty Get a Job

*In which Julius and Sal get off their
plump butts and look for work.*

As time passed and Sal settled into Moira's house, she tried to hatch a plan to reach Joey Hondo. As the cat in charge of the protection of City Hall and its environs, he would be the one to offer the most insight into Frenkel's assassination—and who might have hired Carmine. However, her recent burglary and the mayor's disappearance meant a security clampdown. Meanwhile, the hard facts of life were getting in the way of her detective work.

Moira's bank account was in the red, and her credit cards were maxed out. For animals that were permanently hungry, a bare larder was a scary thing to contemplate.

Moira called a household meeting.

"I'll handle Hondo," she said, paws crossed on the kitchen counter. Julius and Sal sat on stools opposite her. "You two need to get back to work somehow."

"You mean back to work looking for clues, right?" Sal placed a paw on a jar of brekkies; Moira snatched it away.

"I mean a paying job," she said. "What, you think we should stop everything just because you have a mystery to solve? This is the real world, Sal, with real bills to pay. Our fridge is getting empty, and that makes me unhappy. When I'm unhappy…"

"We're not allowed to be happy either. We know." Sal looked suitably guilty.

"I'll look for a new job tomorrow," said Julius.

"No more of this freelance nonsense," Moira chided. "Something that actually helps pay your way."

"At least you'll be safe here," Julius sighed.

"What makes you think I'll be here? I'm getting cabin fever as it is. Besides, you don't seem to realize how serious our financial situation is. It's so bad, I've got to go beg for my old job back."

A pale yellow sun rose the next morning, giving Bast a jaundiced hue. Down by the river, houses and office blocks were being demolished, with shiny new skyscrapers taking their place. These magnificats would symbolize a new beginning for the city, a sophisticated escape heavenward from primal urges and mob mentalities. From the skeletons of the structures that were already being built, ramps and scaffolding poles sprouted like whiskers drooping in the summer heat.

Did I cause all this? Julius wondered as he traversed Champawat Way. Julius had made an announcement on the radio warning listeners about the bad dogs and crafty cats that wished them harm. This had given many citizens an excuse to loot and destroy the city center. Julius had never been punished for his disturbance of the peace; his guilt was penalty enough. Bast would recover from the incident, rebuild, and forget. Julius couldn't do that.

Moira gave him a reason to live, to do good. While he sought answers and looked for a new career, his mate supported him. Not everyone can afford the luxury of soul-searching.

I owe her so much. She's sacrificed a lot for me. Julius couldn't be sure that her neighbors were snubbing her—the Doghouse wasn't known for its friendly atmosphere—but they made a point of crossing the street to avoid her, their noses and tails stuck high in the air, a wicked glint in their eyes. Moira was selling out, mixing with the wrong kind of cats: public officials, snobbish longhairs, and Julius Kyle.

Moira didn't mind. Her work kept her busy, and she still reveled in her relationship with Julius. They cared for each other, whatever the neighbors said behind their backs.

Passing on a tram ride, Julius walked into town on his mission to save a few bucks and make some more. There had to be a job he could take and keep for more than a few hours. He wasn't in any hurry to get downtown, though, ambling out of the Doghouse and sticking to the main streets so that he didn't encroach on another cat's territory.

"Mr. Kyle! Wait up, Mr. Kyle!"

Julius tried to ignore the grating calls, but Sal was persistent, loping across Miro Street to catch up with his host. "You forgot to wake me, Mr. Kyle."

"Uh, yeah, well, you looked like you needed your sleep," Julius mumbled, not looking the snowshoe in the eye.

"I'm going to need a new job if I want to stay with you, which I do. I feel bad, Mr. Kyle."

"You do?"

"I messed up, back at City Hall."

"Really?" Julius's sarcasm was lost on Sal.

"I've never been fired before. Mind you, I've never had a proper job before, so maybe working stiffs are always let go like that."

"I doubt it."

"That was some adventure we had, eh, Mr. Kyle?"

Julius winced in reply, the comment reminding him of his painful bruises. Sal kept pestering him, saying, "You gave that strange cat what for. You should have seen him fall from that rooftop. Crash! Right in the garbage." Sal giggled. "You looking for a new job today, too, huh?"

"Yes." Julius regretted the response as soon as it had left his mouth.

"Great! I'll tag along. We could be workmates!"

"I don't think I could handle the excitement."

A wide road separated the Doghouse from the downtown area. This smarter stretch of Bast was the cornerstone of feline civilization. Cats walked upright on their way to work, noses in the air, forepaws clutching brollies or briefcases. The males wore gray suits with quiet silk ties; the females wore flowing, autumn-colored dresses or no-nonsense business apparel.

Everything downtown was geared toward the furtherance of catkind—rebuilding the city, amassing wealth, pursuing leisure. Despite the concern they shared for Bast, the cats rarely looked each other in the eye. To Julius, the commuters looked lonely in their aloofness, cool and professional, focused on their daily goals but unhappy all the same. The city folk kept to themselves. They had little time for each other; it was every cat for himself.

Julius and Sal passed a store selling Bakelite radios by the bushel. Julius stopped in his tracks when he heard a tremulous voice say, "Out with your claws!"

"That's my line," he said, darting into the store.

Customers browsed shelves stacked with radios, speaker systems, and other home entertainment gadgets. Some of the radios were art déco centerpieces; others were functional brown boxes. Julius passed a row of midget tube models with large white knobs and horizontal ridges. The most expensive sets had long antennae whiskers for extra range.

A colorpoint clerk demonstrated one of the shack's state-of-the-art wireless models. A radio show blared from its honeycombed speakers, hosted by an excitable narrator.

"A lazy housecat by day, no one can guess that the fearful feline moonlights as Wonder Cat, the clawed crime fighter who is the scourge of evil-doing dogs everywhere! Faster than a field mouse, more powerful than a jet-propelled porpoise, able to leap tall boxes with a single bounce!"

"I didn't know they'd adapted your stories for radio," Sal said in awe.

"Neither did I." Julius asked the clerk to raise the volume.

"Immediately, sir," said the clerk with an efficient twiddle.

Julius listened intently as Wonder Cat uttered his trademarked catchphrase. "Out with your claws!"

"This is our favorite seller," the clerk explained. "High fidelity, adjustable balance, changes channels with a flick of your paw." The colorpoint reached for a knob. Julius and Sal snarled.

"No! Don't touch that dial."

"We want to listen to the show," Sal explained. "Not to you."

"I'll leave you guys to make your decision," said the colorpoint, trying his best not to bristle. "Give me a mew whenever you're ready."

"That was a bit rude," Julius told his friend, still listening intently to the radio. "But it was fun."

"I hate pushy salescats, that's all," said Sal.

The narrator gave credence to an array of sound effects. "Only W.C. can stop the dastardly Draxar in his tracks! The evil white-haired genius, cunningly disguised as a priest, intends to turn the entire city into one gigantic pet cemetery!"

"If they're going to rip off my work, they could at least write some decent dialogue," Julius said sadly.

"Who's 'they'?"

"That's what I've got to find out."

Sal caught the determined look in the tabby's eyes. He was about to ask another of his trademark monosyllabic questions when the sales clerk returned.

"Wonder Cat fans, right?" the clerk beamed.

"This dude created Wonder Cat," Sal said with due reverence.

"Yeah, right," said the clerk. "And I'm Mimi Mimu."

"No, really. Tell him, Julius."

"I didn't write this pap." Julius listened intently to the outlandish radio adventure. Wonder Cat was investigating mysterious goings-on in a cemetery, following clues that invariably led to a shadowy figure with a maniacal laugh. Just as the hero was about to catch up with his nemesis, Julius lost his temper, complaining at the top of his voice about the quality of the script.

"This writer's an idiot!" Julius yowled, with Sal nodding in agreement.

"Are you gonna buy this or not?" It was the clerk, his tail switching from side to side with impatience.

"Not." Julius huffed past the colorpoint, Sal right behind him.

"Time-wasters," the clerk grumbled as he turned down the radio. "Right at lunchtime as well." He hesitated before switching off the Bakelite, then turned it up again. Like so many of his fellow felines, he had to know what happened in that week's episode of *Wonder Cat*. Later, he'd discuss it with his colleagues around the milk cooler. He didn't want to feel left out.

"The nerve of those publishers! Selling my ideas like they can just reach a paw into my brain and scoop out whatever they like!" Julius moaned as he reached downtown Bast.

"It makes a lot of people happy, though," Sal piped up. Julius looked at him and Sal flattened his ears a little. "They need a way to forget their problems. Your stories take their mind off things for half an hour. You should be glad."

"You know what really hurts?" asked Julius.

"Catching your whiskers in a window?"

"I'm talking about this radio business. Those leeches are making money off of my characters, and they don't even deign to consult me. That's what really yanks my tail."

It was hard to move through the crowded streets at lunch hour. This was the time when most cats stopped their hustle and bustle, their shopping and snooping and wheeler-dealing to take a break and eat their midday meal. Many had pack-ups and hunkered down in the street to unwrap a tinfoil delight of processed meat. Others caught their food where they could find it, pouncing on pigeons or stalking scuttlebugs.

All this hunting and lunching made it difficult for Julius and Sal to cross the street. It was a strange sight, Julius realized, when you weren't part of the throng. A mass of furry bodies filled the main square, chewing, crunching, and playing. There were inevitable disagreements, scraps concerning leftovers, chocolate bar brawls. Outside a junk store, two rangy moggies showed that there was still hope for felinekind by sharing a hunk of ham. A less generous cat had got himself stuck up a tree on purpose so that no one could get to his fresh sparrow.

Picking their way through the melee, Julius and Sal marveled at the sounds they heard—a thousand jaws chomping in time with each other, with a bass line of the growling, girdling sounds that are made when a morsel slides down a cat's throat.

"I'm famished," Sal admitted, eyeing up a cockroach.

"This is the best time of day to apply for work. The hirers will be available to talk to us and the lines'll be non-existent. Trust me, I've had a lot of experience in the past few months."

"Fine," Sal nodded. "But when do we eat?"

"Determination will override our appetites," Julius told him, but he didn't sound convincing. "To tell the truth, I read that gem on the back of a tuna tin."

"A tuna tin?"

"It's an old mercat motto."

"A tuna tin?" Sal asked. "Really?"

"Yes," Julius nodded, "a tin of tuna."

"Don't mention tuna to me right now. How much farther to the docks?"

"Not long now."

Bast was split in two by a grubby river that trickled down from the Northern Mountains and eventually spewed into the ocean down south. Otto Street ran straight through the middle of the downtown district, from the Doghouse to the river wharf. On the banks stood an oppressive collection of warehouses and factories, all red brick and gray tin.

As Julius and Sal got closer to the docks, the crowds of pedestrians thinned. The citizens were washing themselves now, wetting the backs of their paws and smothering their fur with their scent. Julius tried not to look; he didn't approve of public bathing. Nevertheless, he and his companion felt the urge to join in, fighting a communal impulse to belong that seemed to be present in any large gathering.

"What's that pong?" asked Sal.

"The river. Silt. Marsh mud. Usual stink. Almost there."

Sal nodded, but moved upwind of Julius all the same. "I can't believe you mentioned tuna."

"We'll try over here," Julius told Sal, leading the younger cat along the dockside. "They've just received a new shipment." A freighter was moored outside the Tsavo Warehouse, with crates still being unloaded. One particularly large item of cargo was being lowered onto the dock by a crane, with a brawny, old calico supervising the operation. A crowd of cats sniffed around the crate, mewing pitifully.

"A shipment of what?"

"Let's go find out," said Julius.

The two cats approached the crate but were shooed away by the calico, who was chewing on a fish head.

"Got no work for you," he told them with a low yowl. "You expect to waltz up here and get a job handed to you on a platter?" Julius and Sal shook their heads. "Times're hard y'know." The calico's mouth curled downward as he looked at their sad faces. "Tell you what. I might be able to find a place for one of you. Stacking crates." Behind him, the other cats were climbing onto the precious cargo, pressing their noses against the wood.

Julius exchanged a glance with Sal. "Both of us and nothing," the gray cat said. The calico shrugged and dismissed the pair with a flick of his furry paw.

"You stick your neck out for people," the calico sighed, "and they don't give you so much as a thank-you. Why do I bother?" Then he shouted after the pair, "Try the factory!"

Turning, he noticed a mass of felines clinging to the crate, making it too heavy for the crane. He raised his arms and yelled in dismay as the crate came crashing down, releasing a ton of fresh fish. The cats scrambled for haddock, cod, and redfish, scratching, howling, and hissing at each other for their own private scraps, spitting between chomps, and dragging away their scavenged meals. It was a noisy mess of fish, fur, and splintered packaging.

"Ah, the smell of tuna," said Sal, not even bothering to look over his shoulder at the mess. "Music to my nose."

They seemed tiny in comparison with the Tybalt Inc. Factory, a monstrous structure leaning slightly toward the river. It cast a shadow over the water, with sewer outlets adding their contents to the murk. Sal cricked his neck back to look at the eaves of the building, dark and ugly like the brim of a bad guy's hat.

"Shall we go in?" Julius said with a reassuring grin. As soon as the two cats stepped into the echoing expanse of the factory, they flattened their ears, trying to shut out the racket that rocked their sensitive hearing.

Sal asked a question, but Julius couldn't hear him. The tabby waggled a paw upward, hoping that Sal would understand.

"I said, WHERE DO WE GO?"

Julius shrugged, then indicated a small office. They pushed past sour-pussed workers with narrowed eyes and pursed lips, through a labyrinth cluttered with metal parts and oily hairballs.

"Why aren't they napping?" Sal yelled. "This is primo nap time they're missing. Us too, for that matter."

"They don't get paid to nap," Julius replied, shaking his head sadly. "They get paid to work."

The employees stood in rows, heads bowed, focused on their work. Julius was surprised to see so many felines standing so close to each other for such a length of time without a territorial spat amongst them. They were like fur-lined, dull-witted machines, and he was about to become one of them.

The floor was littered with claw sheaths and clumps of fur; the workers weren't permitted to break from their tasks just to cough up a stray hair or two.

The smell of damp cardboard and sweaty felines filled the air.

Sal stopped as he saw a longhair get caught in a cog. The cat was ungroomed, strands out of place on his head, his legs scraggled with excess fur brimming out of his pants legs. The poor creature yowled, snagged in a remorseless packing machine, until a large clump was ripped from his hide and the cat fell free. His work-mates ignored the kafuffle, continuing with their work as if nothing had happened.

Julius ran over to the longhair, placing a paw on the worker's brand-new bald patch. "Are you okay, son?" he asked, eyes wide with concern. The worker ignored him and got on with his task.

Julius stood next to the machine for a moment, then took a step away from it. "Don't hurt yourself again thanking me so much," Julius grumbled, then led Sal to a small office at the back of the factory.

"Charming," said Sal. "Are you sure you want to work here? It's a bit busy in here for me."

Julius scowled. "Have you done a day's hard work in your life?"

"Of course not ... look at all those conveyor belts 'n hook things." Sal grimaced. "I could lose my tail—or some other extremity. It has been known to happen."

"Sure, Sal, sure. But you can't expect us to put you up and feed you forever. You need to earn your keep."

"I didn't expect you to put up with me for as long as you have," said Sal. "I tend to wear out my welcomes fast."

An obese Egyptian mau almost filled the office, his spotted smoky coat sagging over a messy desk. "Can I help you?" he asked in a curiously gentle, melodious voice that didn't match his form.

"We understand you're hiring," Julius said, glad to be in the supervisor's quiet office, away from the noisy factory floor.

"I'm not hiring nitwits." The mau stared at Julius with intelligent green eyes. "You've never done factory work before, have you?"

"I'll try anything twice," Sal told the supervisor.

"I get a lot of losers in here since times got tight. I'll tell ya this, they don't last a week." The mau chortled to himself. "Can't make their quotas."

"We'll do whatever's required of us," Julius assured him, rubbing against his leg.

"We'll see. I'll tell ya this, I'm a family man. I love my sons and brothers so much, I let 'em work here for free. My father too. If I didn't have such big quotas to keep, I'd stick with 'em, and I wouldn't need to be hiring anyone else. But I do." Julius and Sal sniffed at a contract and added their marks to the document. "Do a good job for me," the supervisor told them, "an' I'll treat you as one of my own."

The supervisor led Julius and Sal back out onto the work floor.

"Where do we start, Chief?" asked Julius, wondering if being one of the mau's own would be such a good thing. The pay sounded lousy.

"You start by not calling me 'Chief.' Name's Faki, don't you forget. Now stop your gabbing. It's time to get your lily-gray paws dirty. I'll make this simple for you since this is your first day and you're obviously thick as shiatsus. You take these," he picked up a quivering mouse, "and put them in these." There was a stack of small, clear boxes with pinprick holes in the top. Once inside, there was barely room for the mouse to move.

"Where do we put the boxes once we're done?" Julius asked, trying to sound intelligent.

"Give 'em to your neighbor," said Faki.

"I just moved into my friend's house," Sal explained slowly. "I don't know who my neighbor is yet."

"I mean the cat standing next to you."

Sal gave a box to Julius. The supervisor narrowed his eyes and walked off, looking for another employee to patronize.

"He certainly earns his keep," said Sal.

"Just put the mice in these empty boxes. I can't believe we're getting paid to do something so simple."

"Yeah. We hardly have to use our brains at all," the snowshoe replied, his mouth stuffed full of mouse.

Moira had a lot more trouble getting into City Hall through the front entrance than she had sneaking in the back way at night. Her numerous requests for a meeting with Otto had all been ignored. Her only recourse was to go to the building in person and wait. After a considerable linger on the marble stoop, she was finally granted an audience with Hondo in the surveillance office. Since he was the top official in charge of planning security, it was his duty to confirm the purpose of her visit.

"I want to speak to Mayor Otto," Moira insisted. She felt awkward returning to the scene of her crime.

Hondo shook his head. He liked the Siamese and hated to say no to her, but his job came first. "He's still indisposed."

"You mean he isn't back yet?"

"No. Something bad may have happened. And that's not all. We had a theft at City Hall recently," he explained. "And I'm not talking brekkies from the break room. Some cheeky toot got into security and made off with confidential information."

"Makes me glad I wasn't an employee at the time." Moira fluttered her eyelashes. "I could hardly be a suspect, could I?"

"Suppose not." She could hear a tinge of suspicion in Hondo's voice. He was slim and handsome with a streak of silver running down the middle of his head, but Moira's attraction for him was subsumed by her fear.

"Anyway, what with the mayor vanishing and the breach in security, I don't think Woodrow wants you around, hen."

Woodrow burst into the room. "Moira! Thank Bastet you've come back! We need you at once."

Moira was astonished by the warm welcome. Was Woodrow doing this to keep a suspect close to him? Or even to put her in harm's way? Moira needed to know, and she needed a paycheck as well.

10

A Day That Will Live in Industry!

In which a tycoon mourns the present dip in full-bore consumerism.

Thaddeus Gregory Tybalt tried to do a good deed every day. It was usually a small gesture, giving some change to a begging Burmese or directing hungry tourists to the nearest deli. Once a year, he'd donate an albacore to the local stray shelter. He needed those deeds to put a spring in his heart, make his middle-aged life more worthwhile and mainly to counterbalance the darker side of his existence.

Tad was a survivor, an entrepreneur who had used his active mind to rise above misfortune. Through determination and greedy dealings, Tad had built up a business empire despite a poor swampland upbringing.

His stores and their catchy commercials were known throughout the city. Other entrepreneurs looked up to him as a template, a guru, a power-napping potentate of capitalism. It wasn't enough.

Without his constant power plays, product developments, and boardroom hissy fits, he would have run out of steam. He needed to invent and create, demolish and rebuild, to avoid his greatest fear—stagnation. That meant dumping employees without notice, hiring and firing willy-nilly, closing successful stores, and establishing new, riskier sites; it all helped to keep Bast alive, vibrant, on edge. Tad loved it.

In some strange way, the dreadful riot in Bast had helped too. With blocks razed to the ground and many cats left homeless, Tad had been the perfect choice to oversee the reconstruction of the city.

The poorest, flimsiest neighborhoods had been hit hardest, but Tad had focused on the city center—now he and the mayor had been provided with an excellent excuse to impose their architectural ideals on a bewildered populace.

The new flurry of construction had given Tad further opportunities to expand and exploit. The cheap building materials he was supplying to create a mighty Tybalt Tower wouldn't last long; for that matter, the methods of construction weren't particularly safe. But Tad's business partners would absorb any liability when the foundations crumbled.

Today, Tad was tired. With the mayor presumably indisposed due to pain and speech loss from his visit to the dentist, the council was being unreasonably cocky. Tad had spent the morning in the City Chambers, arguing that one of Bast's largest temples, destroyed in the riot, should be rebuilt on the outskirts of the city. Its original site—slap bang in the center—would be the perfect place for the new mall he was hoping to construct. For some reason, the council wasn't happy with his reasoning.

"Blasted bureaucrats," he grumbled to his chief exec, Chuck Kingsley, as he paced around his plush office. It was situated on a gallery level that allowed him full view of the Tybalt Inc. Factory floor. Through a large window, he could see his flyspeck employees far below, and they were fully aware that he was watching them. "Just because those officials don't like being told what to do. They panic when they meet a superior intellect. And as for my workers ... they never seem happy with their paychecks. Give 'em a million and they still wouldn't be content."

"We've tried everything we can to get them working harder," Kingsley sighed. "But there's nothing to motivate them. With the long shifts and the heavy labor, we've left them with no time or energy to enjoy the fruits of their work."

"Alright," said Tad with reluctance, "give 'em another raise."

"Beggin' your respect, sir, but a raise is not going to help. The union wants reassurances. A higher salary is no good to them if they're let go in a year, or six months, or three."

"So, what do they want? I'm here to listen."

"They want security. Annual leave. Pensions. Grooming privileges."

"I worked my tail off getting to where I am," said Tad. "These guys want everything handed to them on a saucer. If they want a free lunch, they're going to have to earn it."

"And security?"

"I can't promise anything. The city's in pieces. Now that the blue-collar dogs've been rounded up and sent back up north, I've lost all my cheap labor. Who knows whether we'll have another riot? Or another canine incursion?"

"I don't think that's very likely, sir. The mayor knows what he's doing."

"Really? Have you seen the mayor lately? Because I haven't. We're on our own, Chuck; that's the only thing that's certain."

Tad had reason to be negative. At the moment, Bast's inhabitants were concerned with the necessities of life—rebuilding their homes, restocking their pantries, and resetting their mousetraps. They weren't devoting a lot of thought or money to luxuries like Tad's gourmet products. He had two choices: wait for his customers to regain their old, complacent composures, or cut and run, and he wasn't about to do that.

"No more new hires. If things don't pick up, I'm going to have to trim the workforce. Tell them the harder they work, the more likely they are to keep their jobs. That's the best I can do in the present circumstances."

Back at her old job, Moira was an unashamed workaholic, pouncing on her papers as soon as she reached her office, packing as much as she could into her schedule. She didn't feel fulfilled unless she achieved something every day, eating lunch at her desk with one eye on her monitor and, unusually for a cat, only taking three morning naps (the two she took in the afternoon were mandatory). More than anyone else at City Hall, she appreciated having a job and strove to keep it. She'd experienced hardship growing up in the seedy side of town, mixing with dogs and nip addicts. But now the area known as the Doghouse was scheduled for a facelift. She was on track to own her own home after years of mortgage payments, and she'd built a reputation as a dependable member of the staff. Best of all, her background made her perfect for some tasks that her better-bred colleagues refused to perform.

Today, her schedule was disrupted by the mayor's absence. The city staff had expected him to be out of touch while he got his tooth fixed, but as the week drew on and he continually failed to return calls, they began to panic.

Moira wasn't the panicking type and did her best to soothe her workmates' concerns. Otto was probably sleeping after a dose of heady sedatives, with the phone unplugged and a muzzle of medicated gauze.

"He's not at home," fretted Woodrow, after receiving an update from a team of prowlers. "And he's definitely not at the dental clinic. It's closed, no sign of Dr. Futum."

"Where else might His Honor be?" asked Moira, trying to be helpful. She wanted to tell him about her encounter with the puma, but there was always the possibility that she'd be asked why she'd been visiting the dentist. She never had access to the mayor's highly secure itinerary, and there was no way she could afford to be one of Cal's patients; his fees were exorbitant. She would do anything to prevent herself from being implicated in the City Hall break-in.

"I don't know!" Woodrow shrugged. "Maybe he's delirious. Or he's fallen and hurt himself. Check the hospitals." Woodrow told his aide. "The meat market. The restaurants—the *Grand Canary* is his favorite. Everywhere!"

"He's a grown lion," Moira reminded him. "He can take care of himself."

"This isn't just a breach in protocol. It's a breach in security too," said Woodrow. "I've always known the whereabouts of His Honor, day and night. Since he was a little Honor-in-training."

"Don't tell me you want to cancel the rest of the day's itinerary?"

Woodrow took a deep breath. "No, no. The city can't grind to a halt just because its civic leader has gone AWOL. I'll have to act in his place until we find him. Get back to work, everybody. I'll manage this crisis on my own."

With several assistants in tow, Woodrow left Moira to continue her duties. To Woodrow, life was one big crisis after another, and woe betide anyone who didn't sympathize with his sorry lot. But this was a bigger upset than most. Moira wondered fleetingly if her mysterious attacker had had a go at Otto as well.

As she considered telling her colleagues about the puma, Woodrow was contacting the prowlers, Bast's expansive police force. He was presently visited by Lieutenant Cowl, a trusted friend of Woodrow and a veteran prowler who usually handled the constabulary's media relations.

"Haul in the dentist," Woodrow told him. "If you can root him out. Find out whether the mayor mentioned where he was going before he left Dr. Futum's clinic. I'll keep the press at bay."

"I'll grill the dentist." Cowl nodded. "Where else should we concentrate our efforts?"

"If His Honor's gone walkabout, then it'll be in the uptown area. Get out there and find our mayor, Cowl. This city's in a lot of trouble without him."

The mice stayed quiet in their boxes, cowed by the factory's noisy machinery and the smell of cats with sweaty paws and dirty dungarees. The tiny packages were taken to a loading bay and shipped across the city to grocery stores—

"Today only, BOEO bargains. Buy one, eat one!"

Food courts—

"Mall closing! Every mouse must go!"

Scratch matches and canvas climbing events—

"Live mice! Get your scurriers here!"

And restaurants.

"Come on in for the early mouse special. This ain't your first rodent!"

Bast needed a constant supply of live snacks; the population was never sated. Tad's factory was the only one in the city that could meet the demand, thanks to its hard-working, dedicated labor force.

Then there was Sal, who was singularly averse to hard work and dedicated to goofing off.

"They're moving too fast," Sal complained, his eyes flicking from side to side as he watched his colleagues' paws blur along the production line.

"You've got to keep up," Julius urged. "Keep going." Hunting for a job was tougher than holding this one down. Sal would have to work harder, more efficiently, or he'd make his friend look bad. Julius knew how important first impressions were in a new job.

"The supervisor's watching us, kiddo. C'mon, you can do it." The tabby's rally failed miserably. Sal seemed distracted, shifting from one paw to another, and it wasn't long before he disappeared into the restroom for the umpteenth time that day. Julius followed him, leaving the conveyor belt running full-tilt.

The john was damp and grease-stained. A line of sand-filled stalls smelled like they hadn't been cleaned out in weeks, but Sal wasn't using any of them. He stood at a bog-standard Guy Peters-brand sink, dipping a paw into a paper bag. He withdrew a small pouch that he held up to nose, inhaling deeply. An ecstatic look transformed his face, and Julius's appearance did nothing to spoil the expression.

"What do you think you're doing?" Julius snatched the pouch from his friend. "What've you got there?"

Julius sniffed at the prize and was transported into another realm. He lost control of himself, writhing, clawing at the pouch, trying to get at its contents.

"Strong stuff, ain't it?" Sal giggled as Julius fell to the floor, curled so he could clutch the pouch in all four paws. "Got it from a colorpoint on Eno Bridge. He says it's primo stuff."

Julius struggled to regain his senses. So Sal was a catnip addict. Julius cursed himself for not recognizing the symptoms—the snowshoe's wide-open pupils, his laid-back attitude, his addled mental faculties.

With all his will, Julius kicked the nip under a sink, skooching away from it and shaking his head to wake himself up. He'd allied himself with a "nipper"—a fool with a serious addiction to catnip—and someone could come into the restroom at any minute and get them both arrested for possession.

Holding his breath, holding the pouch an arm's length way, Julius dumped the nip in a litterbox and covered it over quick. Then he washed himself fastidiously, powerless to prevent himself from savoring the taste of the drug on his pads.

"I wasn't taking it," said Sal. "I mean, I haven't, not for a long time. Not since the riots. I was looking at it, that's all."

"I don't believe you," said Julius, gulping in deep breaths of latrine air. "Now, let's get back out there before we lose our jobs."

"No." Sal looked at his paper bag sadly, examined it with his nose, then stood at the exit, barring Julius's departure. "I'm not a user. Not anymore, believe me."

Never trust a nipper, that's what Julius had always been told. Addicts were unpredictable, prone to mood swings, selfishness, and are often hysterical. In his years as a reporter, he'd covered many a cat-fight over the demon drug, seen average cats turn to a life of crime to fund their habit, and watched as the health of young cats deteriorated, victims of addiction. He'd seen many addicts abandoned by their friends and families too. It was the feline way, he supposed. Take care of yourself first, drop anyone who slowed you down. Julius wasn't like that, or at least he didn't want to be.

Julius was about to drag Sal out of the room when Faki the forecat came in, grabbing Julius by the scruff of his neck and dragging him past a notice that said NOW LICK YOUR PAWS. Before Julius could protest, he and Sal were shoved onto the factory floor.

"Dawdlers," said Faki. "I knew it. Wasting the company's time and causing me headaches. You're not paid to mess around in the bathroom, you know."

While Faki was busy with Julius, Sal retrieved his pouch from the litter box, dusting it off and stuffing it in his overalls. Julius was too cowed to notice.

Heads bowed, Julius and Sal returned to the clanking conveyors of the factory floor.

11

Caged

Moira was up to her whiskers in work, trying to catch up on the days she'd been gone. Her desk was piled high with memos, folders, and notebooks. She didn't mind the load, even though her Post-Its kept sticking to her fur. The grind kept her mind off the terrible events of the past week: the ambassador's murder, the puma attack, the mayor's disappearance. She wondered if they were all linked in some way.

Buried in her paperwork, Moira didn't see Hondo approach but she heard him, recognizing his gait immediately. "Why'd you wait so long to pay me a visit?" she asked, still beavering away.

"Still taking inventory after the break-in," Hondo replied. His voice was soft and youthful, despite his strength and maturity.

"Did the burglar leave any clues?"

"Clues? Sounds like you've been reading your mate's mystery books again." Hondo pushed a couple of files aside to get a close look at Moira. She felt drawn to his deep and dreamy emerald eyes, then blinked to clear her thoughts.

"Who's got time to read that guff?" She laughed. Hondo smiled back. "So no clues, then."

"No padprints, no saliva," Hondo said with a shake of his head. "Just a few stray white hairs that could belong to thousands of cats in this city."

"White?" She felt suddenly conscious of her own snow-pure fur.

"Might even have been a Siamese." There was nothing threatening in Hondo's tone, but Moira's breath quickened anyway. She wondered if she was scared or excited. At that moment, it was impossible to tell.

"Good to have you here where you belong." Hondo backed off, replacing the files so that Moira was sheltered behind them.

"Yeah," Moira said quietly. "Good to see you."

Alone, she took a deep breath. Hondo had sounded friendly throughout their conversation, but she was sure she was one of his suspects. She wanted to bolt, but the security guards would be on full alert now, and she would have had no chance of escaping. She would have to sweat out the day and leave as calmly as she could.

Moira looked down at the desk. She'd unknowingly scratched grooves in its wooden surface, right there in front of Hondo. How suspicious was that?

The paper towers around her weren't getting any smaller, but she didn't feel like working anymore. She watched the clock instead, waiting impatiently for the end of the day.

Chico had suffered through some tough jobs in his time. His malting, ashen fur and jaundiced eyes were a testament to that. He'd joined the clean-up crew at a hairball hacking contest, bathed testy tabbies at the Senior Center until his tongue was fluff-covered and sore, emptied litter trays at the local incontinency clinic, and on rare occasions, when the family finances were really tight, he'd even schlepped alongside dogs.

His latest post was the worst of all: dangerous, treasonous, and as scary as could be. In a strange, dark space far from the city center, he was charged with what his latest boss described as a VIP—Very Important Prisoner—and Chico didn't want to be there any more than his captive. He had a home to go to, a hobby to pursue, and a life to preserve. As far as his boss was concerned, Chico's life wasn't all that precious. Chico disagreed.

Shivering in the gloom, he stared at the prisoner: regal nose held high in the air, fat nostrils flared, pacing about as if the very momentum of his walk would crack his cage open and allow him to leave. Each paw landed on the sawdust-covered floor with a muffled thump. As far as Chico knew, a creature like that could have the strength to bend the cage bars and leave at will.

"You're still here though," Chico said under his breath, watching the continuous pacing. The prisoner's swaying movements were considered and majestic, as befitted his blue-blooded background.

"Not for long!" the prisoner roared, shaking his mane. Otto was not a patient lion—if anything, he had less self-control than his mother. "And as soon as I get out of here, I'll use your spine for a toothpick, you whelp." Otto opened his mouth wide, showing off his dreaded chompers. Chico wanted to quit there and then.

He couldn't, though. He'd made a promise. If he broke it, he wouldn't be the only one to suffer; his wife and six kittens would be punished as well. That was how his boss worked—through fear and threats that extended to every family limb. So Chico kept his promise and kept his legs, for the time being at least.

12

An Unwelcome Guest

Down on the factory floor, Julius was getting bored with his repetitive task. "I forgot! I promised I'd walk Moira home from work—that is if they gave her her job back," he whispered to Sal. "I need to make sure she's okay."

"You want to check on her?" asked Sal.

"We can't. Not until we've finished our shift."

"Chatting instead of working again, eh?" Faki strode up to the two cats, noticing the smatterings of sand on Sal's clothes. Before Julius could make a move, Faki swiped the pouch from the snowshoe. Sal stepped back with a gulp, opening his mouth wide to protest his innocence again.

"It's his," he said, pointing a paw at Julius, "I told him not to bring it here."

Faki hauled Julius up with a how-dare-you look in his eyes. Sal kept babbling: "It's not his fault. This stuff is habit-forming. He's addicted, poor guy. You've got to feel sorry for him, the pitiable wretch."

Faki looked Julius up and down. "Yeah, he looks like a niphead to me. Don't know why I didn't spot it before." He took Julius to the warehouse exit, Sal toddling along behind. Their colleagues were so browbeaten, so intent on their work that they didn't notice. "We can't have your sort working here. You'll make a mistake. Mistakes cost money. Stay out of here." Faki threw Julius out of the building and glowered at Sal. "You stop gawking and get back to work."

Sal shook his head, standing by his friend. "This isn't fair," he said in a high-pitched whine.

"Welcome to the real world, runt," Faki turned his back on the sorry pair. "Fair doesn't exist around here."

Sal looked at the factory. He'd worked all day, and now he wasn't going to get paid unless he joined Faki back inside. Maybe if he did, he could get his nip back.

It was so noisy in there, though. So dark. And the work was laborious. He couldn't do it without Julius. Sal turned his back on the offending building and flicked his tail up in defiance.

Julius was fuming. "Last chance," he snarled at Sal. "If I so much as catch a whiff of that rot on your person again, our acquaintance is over. No more free bed and board, no more daft banter, no more helping you to get work. I have enough grief in my life without this kind of nonsense. Understand?"

"No more nip." Sal bowed his head, staring at the floor. "I've been clean for weeks, Mr. Kyle."

"I don't want to hear it," said Julius.

"At least now we can check on Moira."

Julius didn't respond to Sal's comment. "Coming?"

The two cats walked away from the factory without another glance back. After a few minutes, Sal asked, "You gonna stay mad at me?"

"I promised Moira I'd get a job. I never said I'd keep it."

All the city cats were taking a siesta now, warming their satisfied bellies in doorways or on street corners, anywhere that a patch of sun fell. They napped, tails twitching flies and fumes away. Julius and Sal weaved around the dozing bodies, tripping over outstretched paws, stifling their own yawns.

"There it is." Julius gestured at the domed opulence of City Hall looming before them, dominating the center. Sal swallowed hard.

"Mebbe I shouldn't go in there."

"Nonsense!" Julius blinked. "You're with me. I'm just as unwelcome as you are."

"Wouldn't it be better if we didn't visit Moira in the middle of the day?" Sal wheedled. "I mean, are you going to tell her you got yourself fired?"

"I am awful thirsty," said Julius thoughtfully. "I suppose Moira will be alright in her office, with leopard guards out front and pixie bobs working security inside..."

"There's the Milky Bar on Seventh and Elliot."

Julius nodded. "You're a smart cat, Sal."

"I am?"

"Let's go wet our whiskers."

Since he'd run away from home to become a tycoon, Tad had lost at least three fortunes, blowing all his riches on caviar and dodgy commodities. Now he was about to lose another.

In the short time he'd spent growing up, Tad hadn't been like other kittens. His idols hadn't been wrestlers or scratchers or prowlers. He'd looked up to fat cats: the ones who sat in executive suites, gave all the orders, and raked in the dough. He'd been a fast learner too. While his elementary schoolmates struggled through *See Spot Drool*, he'd tucked into autobiographies by the great business successes of the day: Seth Curcio's *Make Your Mice Pay* and the sequel, *Millions in Mice*; Perry Cartel's *Getting Financially Fat*; and best of all, restroom plumbing magnate Guy Peters's *Thinking Outside the Litter Box*.

For most students, the chief currency of middle school was lurid *Wonder Cat* comic books, not money or IOUs. But Tad had stuck to the *Furnancial Times*, bedazzled as he watched shares dance up and down the stock exchange from week to week. He regarded the bank district as his real school, the tabby traders his true teachers.

Overnight, he'd gone from being a pariah to the envy of his fellow pupils. He'd walked out of high school into a job, and within months, he had everything a young cub could want: a maid and personal chef, a house with wall-to-wall carpets and curtains to shred, a walk-in wardrobe with mirrors from floor to ceiling, and a notable private collection of dangly ribbons.

The only thing he lacked was a soul mate, someone who understood him and shared his proclivities. Yet even he never comprehended his compulsion to make money and succeed in business. All he knew was that his latest crisis was upon him. All of his current ventures had tanked, and he was desperately unhappy. He was driven by his need to avoid the terrible feeling that accompanied loss, rather than seeking some elated state.

Emotionally, he found his wealth and status almost as hard to live with as it was to lose. No one his age shared his affluence; the boardrooms were always filled with older, grayer, plumper felines. Their venerable condition alone was a measure of their success. They'd survived years of cut-gut corporate activity and lived to tell the tale.

At least he was in a position to call the shots and delegate and justify his lavish executive suite. He was part of the civilized set, an elite maker and breaker of big deals, the mastermind of company putsches and profit-pumped urban sprawl. Lord of all Vetoes, a force of fiscal nature, he was feared in the factory where he'd set up his headquarters.

He had a soft spot for the large, noisome building, always cranking out products and heavy with furry bodies. Tad liked to look down on his workforce, watching them toiling and wearing themselves thin. Never mind their homes or families or hobbies, their true function was to make him richer. Without that purpose, they would be useless, listless, and they knew it.

Since his latest financial loss, the factory had become the backbone of Tad's business. If the production line was disrupted, then he'd be in real trouble; bankruptcy was a distinct possibility.

Tad wasn't worried, though.

The factory had been busy since it had opened a decade ago, churning with packages produced in shifts that covered morning, noon, and night. Only once had the conveyor belts ground to a halt, singing replacing the cranking and shoptalk:

"We will, we will work for food
"But only when we're in the mood
"We want pay when we are sick
"Rest our paws worn to the quick."

It was a dark time in the factory's history that was never mentioned in company documents or in Tad's presence. Tad still had the occasional nightmare where his place would be empty—no workforce, no product, just a song echoing across the dusty floor.

"We want lengthier lunch breaks
"With free ham and salmon cakes
"We're not wishing to be crude
"We're not trying to get sued."

The reality had been worse than any of his bad dreams. The workers hadn't left, but they'd downed tools, curling up next to their stations; some purring, others chanting. The union had put them up to it. Tad hated the union.

Tad had stood before the huddled rabble, telling them he did not respond to threats and that they were going about their negotiations in a very poor manner. Hard work would be rewarded with extra responsibility; sitting on one's duff with one's eyes half-shut would mean zilch.

"We're tired and we need a rest
"Had to get this off our chest
"We will, we will work for food
"But only when we're in the mood."

Eventually, hunger, along with a fearsome guest appearance by the mayor, had broken the strike. The stoic cats had lasted all of eight hours before they caved and went to get fed. But Tad had never forgotten that day, and the workers had never forgotten that song.

"We're not trying to be slack
"We don't want to break our backs
"So when we are in the mood
"We will, we will work for food."

He couldn't rely on Otto to deal with any future strikers, so he'd devised his own plan to fix them for good. He couldn't wait to see its fruition—the very idea of it made him feel young and ambitious again. At last, he had a brave new goal to aim at.

With a faint smirk on his face, Tad stood up and looked out of the window. His smile disappeared; there was a commotion down on the factory floor.

A pile of backed-up boxes obscured the main production line. Tad's chief foreman, Faki, was yelling at a couple of cowering workers, ordering them to switch a conveyor belt off. The boxes kept coming, nudging each other along the belt and onto the floor. Remembering why he hated to delegate, Tad stomped out of his office to reprimand Faki. Someone obviously hadn't been doing a job properly.

The evening sky gave the crisscrossing power lines a caramel tinge as Moira trotted home from work. She'd waited for Julius for a while, lingering on the City Hall steps while her colleagues passed her by, all done for the day. She'd watched them and every passerby, looking for Julius's trademark crinkled whiskers, his fedora, his endearingly wobbly walk.

No joy. Her great protector was probably back home, working on some dumb new Tiger Straight project. How could he exist, thrive even, with his head in the clouds, writing novels that made no money? Why couldn't he stop wasting his life, his intelligence, and start earning a steady crust like she did? *A Clockwork Mouse*, that's what his latest mystery book was called. As if folks wanted to read such tosh. If not for her, he'd be hungry and homeless, without so much as a cardboard box to call his own. She was a soft touch, and he knew it, though not enough to propose to her. Perhaps their age gap made him hesitate; she was ten months younger than him, a big deal in cat years.

But that gap was no excuse for his infuriating behavior. The way he'd pretend not to hear her when she asked him to do something, and when he did hear, pretending not to understand her. Or the way he'd take a week to get around to a simple chore that only took two minutes to complete. Or the way he could leave trash and newspapers and empty milk cartons lying around the living room, stinking up the place as if they weren't there at all. He was a hero, a nuisance, and a slob all rolled into one fat package.

"I could do worse." Moira smiled to herself, turning her thoughts to her workday. "I could be stuck with a preening idiot like Woodrow." With the mayor temporarily out of action, Woodrow was making changes. The puffed-up politician was enjoying his moment of glory, ensuring that everyone knew he was in charge and firing anyone who wasn't happy about it, reshuffling official positions and ruining old enemies. It was as if the devious feline thought Otto wasn't coming back, which was crazy, of course; Otto always came back.

With her doggy-stained pedigree, Moira's job was secure, so she wasn't worried about that. She sincerely wanted détente with the dogs across the mountains, overseeing the voluntary repatriation of their breed to their old homestead. Many dogs had moved to Bast looking for work, but the recent riot had shattered any illusions of job security for them. At present, there was an incredible amount of tension between the two species, and no amount of positive community action could fix that. Up past Carabas, in the far North, the few cats still living on dog territory were carefully monitored and treated with suspicion. There weren't many dogs left in Bast, either; most of them had fled the city, their kennels wrecked. Moira was doing her best to improve relations, helping the hounds who wanted to go back across the mountains, diverting public funds to cover the cost of their arduous journeys. She hoped that they'd come back once anxieties had eased.

Though the city officials had hampered her work, at least she'd brought Julius around to her way of thinking. Dogs were worthy of the same consideration afforded to cats in Bast and beyond.

As she passed a shop doorway, she bristled, thinking she'd heard something. The store was boarded up like so many on Miro Street, abandoned, economically whipped by the big multipurpose places downtown. Convenience stores placed far from many citizens' homes in a most inconvenient manner.

Why am I jittery? Moira wondered, walking faster now. *I can take care of myself.* There was no one there, not even a shadow to scare her. Only the sound of the wind playing chase through the holes in the awnings. *Yeah, like I took care of myself last night, sure.* Where was Julius?

She had to talk to Woodrow, confront him whisker to whisker, gauge his intentions. What she was doing was too important to be stymied by his macho posing.

Cats and dogs had to get along; the alternative was all around for everyone to see, horribly embodied by the tatters of the riot.

Tomorrow. She'd do it tomorrow. First, she'd give Julius a good piece of her mind. She'd reached her own block now, had a nod to her neighbor Lovie, wrinkled her nose at the stinkweed massing in her front yard, entered her house, and allowed herself a slight laugh. She'd made it home without being stalked or attacked or yowled at by some randy tom.

A furry lump sat on her sofa, lights out, the remote control nestling in its usual place, tucked between two cushions. Moira dropped her briefcase and fired both salvos.

"Where were you? You said you'd come get me. I waited for ages. I was worried about you, you daft—."

She was struck silent as the shape rose from the sofa, impossibly large, reaching toward her. The puma had been waiting for her.

13

Stray Cats

The puma reached out toward Moira, and she backed up, fumbling behind her for the flap. Instead, she grabbed her precious scratching post, raised it, and swung for her attacker. He brought his paws together, clenching at thin air, mesmerized for a moment by the fast-moving object. The enchantment ended when the post crashed down on his head.

Flattening his ears, he shrugged off the blow and pushed Moira against the flap. The latch dug into her back—she was so close to escaping, but the puma was upon her. Clamping his greasy pads over her face, he dragged her across the living room with the Siamese scratching and snarling all the way.

In the evening gloom, she hadn't seen the small carry-case next to the sofa. As Toxic angled her toward it, she fought fiercely, pulling away from him, getting snatched back and crammed into the case.

"Don't make a sound," Toxic hissed, "or I'll skin you alive." Moira believed him, yet as he fastened a black cloth cover over the crate and hauled it out of the house, she heard herself emit a sad mew.

The crate smelled of new plastic. Her limbs were cramped, and she needed to pee. Surely someone would see the suspicious character, challenge him? No, no one did that in Moira's neighborhood. They remained aloof, protecting their own territory, wishing each other well while remaining on the defensive at all times.

"Where are you taking me?" she asked, scratching at the plastic.

"I told you I'd skin you and I meant it," she heard Toxic's menacing reply and clammed up, wondering why she was still alive.

With a straining, wrenching clunk, the conveyor belt seized up, its gears crammed with cardboard. Boxes had been spewed across the factory willy-nilly, their labels confused and merchandise bruised. Tad was his usual calm self, not allowing himself to freak out in front of his workers.

Faki was doing all the shouting for him, getting the drones to pick up the packages double quick time.

"It was two new twerps, sir," Faki told his boss. The foreman was out of breath from all his bellowing.

"Deserted their post. Left early. Didn't even clock out." He held out their punch cards for Tad to inspect.

"You hired these shirkers?" Tad asked, carefully reading the names on the cards: Julius Kyle and Sal Finney.

Faki bowed his head in confirmation.

"Don't leave here until all these goods are back in their proper places," Tad told him, eyes narrowing. "No overtime. Just get it done."

Tad returned to his office up on high, leaving Faki to seethe with anger. He wasn't mad at his boss for giving him extra work; he had other targets at which to aim his hate.

"Get on with it!" he told the drones. "Clear a path through these boxes so everyone can get by!" Once a little space was clear, he began to inspect the conveyor belt, disgusted by the damage Julius and Sal had caused with their negligence.

Moira could hear a loud, metallic rattling—they were near the tramline. *Now someone will see me,* she thought, throwing herself against the sides of the crate, jostling, pounding. The puma kept moving, not even bothering to threaten her again.

She couldn't keep the joggling up for long. Tiring and short of breath, she sat still with her paws tucked underneath her body, determined to start up again as soon as she was able. She wouldn't give up.

If she'd known that Toxic was entering the Central Station at the time, she wouldn't have taken a breather. The place was full of commuters, porters, vacationers laden down with cubs and other baggage, security staff, and vagrant shorthairs. Although they were all focused on their own business, doing their jobs or finding their trains, getting to their destinations, one of them would have noticed a rattling box dragged by a burly puma. But no one looked at him twice as he hauled the crate onto the 08:00 to Carabas; it was just another piece of carry-on luggage.

Toxic shoved the crate into a private compartment and removed the cover. "Come on out," he growled, opening Moira's poky cage. She didn't move.

After all her struggling and complaining, Moira didn't want to leave the crate. She could see that the compartment was locked; she would be moving from one confined space to another. She felt safer in the crate and didn't feel like cooperating with her captor.

"This is the only break I'm giving ya. Get out or ya stay in there the whole trip." Slowly, her face shining with defiance, Moira left the crate and stretched her limbs.

"We're going north?" She placed her forepaws against the window, recognizing the countryside. Toxic pulled the shade down and motioned for Moira to sit down.

"Express to Carabas. No stops, no escape. Behave yourself, and you can stay outta the box. If anyone comes to check our tickets, say nothing. Let me do all the talking."

"Sure, you're a real conversationalist. Friendly sort, too."

The puma looked at Moira as if he was about to take a swipe at her. Then he smiled, showing rows of jagged teeth. "Yeah. I'm a regular Puppy Happy."

"Who are you doing this for? Anyone I know?"

Toxic pushed his nose up against Moira's. "You think you're so much better than me? I know where you're from and where you're bound. So I'm in charge now." He sat down in a seat opposite his captive. "No more chit-chat."

Moira tried to conceal her fear, breathing hard through her nose while retaining eye contact with her catnapper. If she wasn't allowed to talk, then she'd curse him with her stare instead.

Her mind spun with escape plans: the window wasn't latched; the ticket collector would soon pay a visit to the compartment; if the train was full, other passengers might try to get in, looking for a seat. The puma would be distracted, and Moira would take her chance. Only two words quelled her hopes:

No stops.

<hr>

Julius and Sal's whisker-wetting had turned into an all-nighter of drinking, sorrow drowning, and terrible singing on the wall behind the Milky Bar. When Julius saw the sun rise and finally dared to check the time, he was filled with dread. It was in his nature to be self-centered, but he knew that evading Moira was wrong. She had always accepted his flaws; why try to hide his latest failure from her?

"Why do I ever listen to you, Sal?" he said, his stomach churning with a sour milk hangover.

"Because I'm a smart cat," said Sal.

Moira was not at City Hall that morning; it wasn't like her to oversleep. Julius's sense of dread worsened.

"Let's go home. No more dawdling," Julius snapped as the two cats took a shortcut behind a fishmonger's. The alleyway was littered with rotting fish skeletons, discarded by other citizens who'd used the shortcut and got waylaid by a finding in the dumpster. Julius kept going, though. He wasn't distracted by the strong smell of herring wafting from the trash, or the heaven-scent of fried chicken from the fast-food joint next door. Instead, he was stopped by a Coming Attractions poster outside the downtown theater, advertising *Wonder Cat! The Musical.*

"Impossible," Julius grumbled. "How come I never heard about this?"

"You should read *The Scratching Post*," said Sal, peering at the small print on the poster.

"Can't." Julius shook his head. "Makes me angry."

"You're jealous 'cause all your friends are still writing for the paper and you're not?" Sal suggested, batting his eyelids.

"How could they do this?" Julius fumed.

"Well, they get some singers, and some cats that can dance, and they dress 'em up in costumes and people pay—."

"Right. Audiences pay to see this froufrou garbage. Advertisers pay for those blooming radio shows. I deserve a piece of the take."

"We'd never have to work again," said Sal.

"*I'd* never have to work again. You need to work on your ... problem. Follow me."

Julius decided to make one more detour before he met up with Moira. He led Sal across town to a fancy office building near City Hall—the nicest part of Bast. To his surprise, his old publisher, Boston Tarjé, agreed to see him straight away.

Boston's office had undergone a total redo after the riot when crazed kitties had run amok among the books, shredding records and stealing his favorite antique paperweights. There were still a few faint claw marks on the ceiling, where a margay had clambered up to the cornices in his frenzy. Fortunately, a must-buy book about the uprising had paid for the renovations. Now the room was fully carpeted—not just the floor but the walls, too, ready to scratch at or brush against, soft as a mother's belly, comforting as warm milk. There was nothing comforting about the red paisley patterns, however; the brazen décor matched Boston's personality.

Book awards adorned Boston's desk: some gold, some clear plastic, all ostentatious. Julius didn't have any awards; he didn't have an office either. This confrontation was long overdue.

"No meetings to run off to?" Julius asked. "Not like you, Boston."

Boston was heavy-set with graying ears, rose-tinted glasses, and a fake-smile mouth that seemed to have too many teeth. He gave Julius a friendly sniff and tried to do the same to Sal, but wrinkled his nose and backed off at the snowshoe's body odor.

"This is a far cry from your previous digs," Julius told him, shedding on an expensive leather couch.

"The past year or so's been quite kind to me, J. Gone into the broadcasting biz. There's a whole city-load of rubes desperate for a form of escape. A good radio show to take their minds off their real-life troubles."

"The spin-offs from my novels haven't hurt, I'm sure," said Julius.

"Now, you know full well that you sold me the rights to those works long ago. I secured them in good faith, for perpetuity and beyond, in all the known universe, for all media invented and not invented yet ... You were in a tough spot, and I helped you out, right?"

"I was desperate," Julius said, as much for himself as for Sal. The snowshoe had taken a rare, leather-bound book from a shelf and was slowly turning the pages, his lips moving to the rhythm of the words within.

"You always used to say you had plenty more ideas where those came from," said Boston. "*Mea culpa*, the last thing I want to do is alienate a nest egg like you. But what's fair is square."

The ideas had stopped flowing long ago, and Julius found it much harder to write now than he had as an idealistic cub. He'd lost that innocent belief that everything he wrote was worth reading, stymieing himself in the process. He wasn't going to tell Boston that, though.

"What about my idea for a juvenile mystery book?" asked the peeved puss. "That was perfectly viable. Why did that get shelved?"

"You used too many big words, baby." Boston shrugged.

"Patronize much?"

"It was too scary for the little 'uns," Boston added.

With a loud rend, Sal caught a claw in one of the rare book's pages. He put it back where it came from, hoping Boston wouldn't notice.

"Too scary? They *love* to be scared," said Julius. "It's the adults who can't cope with anything out of the ordinary. If the mommies and daddies had their way, all stories would be mundane, sanitized into redundancy."

"Come on now," said Boston. "There's a lot to be said for a predictable tale that sticks to a reassuring formula. I've made my fortune that way."

"And what about *my* fortune?" asked Julius.

"You had your opportunities, back in your best-selling days. What you did or chose not to do with them is your business."

"Maybe there's something in your contract that says you can stop them using your characters," Sal suggested.

"What contract?" Julius sighed. "We just spat on our paws, shook, and that was it."

"It was a furball agreement," said Boston.

"Very funny. You think I was naïve? Well, you're right. I wanted to learn everything about your business from working with you. Took a cut in royalties, offered to help you out with whatever I could—the amount of publicity I gave your books in my *Scratching Post* columns!—and agreed to whatever you wanted me to. All the troubles in the world are due to contracts..."

"If you so say. What do you want with wealth? If you wanted money or power, you wouldn't be a writer, right? All these years spent fretting and jotting could have been spent building a career in a mighty corporation. Smart cat like you could be Boss Almighty by now. Manager of a smoked salmon cannery, a feline freedom-fighting wheeler-dealer in radical politics ... Bastet above, you could have been mayor. You chose a different path, didntcha? One where the pay sucks, but you get to do what *you* want to do."

"I was hoping to make enough off my books to retire."

Boston laughed. "Writers don't retire!"

"No, they don't, do they?" Julius replied sharply. "They just keep on making money for their publishers."

"Why don't you write something light and frothy? That's what our readers really like. Nothing too taxing. Say what you like about dogs, but they love their *Puppy Happy* books. Stories full of cute mutts with waggy tails and sugarplum hearts. Why can't you write a cat equivalent of that?"

It had grown dark, and the trams had stopped running. "We should be getting back," Julius said to Sal.

"Moira will be going pure mental." Julius wondered why he'd offered to visit her at work. "She probably expected me to pick her up and everything. I'm toast." He turned back to his publisher. "Boston, you can keep your money. I have more important matters to worry about."

Without bidding adieu to the bemused businesscat, Julius and Sal rushed out of the Boston Broadcasting Company, across the street, and up the steps of City Hall. There were no lights in the windows, no scratching sounds from within.

"I think we missed her," Sal said quietly.

"You reckon? We'll catch up with her at home. Don't be your usual random self, okay? Moira will be on the warpath."

"Take my private tram," said an apologetic Boston as he stepped out of his office building. "My secretary will show you the way. Take the jewel-encrusted passage to the ornately carved archway at the back of this place. My personal driver will get you back to your house."

"Good to see he's spending your profits wisely," Sal muttered as he and Julius scampered down the stairs. "All those shiny jewels do look pretty though, don't they?"

Their pads were sore with a day's walking and working, so the two cats were glad to get a ride most of the way home. Tramlines led to the outskirts of the Doghouse, where they disembarked, thanked Boston's well-bred driver, and ran to Moira's house.

The house was a mess—ornaments smashed, furniture upturned, milk dribbling from a gaping wound in the fridge.

"Maybe she's in the middle of a makeover," Sal attempted to reassure his friend.

Julius knew what had really happened. He felt terrible. He couldn't blame Sal for dragging him off to a bar when he should have been watching out for Moira. He was a grown cat who took responsibility for his actions. But he was too worried about Moira to wallow in guilt. "We need to tell City Hall. Call the prowlers. Better yet..."

"Take a nap?"

"Where do you go if you've lost something?" Julius asked, looking at the marks on the floor left by the carrying case.

Sal thought for a moment, his eyelids drooping with fatigue. "Lost and found," he yawned.

"You got it. I'm going to the Stray Cats Bureau."

The entrance was too narrow for comfort, a skinny, little slot in the wall. Julius almost missed it entirely, slinking by, then turning around to sniff at a tiny black sign that read:

STRAY CATS BUREAU

Julius's whiskers helped him to judge the width of the entranceway as he squeezed through.

Inside, a loose straggly line of cats waited in an antechamber. The cats were bred with being orderly, rolling on the floor, licking their particulars, or scratching at the wooden statues that stood on each side of the room. The statues depicted famous cats who had wandered off, away from the civilization of their respective neighborhoods, never to return: Twitch Shackleford, lost in the last slightly chilly ice storm; Guglielmo

Macaroni, gourmet chef and inventor of the codnut, a fish-flavored donut—he had vanished along with his secret recipe; Amelia Hairheart, a traveler so intrepid, she'd explored herself off the map.

Since the statues were based on sketches and photographs, some likenesses were more accurate than others. The bureau didn't care; it wasn't as if the originals would come back to criticize.

When Julius and Sal walked confidently to the head of the line, none of the waiting cats complained. They'd been waiting so long, it seemed, they'd lost all sense of time and judgment.

Julius and Sal took the first turn they came to. There were no more signs to help them, and the corridors were poorly lit. They eventually found an office where a sphynx was leafing through a stack of papers. He wore a black name badge and a haughty expression.

"I need your help, Weems," Julius said, reading the badge. "I've lost someone very dear to me."

"We'd love to help, sir, we really would."

"Should I describe her?" Julius asked.

"What?" The sphynx kept leafing.

"Do you want a description?"

"Of what, sir?"

"Not what. Whom. Moira Marti, average height, stunning green eyes, a heart-shaped face, and an attitude."

"No, I don't need a description." The clerk finally looked up from his work. "Siamese, did you say?"

"I sure did."

Sal scrabbled at a filing cabinet, using a tentative claw to poke at a drawer marked "W." Weems shook his head, and Sal slowly pulled his paw away.

"And where was she last seen?" Weems asked with an impressive lack of interest.

"City Hall. Her office. She works hard."

"I'm sure she does. I'll need you to give a description of her to the lad curled up over there."

"But I've told you what she looks like!"

"Not my job, sir. Everyone in the bureau has his own role. I take note of places, addresses. My colleague marks down any distinguishing physical characteristics..." Julius showed the official his distinguished rear end, striding over to the curled-up colleague who reposed within earshot of Weems.

"Not disturbing you, am I?"

"Why, no," said the colleague. "I was resting my eyes is all."

"I was wondering why you don't write down people's information in one go," Julius to the clerk, whose badge said "Curly." "You must've heard me describing Moira."

"I wasn't ready."

"Are you ready now?"

"One moment, please." Curly hollered for a secretary, who hurried from a desk in a dark alcove. The secretary stood poised, ready to take notes with a stylus.

"Okay, she looks like this—."

"Description of Moira Marti," Curly dictated to the secretary, "reported missing this morning by one Julius Kyle of ... where are you from?"

"We both live in Miro Street."

"The Doghouse?" Weems asked with a twitch of his whiskers.

"Yeah." Julius nodded. "Number Three. But she disappeared downtown."

"Julius Kyle of Three Miro Street, The Doghouse," Curly continued his dictation. "Described as follows."

"Look, we're wasting time." Julius, who had lost his patience by now, snatched the stylus from the secretary. "Why don't I write down Moira's particulars so we can move on?"

"That's not how we do things here," Weems grumbled, retrieving the stylus and giving it back to the secretary. "I'm sure you're concerned about Mertha—."

"Moira," Julius snapped, his eyes narrowing.

"But we care deeply about these problems," Weems continued.

Julius didn't feel reassured, but he did as he was told, giving the officials all the information they required to complete their hallowed forms.

"So, you gonna put out an all-paws bulletin for her, or what?"

"It doesn't work quite like that," Weems explained. Was it Julius's cynical imagination at work, or was the snot *smirking*? "This form has to be checked and signed off by our superior."

"Why can't you do it?" Julius wondered.

"I haven't been trained to do that," Weems told him, as if he was sharing a national secret.

"Well, where's this superior of yours?" asked Julius. "Can he do it now?"

"He won't be here for a while," Culy said in an apologetic tone. "Rest assured, Mr. Kyle, the wheels have been set in motion."

"I need you to take some action!" Julius raised his voice. "I'm not leaving until something gets done." He sat on the other side of the office, seething with frustration. He chewed the leaves of a potted plant, trying to calm himself down. After a while, he noticed a portly, smoke-colored nebelung, luxurious fur forming a ruff around his neck. The nebelung watched Julius closely.

"They're wasting your time," the nebelung told him softly.

"You one of them?"

"I work here." The nebelung flashed a badge that read, "Johannes." "But sometimes if I'm really good, they let me perform some simple, idiot-proof tasks across the street."

"In City Hall?"

"That's right." Johannes joined Julius in his plant nibbling, choosing a leaf opposite. "Now and again, I come across an outspoken young filly called—."

"Moira! Have you seen her?"

"Not recently, no." Johannes lowered his voice, risking a sideways glance at the officials. They were busy processing their forms, making a point of ignoring Julius. "But I do know that she's one of the few cats who can calmly and effectively communicate with dogs. It's almost as if she's one of them sometimes."

"What's happened to her?" Julius asked.

"I don't know. But it could be something to do with her diplomatic skill. I'd start my search northwards if I were you."

Curly stared over at the pair of whispering cats, who stopped mid-chew.

"I've said too much," Johannes said as he swallowed his saliva. "You should go now."

Julius left in a huff, as frustrated as most of the bureau's visitors. He had one last stop to make, a last straw to grab before he set off north after Moira. It was the last place he'd ever expected to find himself again, one that he'd spent many long years of drudgery—the offices of Bast's longest-serving broadsheet newspaper, *The Scratching Post*.

14

Inky Wretches

THE CUB DETECTIVES

BY JULIUS KYLE

Bryce was a scaredy cat. Every time he saw a shadow in his bedroom, he'd cower under his bedclothes, imagining a dog in his closet. Of course, it always turned out to be a coat or a lampshade instead. Whenever he heard a bump in the night, he'd mew for his dad, quivering with fear like a jelly in an earthquake. Of course, the sound was made by the rusty old pipes in the pantry.

When Bryce smelled a bad smell, he'd start to cry, sure that he'd whiffed the oozing ectoplasm of a wandering ghost. Of course, the smell came from his brothers and sisters passing gas in their sleep. So Bryce was a scaredy cat. He couldn't help it; it was in his nature to be petrified by the slightest pin drop.

One night was particularly dark and spooky. Clouds obscured the moonlight and Bryce couldn't sleep. It was his own fault; he'd slept in a patch of sunlight the whole day long, and now he was wide awake.

When his closet door swung open, it made a loud, hideous, creaking sound that almost frightened the fur from his body. He scampered under the bed and stared at the closet, his bright green eyes piercing the gloom.

Moira felt sleepy, rocked gently from side to side by the train, and tired from her ordeal. She rubbed her paw slowly across the carriage window beside her and her eyes were half-closed when a ticket collector scritched his way into their carriage.

"Tickets please."

Toxic stared at the insistent staff member.

"No ticket?" the collector asked sadly.

"I'm a fare dodger. You'll have to take me in." Moira pushed past the puma before he could stop her and moved to the corridor so that the ticket collector stood between her and her captor.

"Is there something going on here I should know about?" asked the conductor, still cheerful. Toxic offered him a bribe, producing a dead vole from his pocket and dropping it on the floor, but the official was having none of it. "Come with me, miss," he said, concerned now, turning his back on the black cat.

That was a mistake. The catnapper sprang, dug his claws into the ticket collector's shoulders, and threw him against the window, the glass cracking at the same time as his skull.

Moira was already running for the next car, looking for a bolt hole. She reached the end of the carriage and looked out at the fast-moving grasslands beyond the tracks. No stops, eh? She let go of the carriage, falling through space, then righting herself as she landed, shaken but intact.

She didn't even have time to catch her breath. A few yards farther down the track, something slammed into her side, knocking her flat. Moira looked up to see that the puma had followed her, and now he was jumping in front of her, panting and ticked off. Even in the open countryside with nothing in view but the far-distant mountains and the whistling, accelerating train, she had nowhere to run.

"Follow me." Toxic was following the train's rusty trail. "Civilization's this way."

"What would you know about civilization?" Moira hissed. "I'm not following you anywhere."

"You can stay out here and be a piñata for buzzard beaks if you want to. Me, I prefer survival." Toxic could tell that he'd won his argument. This female was stubborn, but wickedly sharp as well. "Let's go. The sun'll be right above us soon. Don't want to get stuck out in the noonday heat."

Reluctant, still sulking, Moira traipsed after her captor, listening for the whistle of the next train and possible rescue.

Bridget wasn't usually the kind of lady who'd cut and run, but with wild dogs on the streets of Bast and a treacherous son capable of culling her, she'd decided to take a wee holiday away from angry mobs, burning buildings, and the intense heat of media politics. As head of the MMA (the Monitoring of Morality in Advertising), she'd given countless speeches about decency and pure breeding.

This vacation had been longer than most. Any concern that her power base might be weakened while she holidayed was outweighed by more practical concerns—primarily preserving her own skin. So she sailed on, admiring the ocean's glorious blue hue, feasting on fresh cattle carcasses delivered by supply boats, and venting her frustrations on her captive underlings.

Her dining done, she turned her head slowly from side to side with a lazy aerobic roll, then lay down on a pile of satin cushions. Eyes closed, she listened to the salt water lapping at the ship's hull. The faint rocking motion reminded her of her cubs snuggled in their cribs, oblivious to their great destinies.

Her own destiny was uncertain, but she was sure that lying low had worn her patience to the quick. It would soon be time to order an about turn, go back to her home city, and reclaim her place as ruler of Bast. A lioness could settle for nothing less.

Moira didn't know why the puma had stopped following the railway; she assumed it was something to do with safety. She'd heard rumors of bandits and scavengers picking off broken-down trains, savages who'd steal scraps and eke out a scrawny existence in the Wildside. She appreciated the sense of freedom she felt in the grasslands, far from city grit and clamor. But Moira was glad that the puma was near, despite his cruelty, when she heard strange growls in the night. They sounded so hungry.

Toxic had found a hollow for them to sleep in, edged with thick, tall grass stalks perfect to peek through. Ears locked for approaching predators, he dozed, confidant that Moira wouldn't try to escape from the haven.

Moira couldn't help herself. As the moon rose and bathed the ground in a cool blue light, she had to leave the foxhole and take stock of her surroundings, try to find out where she was. The long grass made it hard to see anything on the horizon, but she kept moving, placing one soft paw after another on the moon-mottled earth.

Toxic stirred, making a smacking noise with his mouth. Moira froze, holding her breath. Her captor didn't pounce on her this time—he kept sleeping. So she took a few more steps away from the hole, sniffing at night scents borne on the breeze, every sense switched on and cranked high.

The farther she went, the braver she felt, relying on her strongest sense of all, her instinct, to keep her safe. Before long, her eyes made out a glint in the distance, something solid and metallic. She headed straight for it, moving forward until her paws connected with a shiny section of the railway track.

Now all she had to do was follow it in either direction and she'd get to Bast, or Carabas, or maybe a little station in between where she could call for help. Just because *her* train hadn't made any stops, that didn't mean that other trains didn't pick up passengers at certain points.

She trod softly on the sleepers with her sensitive pads, heading to her left in a direction she hoped was south. She cursed herself for not making note of how long the train had been moving when she'd disembarked; she'd been preoccupied.

After a while, Moira got used to feeling the regular slats beneath her slow down and speed up, the moonlight fading and reappearing as clouds crossed the sky. She moved even faster when she became aware of a rustling in the grass on either side of her, a constant movement as if something was keeping pace with her.

She hoped it was a curious rodent or some other nocturnal nuisance that wouldn't dare challenge her. Surely if the puma had woken up and traced her, he'd simply jump on her and drag her back to his shelter, not track her and sneak along so close to her.

Satisfied that she was safe, if not alone, she dared to look over her shoulder. That's when she saw the eyes. Dozens of pairs, yellowy green, too spiteful to belong to any cutesy bunny. They belonged to cats that were hungrier than Moira, craftier, and more used to the terrain.

The next time the moon popped out from behind a cloud, she was ready. She changed course, moving westward away from the tracks, keeping her head low and racing through the grass. She heard a patter as her pursuers followed her over the railway, closing in and trying to outflank her.

Ahead, Moira could hear rushing water. Behind, she heard savage, panting beasts and for the second time since her abduction, she actually wanted the puma's protection. But he wasn't there. She'd ditched him. She was all alone, and whatever happened next would be hers to deal with—and all her fault.

The rushing sound got louder, and she soon found its source—a deep, fast-moving river spitting up white froth as it hit a mass of big sharp rocks. Moira stood on the bank looking down at the cold blue water. As she tried to decide which way to turn, her hunters made the decision for her, leaving her with only one escape route. As they closed in, she got a decent look at her hunters for the first time.

Ferals. Wild, unkempt, uncivilized cats who'd eschewed regular life for a nomadic, unstructured existence. They were savage, unpredictable, cannibalistic scavengers. Moira counted at least twenty before they got too close for her to tell.

"You're not going to eat me," she told them, her voice sounding faint next to the surging river. The ferals laughed; she wasn't sure if they understood her tongue or not. They had their claws out, jutting their ragged tufts of paw fur dirty with marsh mud and old blood. One of them seemed to be the leader, a big-eyed, jag-eared tom, and he got within a whisker's distance of his prey before she snapped her own claws out and took a swipe.

This riled the ferals. They lunged, and Moira took the only way out she could, backward into the water.

Moira landed on a slippery rock, watching the bank to make sure that the ferals weren't following her. Not even the thrill of their chase would convince them to brave the rapids. But Moira wasn't safe—the torrent around her soon yanked her from her perch and she slammed against another rock, struggling to keep her nose above water in the darkness.

She tried to stay conscious. Moira'd spent her life trying to avoid getting wet. As an adult, the nearest she'd come to a river was crossing the bridge on her way to work every day. Now it was only her cherished memories of Pa, her surrogate canine father who had loved the water, and his enthusiastic doggie paddle that kept her afloat.

That's it, Hen. Keep putting one paw in front of the other. Take deep breaths, head for the bank, and think of all the cursed fleas you're drowning!

The ferals weren't following her by land as far as she could tell. They'd vanished in the grass. She wanted to head for the far bank with the water separating her from the scavengers, but the currents prevented her from doing that. So she kicked off from a rock and aimed for the closer moss bank instead.

Her head slammed against another crag obscured by the treacherous white water. Her breath came in short, sharp gasps by now, and she flailed, weakened. She was so close to the bank, but she had no strength left. Panicking, she grabbed onto a thick limb with her teeth and scrabbled for the shore. Moira was hoisted onto dry land where she found the limb was no tree branch. The limb belonged to Toxic, who'd waited for the current to pull her to him. Bedraggled, freezing, and almost senseless, Moira lay on the murky bank looking up at the puma.

"Like I toldja," he gloated, "there's nowhere to run."

In the reception area of the *Post* building, a security guard was reading the new edition of the paper. As he was asked for a visitor badge, Julius snatched a quick look at two front-page headlines:

OTTO IN SECLUSION?
NO OFFICIAL WORD FROM CITY HALL

TOP MAYORAL AIDE MISSING
"INDISPENSABLE" MOIRA MARTI AWOL

Julius left Sal to ponder the mysteries of operating a treat dispenser and headed for an office space that was a soulless shell of its former self. What had once been a bustling hub of noisy activity, full of cats on cushions yowling their stories into dictaphones, was now a carefully cubicled place with a skeleton crew of slow-moving, bored-looking youngsters who couldn't see each other over their partitions. They didn't look as if they could write their own names, let alone a story, and most of them seemed to be more interested in playing with the flecks of dust that floated in shafts of light throughout the room. No wonder the paper was looking so thin.

Lording over them all was Julius's old rival, Roy Fury. As jobbing journos, they'd competed for the same stories and Roy—the more ambitious of the two—had often won. Now he sat in a massive, padded swivel chair raised high off the ground, his back to his slack-happy staff. Julius climbed a set of shiny black steps to reach the newly crowned editor, scowling at the setup.

When Julius reached the top of the stairs, Roy spun around to face him. "I've been expecting you," he told the tabby with a strangely apologetic smile.

"Oh yeah. I was forgetting. The editor of *The Scratching Post* sees all and knows all."

"Editor-in-Chief," Roy corrected him.

"That means there's other editors, all after your job?"

"Enough with the sour banter. Look around you, J. The guy who owns this paper's nowhere to be seen. He's cut our budget more times than even I can recall.

This is a game to him, a piece of string to play with—only difference is, he expects this string to make him a profit."

"And you're dangling from the end of it," Julius interrupted.

"Newspapers do not *make* a profit unless they're well-written and sell lotsa copies," said Roy. "How'm I gonna sell any copies when my staff are cheapo, flea-bitten paper-pushers hired out of some lame recruitment office? I need good reporters. Guys who can string more than one word together, make the least cooperative interview subjects purr on a dime. I need you."

"I wish I could say I've always wanted to hear you say those words. I can't, and I haven't. I'm here because I'm desperate."

"Here's the deal." Roy jabbed a paw at Julius. "You get the full support of *The Scratching Post* and its multimedia offshoots, with all their information networking and ... well, wisdom and experience don't really come into it. But we'll do our utmost to get you on your way and help you find Moira, in exchange for some of your gritty insight into life beyond the city. Folks are so wrapped up in their troubles, they need to be reminded that there's a whole glorious world out there to amaze and distract them. Wire us your insights and when you get back with our babe in arms, we'll settle up, take it from there."

"I don't have a choice, do I?"

"Not if you want our help finding Moira, no."

"So where do I start?"

Roy clicked two claws together and one of the goggle-eyed office cats walked up the steps to join them. She moved slowly, at exactly the same pace that her colleagues performed their tasks. It was as if she was wasting as much time as she could between clocking on and her next milk break. But, eventually, she reached her boss's chair, extended a paw toward him, and gave him a folded piece of paper.

"A letter of travel," Roy explained as Julius took it from him. "A passe-partout signed by Woodrow himself. It will get you anywhere across the continent, gratis. Make sure you smile when you show it to anyone and don't lose it."

"I'll try not to." Julius examined the letter closely and saw that it had been countersigned by Swampy McMahon, the *Post*'s publisher and CEO, the biggest celebrity in Bast and yet another cat he didn't get along with. He wondered where his colleagues had gone, the crumpled sourpusses who had once filled the office with noise and inky odors.

"What about Chip?" Julius asked Roy. "He used to write a mean sports report."

"We laid him off, and he moved to Carabas. Liked their prim and proper ways, apparently."

"And Ace?"

"Retired."

"Ollie?"

"Don't know what happened to him. Wandered off one day, never came back. So I'm left with copycats and wannabe hotshots. They don't cost much and I've been training them up the best I can, but they don't learn much at journalism school these days. Why, half of them don't even know how to clean their claws." He scowled at an intern. "Where do you think you're going? You can't take those files out of here before I've checked them."

"I was just—," the intern began.

"Not before I've gone through them all." Roy's tone suggested that the intern was an imbecile. Julius knew that this was just Roy's way: he had two moods, bad or sarcastic.

"You were always into those chin-stroking, furry-feely pieces," said Roy.

"You mean social issues?" asked Julius, green eyes gleaming. "The everyday concerns of real-life members of the public?"

"Yeah, the soft stuff. Now that's what we need. Thought the low-denominator appeal would bump up sales, and it did, in the short term. But now our readers seem..."

"Dissatisfied?"

"Listen to the cat who swallowed a dictionary. Well, you know what'll bring 'em back. They need a bit of substance to go with their movie star gossip. You are Mr. Substance."

"I'm nothing without Moira," said Julius.

"We'll see. We'll see."

Clutching his letter of travel, Julius turned to leave. But he had one more question for Roy.

"Where is it?"

"What?" asked Roy.

"The noise. The din of the presses. The grinding, the thumping. The kind of clamor that makes my ears sing."

Roy shrugged. "All gone. No more scent stains, no more printing errors. No more stinging ears."

"It's too quiet." Julius wiped his paw across a bank of computers. He licked at his paw but tasted nothing exciting, apart from himself.

"Some cats are never content," Roy sighed. "Remember when we changed our logo? The move from that wishy-washy fishy smell to something more woody and solid, in keeping with the *Post*'s rep as a paper you could count on? The staff didn't like it. Our most loyal readers complained. But my predecessor Morris, Bastet rest his soul, stuck with it. He didn't budge and let's face it, he was so huge that he could hardly shift positions when he wanted to. We all got used to the new logo, even you, Julius. Now it's accepted. Everything gets accepted, becomes part of the oh-so-precious status quo, if it's around long enough."

"And I've been gone long enough for you to get used to my absence?"

"Not quite. The readers still miss you, like they missed that sad, old logo for a while. You never fit in here—you were too positive. You weren't cynical enough to make it as a great reporter. I guess the punters just got used to your hackwork over the years."

"I got my facts straight and the job done."

"But you never really wanted to be here, did you? You just did it to pay the bills. Well, like I say, for some weird reason you're missed. That's why we're prepared to bankroll your goose chase."

"Moira isn't a goose."

"No, you're right. She's a valuable member of the mayor's administrative team. Funny that she should disappear around the same time as His Honor ... did she ever seem attracted to her boss?"

Julius shook his head at the editor's snide suggestion. The thought hadn't crossed his mind until now. Otto's power could mesmerize the most sensible ladies in the land. But no, Julius knew Moira better than that. She had more taste; that was why she lived with him.

"I'll do it."

"Anything for a story, eh, J?"

"Anything for her."

Outside, the citizens hurried about their business. Julius wondered what was wrong with them. Didn't they read the papers? Didn't they care that Moira had been abducted? Couldn't they put themselves in his place? They'd stop their constant to-ing and fro-ing immediately if it was their mate they'd lost.

He passed a rack of gossip mags, saw an ad for a scratch match near the ticket booths. Fashion. Sports. Birdwatching. How could anyone concern themselves with trivia when life was so precious, so unduly short?

According to Roy, the conspicuously meaty puma had been spotted heading north. All northbound trains stopped at Carabas, a bridging point between Bast and the mountains.

"I once met a businesscat just back from a conference in Carabas," Roy had told him. "We were waiting for a tram on a seedy stretch of Freyja Avenue, with nothing better to do than chat with strangers. The traveler was a talkative soul anyway, his gabby gift having seen him through many a business deal.

"He explained why so many corporations liked to hold their conferences there—it was because the staging post was a chaotic mess of pubs, cathouses, and nightclubs, with few rules and less moral standards. Meetings ended early so that bosses could frolic with loose Carabians. It was a place of desperate souls and basest instincts."

"I'm surprised you've never been there," Julius had laughed.

"Change is afoot," said Roy. "A big clean-up thanks to the area's new governor. Communications with that wretched place have become few and far between. I need you to check it out and send back a report."

"What happened to the businesscat?"

"Don't know, don't care. But after the new administration kicked in, he was determined never to go back to that place."

"I'll do what I can."

Julius hoped that his journey would end in Carabas. He'd find Moira and file a report back to the *Post* to earn their passage home. He certainly didn't fancy his chances north of Carabas. Beyond the range lay a wasteland that few cats ever desired to visit; many miles farther on lay a coastal island. The Isle of Dogs. Vast, smelly, and full of toothsome hounds. Even the black cat would hesitate to go there.

A visit to Carabas would mean that he'd come into contact with visitors from the isle, who traded with cats using the bartering system preferred by dogs. Julius could cope with canines. Dealing with Tarquin, the increasingly powerful ruler of Carabas, would be a lot more difficult.

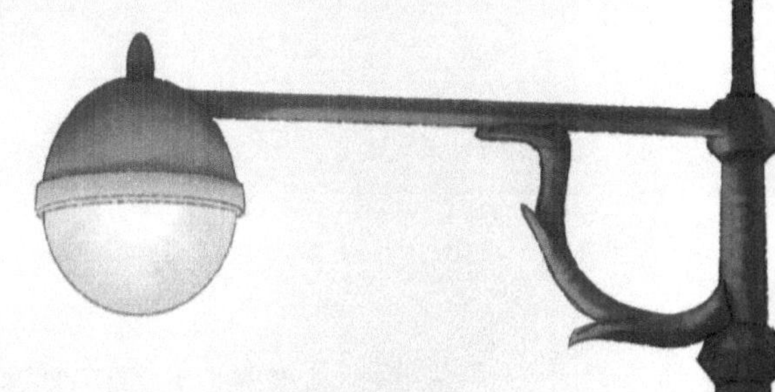

Part Two: Carabas

15

Rats on a Train

*In which Julius and Sal
make a military connection.*

The station was quiet so late at night, every sound echoing around its vaulted gray interior. Julius and Sal pelted toward Platform Eight, the tabby cat gasping for breath, his dopey friend tripping over a bobtail.

"Sorry pal," said Sal. "Didn't see your, uh…" The bobtail's extremity wasn't much more than a stump, so Sal's words merely added to the offense.

"How could you not see my tail?" the bobtail snapped. "What's wrong witchoo? You got hairballs for brains?"

"You could be right there," said Julius diplomatically, taking Sal by the shoulders and leading him away. "We don't have time for your nonsense. We've got to catch that train."

"I don't see what the problem is," Sal complained as they reached the platform. A whistle blew as the northbound steam train, the Windy Thistle, chugged to life. "So he doesn't have much of a tail. So what? You wouldn't hear me moaning if I had smaller feet."

Julius wasn't listening. The Thistle was leaving the station. He leaped for the train, finding a second wind and grabbing a handle, hoisting himself against a carriage. Sal ran along beside him, engulfed in a cloud of steam, trying to keep pace with the locomotive.

"Get in the carriage, quick!" Julius gasped.

"I'm trying," said Sal.

His fur bristling and eyes watering in the cold air, Julius rattled at the handle, trying to force his way into the carriage. Sal was slowing down, head bowed, still running as fast as he could. The platform's end was close now, though Julius was sure that Sal hadn't noticed. He had to choose—stick with the train and risk a nasty fall when he lost his grip further down the line, or jump off and help his clumsy buddy. He gave the handle one last tug, and his dilemma was solved. A conductor opened up for him, grasping him by the scruff of the neck; Julius reached out a paw and helped Sal on board.

The conductor looked down at the two friends, crumpled in a panting heap. "Can I see your tickets, please?"

They scrounged together enough change to pay for the trip north, one way, no stops. Once the captain was satisfied that they wouldn't cause any more trouble, he found them a couple of cushions to sit on and gave them some essential information.

"The buffet's in Car Three, litter trays in the rear," he snooted as he headed off.

"A buffet sounds good," said Julius, his stomach rumbling. "How long is it since we ate?"

"We had a snack half an hour ago," Sal reminded him, but that didn't stop his mouth from watering.

"Far too long. We'll seek out Moira, then get a bite."

"What with?" asked Sal as they worked their way down the train, checking every compartment. "We spent all our dough on my ticket."

"Let's just concentrate on finding Moira."

"Did she have any cash on her?" Julius hushed his friend, placing a paw on his own belly to stifle the gurgles.

As he was rattled from side to side, Julius recalled the last time he'd sought a lady on a train. His closest colleague at *The Scratching Post*, Camilla, had also been his lover. She had embarked on a journey north to cover a story and stir up some trouble. Back then. That time, Julius had hopped off before the train had left the station; there were too many dogs up north for his liking. Funny that back then, he'd been so desperate to get home, and now he'd put his life at risk to hitch a ride.

"Why should she go north?" Sal pushed past a disapproving tonkinese. "Cats are about as popular as a hot hairball up there at the moment."

"I don't think she had much choice in the matter. I'm wondering why the black cat wants to drag her there."

"I shudder to think," Sal replied, his fur bristling to illustrate. "Did I mention I get train sick?"

Julius checked the little compartments, not much larger than grocery cartons, with just enough room for passengers to curl up and take a nap between stations.

"What if she's not here?" asked Sal.

"She'll be here. Some sign of her, at least." Julius looked in the third carriage alone, hoping that he'd have more luck without the hex that was his friend. Sure enough, he found a clue while rummaging around an unoccupied compartment.

He recognized her scent, a heady bouquet of toasted mackerel sandwiches and department store perfume. He sniffed at a stray hair clinging to the windowsill; it glowed white in the sunlight that streamed through the pane. It matched her fur.

As his breath fogged the glass, he noticed the edge of a pad mark. Someone had pressed their paw hard against the window. He breathed hard, seeing more of the paw print and a word scratched with a dainty claw—*Puppy Happy*. Julius wasn't exactly sure what it meant, but it had to be important.

For the first time, he noticed a large sack on the luggage rack. *Even kidnappers need fresh undies,* he supposed as he stretched up on his hind legs, tail flicking with uncertainty.

"What in Bastet's name are you doing in here?"

A broad-shouldered lynx shoved his way into the compartment, his ears barely fitting through the door. A forked, furry beard drooped from his chin. He was dressed in army fatigues, and his sleep-starved eyes were fixed in a permanent squint.

"Uh ... this must be your bag." Julius backed away from the luggage rack and glanced at the window. The fog from his breath was long gone.

"Too right it is." The soldier checked his bag, satisfying himself that it hadn't been tampered with.

"I thought it belonged to a friend of mine. Have you seen a Siamese around here?"

The soldier breathed air in through his hairy nostrils, staring at Julius with deep suspicion. "Buddy, there ain't room enough for us two in here. Where would I hide a Siamese? Up my—?"

"She might have been in here before you."

"I haven't seen no one except you and some tick-et-taking prig. Now, if you're finished snooping, I have to get some shuteye before we reach Carabas."

"You stationed there?" Julius kept half an eye on the sack, watching for movement.

"I wish. I'm in the middle of nowhere, right on the border. Keeping the peace, twiddling my whiskers. We're not allowed to so much as scratch those dogs unless they attack us first. Can you believe that?"

"Hardly. You've been on leave?"

"Picking up supplies." The soldier patted his sack, and Julius thought he heard a faint squeal.

"Listen, if you see a big black cat with a Siamese in tow, let me know, will you? I'm desperate to find her. The Siamese, I mean."

"Staff Sergeant Barr," the soldier introduced him-self. "I'll do what I can."

It was time for Bridget's constitutional. She strolled around the deck, the sun adding errant freckles to pud-dles of sea spray. She passed a row of striped cushions, anchored in place by tiny silver hooks. Even the stron-gest northeasterly gale would fail to budge them.

Bridget kept walking, entering the cool shade cast by one of the ship's funnels. A state edict ensured that their whistles would not blow while Bridget slept, emergencies be hanged.

When surrounded by a vast body of water, most cats would have felt on edge and insignificant. Bridget was different. Larger, meaner, and more ambitious than the wretches around her, she reveled in her powerful reputation. If the sun was too hot, she would order Pollet to cool her with a fan; if the water became too rough for her, she'd command her crew to find dry land. Lakes were hers to be dammed, rivers to be bridged, subjects to be eaten if they grew too troublesome.

This had been Bridget's life, and the only animal who had ever dared trouble her was her eldest son—the mighty, crafty king of the beasts, Mayor Otto. She'd soon take him down a peg or two.

Thinking of her insolent heir made her crabbit right at the moment when she spotted something on the deck that made her fume. She stomped to the bridge, roaring at the captain.

"This is disgraceful!"

"Yes, ma'am." Captain Calvin Lear flinched at the lioness's entrance but tried to take her rage in his stride, determined to look confident in front of his first mate. "I'll have the crew see to it at once." Lear focused on the wheel, not looking Bridget in the face.

"Don't you want to know *what* I find so disgusting?" she asked, her voice still loud and ill-tempered.

"Something to do with your food, perhaps?" Lear struggled to turn around and face his passenger. One of his hind limbs had been replaced with a pegleg long ago, after a wharf tavern altercation with a sour milk-soused naval officer.

Bridget shook her head, her eyes locked on Lear. "Where have I just been strolling?"

"On deck. You saw something on deck that displeased you."

"There is a stain. Your swabs have missed a spot near the deckchairs. Who is responsible?"

"Ma'am, all of the crew help scrub the deck ... they've been working day and night to keep this ship squeaky clean for your pleasure."

"Then all of the crew is at fault."

Captain Lear scraped himself back to the wheel. "I'll see that they're sufficiently reprimanded."

"I will mete out the punishment," Bridget glowered. "Now."

Julius looked out of the window at the grasslands rushing by, wondering what creatures lurked in the rain-soaked undergrowth. It was a world alien to him, frightening and curious. He was glad the train wasn't scheduled to stop until it reached Carabas. He stared at his reflection, marveling at how dapper he looked, even with unwashed fur and a sleepless night. No wonder Moira loved him.

While Julius gazed out the window, wondering if Sal was having better luck, Barr stretched himself out as best he could on his seat, tucking his large, padded paws under his haunches. By the time Julius turned around to talk to him again, he was asleep. Julius watched the lynx's chest rise and fall to make sure he was sound asleep, then used the opportunity to reach up for the sack again. There was definitely something small and furry moving inside. Julius dug a claw into the tight knot and weedled it around, untied the drawstring, and peeked inside.

At that moment, the train lurched to a halt. Barr was thrown from his seat; Julius landed on top of him along with the sack, its contents scattering all across the compartment. As the two cats steadied themselves, their instincts sang at the sight of the mass of rats scurrying around, their pesky, little heads weaving left to right, ducking for cover.

"Don't let them get out!" yowled Barr, but it was too late. A few of the rodents had escaped down the corridor, heading for the engine. Avoiding the soldier's wrath, Julius chased after them.

"She's, er, a she. With white fur, long ears ... she hears everything I say, you know, even behind her back." Sal was trying to describe Moira to the conductor, but his memory wasn't his greatest asset.

"I don't recall taking a ticket from such a passenger." The captain looked closely at Sal, wondering whether he should throw the scallywag off the train. Seeing a blur in the corner of his eye, he looked down to see a fat black rat pelting between his legs. Sal almost collided with him as he sprang, taking a swipe at the vermin with his ticket puncher.

In the buffet carriage, the diners were delighted to see a couple of extra items that had not been listed on their menu—a pair of rats *al dente*, jumping from table to table until they landed in the mouths of two hungry cubs.

Julius raced toward the engine, looking from side to side, scanning nooks and corners until he found the fourth escapee in the engineer's cab. It had set its teeth into the engineer's left hindpaw, and blood already spat from the wound.

Back in the corridor, the black rat had no intention of biting Sal because it was having so much fun confusing the cat, running to and fro with Sal getting dizzy with the chase. The conductor put an end to the game by trapping the rodent between his paws, squeezing tight. Sal watched, hypnotized, as the rat's tail ticked around, writhing between the conductor's pads like a snake in a charmer's basket.

The engineer was faint with the surprise of getting bit, so it was left up to Julius to get rid of the attacker. He sunk his own teeth into the rat's rangy back and turned his head sharply, opening his mouth. The rat flew into the furnace and was crisped in an instant.

"Why did we stop?" Julius mumbled, his mouth full of greasy hairs.

"Something on the track," the engineer told him, steadying himself. Both cats wrinkled their noses against the stench rising from the furnace. "I sent a porter out to clear it. No sign of 'im."

"I'll take a look." Julius stepped out of the engine, impatient to get the train moving again. The landscape was flat and desolate. Through the harsh glare of the noonday sun, he saw cacti, puny trees, and the train track, stretching off into the horizon.

"Nothing there now," he hollered to the driver, who was already getting the train up to steam again. The wilderness was too quiet for Julius, used to the timbres of the city. He was about to return to the engine when he heard a scraping sound.

At first, he thought it was the train clanking back into action, but the noise wasn't metallic; it was organic. He hunched down, belly flat to the ground so that he could see the other side of the track between the wheels. He could also see the body of the porter, lying broken and bloody.

Julius bounded around the front of the engine to check the porter. There was no scent of the puma, so this probably wasn't his doing. From the wounds, it was obvious that the victim had been killed by something larger and more savage than a rat.

"Get this old rust bucket going!" Julius checked underneath the train, making sure that the killer wasn't hiding in the harsh shadows. He thought of Moira, fearing for her life. If her catnapper had thrown her off the train, she'd be at the mercy of whatever had struck the porter. It was a nasty, distracting thought.

Julius'd taken a thorough look on each side of the train and beneath it, too. There was only one place left to go. As the Thistle began to move forward, he scrambled up the side of the first carriage. On top were the most unlikely passengers he'd ever seen—a group of feral cats, fury in their round green eyes, hunger in their bellies.

Displaying their dirty claws and wicked teeth, they snarled at the tabby. Fortunately, the train's resuscitation made them stumble, giving Julius time to unleash his own claws and arch his back.

They attacked with a unanimous hiss, darting across the roof, their hind paws making tooth-tormenting screeches on the metal. Julius backed up as far as he could, marveling at the strong wind that bristled his fur.

The ferals were cats with all the civility, nonchalance, and optimism stripped away. They embodied Julius's wildest side, ferocious ancestral missing links with matted fur and hot tempers. They'd probably seen the roof as a vantage point, not expecting the train to move so suddenly. Julius remembered rumors printed in his paper about passengers ambushed and slaughtered by ferals. They were infamous for giving no quarter, taking no prisoners. Julius had to face them alone and meet their wild ways with his own.

"Excuse me," he asked, "are you sure you're on the right train? This is the express, you know. It doesn't stop 'til Carabas."

One of the ferals, dressed in dark blue rags, leaped on Julius. He kicked the creature away, hearing it roll to the ground with a grinding thump. Julius held out his paws, claws foremost, offering a spiky greeting to any comers. The animals didn't seem to care, rushing him, impaling their chests and shoulders on his claws, trying to get a purchase on his throat with their teeth. He spat, twisting his torso, shaking off a couple more cats.

Giving up the advantage of his solid footing, Julius retreated, leaping onto the pile of dried food, flicking lumps at his foes, trying to blind them. One latched itself onto his back and dug deep. Julius tried not to panic, knowing he'd be overwhelmed if he didn't keep moving.

He flipped over and rolled on his back, using all his weight to grind his attacker into the food while using his paws to protect his soft belly. Once he felt the assailant's grip loosen, he forced his way through the mob back onto the roof of Carriage Three.

"What's going on up there?" Sal heard the commotion above him and stuck his head out through an open window to investigate. "You're not allowed up there, J."

"I don't care, Sal. Clear the carriage quick, then get yourself to the next one."

"I hope you know what you're doing."

"Better than you do." Julius fought off a snarling oaf of a passenger. "Now hurry! These creatures are starving!"

Sal looked ready to climb up and help his friend, but instead, he complied with Julius's wishes. "They're just cats," the snowshoe mumbled, though the marks on Julius's back told a different story. The remaining ferals were wary of Julius now, outnumbering him considerably. Their leader licked his chops, uncertain, then blinked at his brethren and rushed straight toward the tabby.

Julius scratched at the leader's face, giving him a nasty cut on his eye. The leader hardly seemed fazed, and Julius was forced to back away.

"I can't leave them," Barr bellowed, saliva spilling from his mouth. "And you can't make me."

Sal sized up the soldier. All the other passengers in Carriage Three had evacuated as soon as he'd told them what was directly above them. Only Barr remained, still trying to bundle the wayward rats back into his sack.

"Fine," Sal pouted, snatching up one of the rats. It let out a squeal of complaint as the snowshoe ran out of the compartment and along the carriage corridor.

"Come back here with that!" Barr gave chase, loosing the rest of the rats in his haste. Sal disappeared into Carriage Two with the soldier gaining fast.

Behind him, Julius lowered himself through a hatch and dropped sharply to the floor. He pushed Barr into Carriage Two as the ferals streamed into the train. Struggling with the coupling, he asked Barr and Sal to help him.

Dalen, the feral leader, stopped and grunted. He was larger than his followers, eyes wild with paranoia, teeth broken, claws yellow with rot and filth, fur matted into spikey bristles, shoulder blades jutting from his back: there was nothing cuddlesome about this cat. He'd noticed the scuffling sound of the rats in Barr's compartment. The ferals found the rodents and feasted on them, buying Julius time to figure out the latch.

"Sal! Go get the conductor and tell the driver to pick up steam! Barr, you're good with knots, aren't you?"

"Wait—." Sal handed Barr his rat and got going. Julius looked at the critter with its sharp, gnashing teeth and dripped some blood from his forelimb onto the rope. With Barr protesting, he held the rat against the rope, and it began to gnaw.

By the time the ferals had finished off the rats in Carriage Three, the rope was almost severed. Julius added more blood to keep his rat interested.

"That's enough." Barr snatched his rat away. As Dalen prepared to leap into Carriage Two, Julius split the rope with his claw. The rear carriage was left behind; Dalen tried to make the jump, grabbing the frayed end of the rope. Barr shrugged and threw the last rat at him, and the leader was left tumbling down the track.

"Sorry," Julius said, catching his breath.

"You probably saved my ninth life. Don't think you're not in my bad books, city cat." Barr turned his back on Julius and went to find the buffet carriage. The tabby found a quiet compartment and began to wash himself, slowly, thoroughly, as if in a trance.

"I gottim! Here he is!" Sal interrupted Julius's ablutions. The snowshoe was followed by the conductor, who scratched the back of his graying ear.

"Where's my carriage?" the conductor asked.

"The ferals've got it," Sal told him.

Exhausted, Julius looked up at the conductor and said, "They didn't have a ticket."

Dalen shook himself and stood up quickly. He had to keep up appearances in front of his tribe—he had hundreds of followers and any one of them could attempt a coup at any moment. So he had to offer the ferals a sense of purpose, set them on the trail of their next meal.

He picked up the severed end of the rope and sniffed at it. A thin sheath from Julius's claw had snagged on the rope; it was enough to give the feral leader a scent. Leaping from the carriage, he slobbered on the track, pressing his nose against the sun-warmed metal. With a wave of his paw, he ordered his underlings to follow him, stumbling along the track, heading for Carabas.

A group of small, furry figures ran in the opposite direction, clumped together for safety. The remaining rats from Barr's collection headed for Bast, where thousands of ever-hungry cats would welcome them with open mouths.

16

All Cats
Great and Small

So *this is what Bridget does for kicks,* thought Captain Lear, his crew assembled before the lioness. *Humiliates my crew, and in the process, myself.*

"I know that you sailors dwell among legends as you make your living, thrive on marine myths and fish tales to wile away your long voyages. And rumors. A vessel without rumors might as well be empty, so little sound it makes.

"I've heard one such rumor," she purred, not bothering to raise her voice over the pounding waves around the yacht. "That some of you yoiks think it's bad luck to have a lioness on board a seafaring vessel. For those of you who are superstitious ... you're right. I'm bad luck for the lot of you. I haven't been with you for all that long a time, but it's obviously been long enough to make you slack. Slovenly. You're taking your honored duty for granted.

"This morning was the last straw," Bridget snarled at the captain. "I don't know who was the last moron to swab the deck and I don't care. The fact is, he was one sloppy-mopping moggy. All of you will be disciplined. Captain?"

Lear shrugged a shoulder. His crew was tough; few things fazed them. They'd been away at sea so long that they would welcome fifty licks of a cat.

"Send your first mate to that nasty, little secret store of yours. The one my steward accidentally took food from at breakfast time."

"Ma'am?" Lear squinted.

"Don't play the dunce with me. You know what I'm talking about. Bring the rest of that meat up on deck. I want your crew to sample it."

"I don't really think that's—."

"Do it, Captain," Bridget asserted her authority over Lear. "Or I'll make you swallow some as well."

The first mate hurried below to liberate the stores, soon returning with a large chest full of tinned food.

"Eat it," Bridget said between gritted teeth. "Every last bite." At this, the sea roiled and spat froth as if she really did have command over its currents.

With a nod from their captain, the crew sniffed at the meat, turning their noses up at its unappealing odor. "Sorry lads," Lear told them. "Do as the lady says."

As soon as they started eating the tough chunks, the cats began to gag and heave, grimacing as they chewed. Some of them ran to the side of the yacht and vomited into the water; others didn't make it that far. Bridget chuckled, stalking back and forth as they cleaned out the cans. The crew knew that if they didn't comply with her wishes, she'd bite their furry, little heads off.

"Throw those empty cans overboard," Bridget told Pollet, who had been spared the degrading punishment. As he did so, he noticed that some of the rusty metal canisters had labels on them with pictures of a cute Cocker Spaniel puppy surrounded by a cartoon border of intestines, liver, and kidney shapes.

"I hear they put goat guts in this dog food," he mumbled as he finished his task.

"Well, now this dog food has put cat guts on the deck." Bridget smiled. "Clean up the mess, Pollet, and make sure you do a good job. Or I'll cook up something worse for you."

Chico wanted to block his ears when Otto ate. The lion didn't nibble daintily on his gazelle as a typical mayor might; he bit and tore and crunched his way through his raw repast, hurriedly, as hungry for sustenance as he was for escape. He obviously didn't care how salty his food was, so long as it was fresh and bloody. When he was done, he stared at Chico with a look that said he wasn't sated yet.

"Good," Otto opined, his mouth dripping with blood. "Am I being plumped up? Are you nutty cats planning to feast on my flesh?"

"Hardly, Your Honor." That would be a turnabout. "We just want to keep you healthy."

"Then I need exercise." Otto gestured around the dark space outside his cage. The walls flapped slightly, canvas shifted by the wind outside. Above his cage, a net stretched from one wall to another, preventing him from leaping up and out. "All cats, great and small, cannot be denied such a thing."

"We have to deny it," said Chico, watching Otto suck grue off his mighty paws, "for a little while." When the lion was done, he urinated on the ground. The liquid trickled toward Chico, making the cat take a step back to avoid it.

"I don't see any *we*. You. I. That's all the *we* I see, lying before us. Who are your betters, little one?"

"I can't say. But I can tell you my name."

"Does your name really matter?" Otto asked.

"It's Chico," the jailer insisted.

"I understand." With great effort, the lion calmed himself. "Call me Otto, I insist."

Nodding, Chico collected the well-gnawed bones and left the tent. As the guard pushed through the flap to go out, Otto squinted at the tiny triangle of light that momentarily appeared. He opened his mouth as if to suck in the sunshine, swallow it down, and charge himself with its energy. When it was gone and the lion was left in the dark, he could still see the light in his mind's eye and feel a dash of warmth on his hide.

Soon he'd see the sun again, and his captors would be sorry.

***

Chico reported to a small tent, decked out in sumptuous cloths, filled with mats, pads, and woolsacks, and obscured with a haze of cigar smoke. Eyes watering, the jailer entered his master's quarters and gave an update on the prisoner.

"So he's in distress?" the cigar-smoking cat asked.

"Oh, he's troubled, to be sure. Frustrated. Lots of questions."

"Splendid." Chico's master blew gleeful smoke rings about the tent. "Let's keep him in the dark. Bring him to a boiling point. He'll tire himself out, the old tyrant." The smoker took note of the jailer's sad expression. "Getting to know the mayor, Chico?"

"Kind of. We don't have much in common."

"I can understand why you're fascinated. The amount of power that lion wielded—until recently—makes him a creature worth studying. Befriending, even."

"You mean you want to make him your ally?" Chico's eyes were tearing up from the cigar smoke.

"You're the one who's built a bond with that buffoon. Be careful who you become attached to, Chico. It's a terrible thing to lose a friend."

"What do you want me to do?"

"Get tough with him! Show him who's in charge. If he sees how weak you really are, he'll be busting out of his cell and lording it over us all again in no time. We can't have that."

"You think I'm weak?" Chico opened his eyes wide. "Why did you give me this job, sir?"

"Aw, I'm trying to rile you up a little. Get your goat. Stoke some passion. If you keep a clear head and a stout heart, then I know you can perform this task— and the larger one to come." Chico understood the inference. Do a good job, and he'd be up for a promotion. Less work, more money, and the respect he deserved at last. "Go to it, laddie!" The boss clapped him on the shoulder. "Tame that lion!"

17

The Waystation

Huffing to a halt with an elderly wheeze, the Windy Thistle arrived at the Waystation, a built-up area on the outskirts of Carabas. Once it had been the only whiff of civilization in the area, but travelers had taken a shine to the grasslands and had started to build homes nearby. Now urban sprawl had brought Carabas right up close to the station.

Through the window, Julius and Sal could see the Carabas skyline: tall granite tower blocks with flat, featureless walls, a splendid mansion on the west side, and a towering tree-like structure with many limbs.

"End of the line." Sal smiled, hurrying to be first out of the compartment.

"Looks like." Julius blinked slowly, moving with the patience of an older cat. Sergeant Barr barged in front, his massive ears brushing past them as he grabbed his empty luggage.

As they stepped from the train, they were amazed by what they saw. Their fellow passengers had included a couple of country cats and a few squaddies, but this couldn't have prepared them for the incredible mix of different shapes, sizes and breeds of feline that packed the station: almond-eyed Balinese yowling for help from laid-back birman porters; half-asleep ragdolls blinked their bright blue eyes, trailing their long, silky hair along the platform, jolted from a nap by the train's arrival; friendly Somalis in luxurious fur coats handed out pamphlets about the local hostels. Sergeant Barr, mighty ears twitching, joined Julius and Sal with the now-empty sack slung over his shoulder.

"This place is cool," said Sal, happy to be off the train at last.

"Yeah. A dream come true for agoraphobics." Julius tried to sound cynical, but he was also impressed by the miasma of cats around him.

"How ever are we going to find Moira in this crowd, though?" Sal whined. "And we've got to find her soon. The longer it takes, the farther away her abductor will get. The farther away he gets, the harder it'll be to find him."

"We start looking," said Julius. "Ask the porters if they've seen Moira. I'll meet you at the east entrance in one hour."

"An hour?" Sal saw his companion's determined expression. "I don't know if that'll be long enough. Let's hope we get lucky." Julius warily nodded farewell to the sergeant, who wished them all the goodwill he could muster after his loss.

Sal pushed his way through a line of longhairs waiting to buy tickets. Julius slumped on a bench, his head in his paws. They would need a great deal of luck to survive this town with no money and no friends, let alone find Moira. He would try his best—he owed her that much.

Not that playing detective and solving the mystery didn't appeal. Finding answers would be good, a positive step, helping Julius to make sense of his scattered puzzle of a life. Everyone went through the same thing, expecting their experiences to lead neatly from one to the next, each choice a correct one guaranteed to improve their lot; the people around them would always act the way they should, in the expected fashion, in the right mood, and fit in.

These expectations could only be fulfilled in a perfect world, one where every single niggling piece fitted together without a seam.

Perfection's overrated, Julius told himself. *I'd be bored to tears with perfect.* Still, he could have done without the frustration. If variety spiced his life, then the uncertainties laced it with maggots.

Sergeant Barr cursed his rotten luck. He'd never failed a mission before, never so much as served a cold kipper to a superior. Now he was due to report to the military liaison in Carabas, and he had to fill his sack with rats quick.

All day he searched the back streets and rubbish tips of the Waystation. All he came up with was a measly albino rat, barely old enough to bite. He shoved it in his sack, hoping that the albino's parents would come running so that he could snatch them up too; his run of bad fortune continued, and they never showed.

Demoralized, he went to Waystation's central *souq* to cheer himself up with some female companionship.

"Well darlin', how about it?" he said to the first female he found.

"How about what?" The fishwife didn't even bother to bat an eyelash, and Barr didn't know what to do about it. He'd rarely been in this situation before; usually, he couldn't keep the ladies away from him. There was something about the uniform that made them hop on him like eager fleas. A fishwife could afford to be selective—in any cat city, a woman of her profession was held in the highest regard—what could be better than a mate who could secure fresh fish for you and had such a wonderful perfume? But all the same, Barr had never been shunned like this before. And in the Waystation, Barr had been as unlucky in love as he had been in rat-catching.

He decided that there was something wrong with the place. Nothing he tried seemed to work. He'd polished his brass buttons, removed every trace of lint from his epaulets, dusted down his ratsack, and slicked back the fur on the top of his head with oodles of spit. He was sure he looked his best, which apparently wasn't good enough.

He sucked in his chest and stuck out his belly. A chubby cat was a successful, superior cat, so toms always proudly allowed their bellies to sag and sway when they strutted past a lady. It was the easiest trick in the book to snare a mate. In Bast, she-felines couldn't resist a round stomach. Here was a different story.

"Do I have, uh, kitten breath or something?" he asked the fishwife. He pushed out his lower lip and tried to breathe onto his nose. He'd had penguin stew for breakfast, and he hadn't had time to pop a claw and pick his teeth clean.

"Why, no. Should you have?" He had the fish-wife's full attention at last but she still didn't seem too impressed.

"I wondered why you weren't interested in me, that's all," said Barr with the brand of candid grin that had sufficed to win him a tryst with a tabby lass back at military academy. "Thought mebbe there was something wrong with me."

"Oh, no." The fishwife returned his smile. "There's nothing wrong with you."

"Then you'll join me for dinner tonight?" Barr sounded a little too hopeful.

"No." The fishwife turned back to her haddock, leaving Barr stunned by the rejection. Sure, she was a fishwife, but she was also a tabby, damn it all. It wasn't as if she was rich or pedigreed ... How could she turn him down?

In exasperation, he left the stall and stumbled down the *souq*, his trust completely lost, paranoid and confused. He tried a different sexy wink and nod for every female he passed; they all ignored him. Spices and fragrances filled his nostrils, leading him to a perfumer where he purchased honeysuckle. Even if the local ladies found him resistable, the calming effects of the woodbine always gave him an edge when he went on the prowl.

The *souq* was busy with cats clamoring for food, some accompanied by dogs who gladly carried their groceries for them. The shoppers gladly traveled from Carabas to the Waystation for a break from the big city. *From one crammed area to another*, thought Barr. No wonder the fishwife didn't want her personal bubble to be burst. He would use his charm to pierce her armor.

18

A Perfect World

*In which Julius and Sal catch a show
and the ferals come to town.*

A NEW CARABAS

Carabas is a town in flux. Its past is as dubious as a pitbull's. Originally a stop-off oasis for bank traders on their way to the vast chicken farms of Seedsville, Carabas did some trading of its own. It relied on its remote location to build a reputation as a place where travelers could gamble, cavort, and satisfy their animal lust with impunity. Their families back home would never know; what happened in Carabas stayed in Carabas.

As the city's reputation grew, so did its reach. A train station was built and famed establishments like Café Risqué and the Pussy Foot Club—the central hub of all the town's nightlife—sprang up.

Last year, everything changed. The town cleaned up its act, changing slowly from a vibrant delight to a boring chore to pass through. Travelers don't stay there long anymore; they have no reason to. The Pussy Foot Club remains open, but it's now a tame nightspot for young professionals.

Thanks to Governor Tarquin Quintroche, the spouses of those naughty businesscats are happy. They get their mates home sooner. But no one else is pleased. Tourism has suffered, and if Carabas continues its aim to be safe, polite, and unendearingly dull, it will soon disappear completely.

From *Walking in Eternity:*
A Traveler's Guide to Cat World
by Nat Jones

This is weird, thought Julius as he followed a main thoroughfare. ***There's something not quite right here.*** It wasn't the dogs who passed by, dressed in overalls or blue-collar work clothes; they didn't look any different from the ones that used to do menial tasks in Bast. No, the difference was in the Carabian cats' attitude to their canine neighbors. Instead of looking down on them, avoiding them, or spitting on them, they were positively mingling. They seemed to take pride in their tolerance.

"What kind of twisted place is this?" Sal wondered, rejoining Julius with no news of Moira. "No one wants to talk to me." He leaned close to the reporter and breathed in his face. "Do I smell or something?"

"No worse than usual." Julius followed signs for a "Friendship Center," hoping that it would be some kind of tourist information hub.

"For a journalist, you don't know much, do you?"

"About this place?" Julius frowned. "I've been out of the loop for a while. Besides, my beat always stopped within the Bast city limits. Always plenty going on there to keep me busy."

"Why are they so … quiet?" Sal asked.

The citizens didn't push at each other or squabble. They went about their business calmly, without so much as a mew.

"There's something terribly wrong here," Julius whispered. "What has the ruler of this place done to these animals?"

"It's lunchtime," said Sal ominously.

"You're right, that's what's wrong." None of the cats seemed hungry, and they certainly weren't having a street-side siesta; their intentions were all askew. They seemed more interested in getting their work done than filling their bellies.

"I'm hungry," Sal said to no one in particular. They moved farther into Carabas, cricking their necks upward to gawp at the tall, slim, leaning towers of the business district. The shadows of the buildings intersected like a tangled mass of whiskers. The two cats encountered more and more signs; they passed a No Purr Zone (CAUTION! CATS SLEEPING!) and a brightly colored mural depicting pups and kittens gamboling together (LICK THY NEIGHBOR). Within half an hour they'd reached the town center, where a canted, spindly tower stretched into the sky. It was the tallest building in Carabas, and they'd been able to see its spire from the train. Like a giant sundial, it cast its shade across the central square. It was the Friendship Center.

With a name like that, the dudes in here are bound to be more helpful, thought Julius. But once inside, he didn't get a smile out of the desk clerk until he handed over a rat's tail he'd been saving from the train.

"So, what is this place?" asked Sal, never afraid to ask a dumb question. A tour guide was happy to answer.

"Welcome to the Friendship Center, the happiest place in Carabas. It's here that we celebrate the togetherness of dog and cat in our unique community."

"Unique 'cause it's nuts," Sal whispered. His susurrus echoed around a large auditorium, where they were invited to sit and watch a show.

"I'll rejoin you in four minutes. The presentation will begin momentarily. Don't fall asleep now!" The cheerful guide left them curled up on stadium seats, relaxed by the auditorium's dim light. Julius kept half an eye open, watching the seats fill up with school parties, tourists, and elderly Carabians.

On a large stage, a lithe, attractive cat materialized, performing a spirited dance. With an explosion of music and fireworks, a dog leaped from stage left and chased her around in a pantomime frenzy. Before long, the dog feigned exhaustion, fell, and nursed a sore leg. The cat moved toward the dog—cautiously at first, then with more confidence, as the dog didn't bark. The cat washed the dog's leg, helped him up, and they rubbed noses together.

"Lick thy neighbor," Sal said, coming to a realization.

"I think I'm going to be sick," Julius scowled. "They're all puppy happy." Had the message on the train window referred to Carabas, a place where all cats seemed intent on befriending dogs?

To massive applause, the performers bowed and ducked behind a closing curtain. Show's over.

"Nice message," Sal told the tour guide, who startled Julius by appearing soundlessly right beside him.

"Too twee for my taste," Julius told her. "I like my theatrical experiences to have a little more spice."

"Oh, no spice allowed here, sir," the guide told him, her smile never leaving her face. "Would you like to see the rest of the center now? We have so much to show you. The Sculpture Garden of Hope. The Fashion Boutiques of Progress. The Fountain of Understanding..."

"The Carousel of Kiss My Tail," said Sal, then tucked himself behind his friend in case he got told off.

"How about the way out?" asked Julius. "I was hoping to get some information on a friend of mine I'm looking for."

"I don't think I can help you with that. Not my job. I can help you find the Love for One Another Food Court, though."

The guide was talking to thin air. Discouraged, Julius and Sal had left the building, venturing farther into the perfect world of Carabas.

Once the ferals had Julius's scent, nothing could stop them from entering Carabas. Not the ancient wooden portcullis, carved into sharp points like jagged, broken teeth. Not the guards, dumbed by torpor and bored half out of their skulls. Those guards had been trained to spot a troublemaker from a distance and sound the alarm immediately, without swithering.

They weren't ready for a hoard of savage heathens rushing them in the middle of the night. Before they had a chance to hiss or bush up their furry coats, the ferals were upon them, turning them to mincemeat and smashing through the portcullis with barely a pause for breath.

The gates had been designed to impress visitors and deter miscreants with their looming look. The ferals used sticks and flints, teeth and claws, scratching and biting and wrenching their skinny bodies through to the sleepy waystation.

They sniffed their way along the tracks until they reached the end of the line. They prowled around the train, cleaned up from its dusty journey. The ferals didn't like it, in danger of losing the trail. They sniffed at the tables in the buffet carriage, looking for signs of life but finding none. Their leader Dalen motioned them to leave the train, his one good eye bloodshot and roving. He was worried that if they stayed in one place too long, they'd draw too much unwelcome attention. They could cope with a couple of guards, but an armed band of vengeful, organized cats wouldn't be so easy to deal with. Worse, the sun was beginning to rise, tinting the lower third of the sky with a caramel glow.

The ferals disembarked, looking like red-eyed passengers who'd lost their luggage. They fanned out, seeking a familiar smell. Although they found Carabas's neon signs and echoing timbres disorienting, they were starving by now. Desperation overcame any wariness they felt. They were determined to finish off the cocky cat who'd dared to fight them.

19

The Old Exchange

PEACE AND PROSPERITY

This tinpot world is so askew with good intentions that it threatens to lose its balance completely. But what a pleasant world it is to live in.

No bad manners, no serial sneezers spreading their germs in public places; everyone nice and neatly turned out, no navels flashed or paws pierced. No one mewed out of turn or shoved to the front of a queue.

There are no gruff ruffians or bet-hedging beggars to be seen. Life is surface-perfect. Kittens go to bed on time and curfews are always kept. At all times, the citizens strive to think happy thoughts and dream positive dreams. Life is better that way, more constructive, less arduous. Life seems safer for them.

Special to *The Scratching Post*
By Julius Kyle

Julius and Sal explored Carabas, frustrated at the lack of street signs. There were plenty of notices prohibiting them from scratching tree trunks or sticking their tails up in an unseemly manner, but nothing directing them to the heart of the town.

Julius stopped in a carpenter's workshop to find out what part of Carabas he was in. The ginger-hued owner was busy sanding a large rectangular slab of wood, with his employees grafting hard around him on similar products. The air was thick with sawdust and varnish fumes.

"What are you working on?" asked Julius, curious as always.

"It's called a door," answered the jovial ginger tom. "It keeps the wind out, and it's great for security."

"How does it work?"

"Let me show you," the carpenter said proudly. He led Julius and Sal to a back room, where their way was barred by one of the doors. "The governor has had them installed all through the city. He says they give the citizens privacy. Now they can lock themselves in their homes after curfew."

"Why would they want to do that?" Julius peered at the door suspiciously.

"They have to. It's part of the whole curfew thing."

"I still don't get how this—door, did you call it? How this door works."

"Well, you mew until someone opens it for you…" The carpenter let out a loud yowl, and a canine apprentice in the back room opened up for him. "Then you step through…" The tom led Julius and Sal through the door, which was shut behind them. "And as soon as it closes, you cry and scratch at the door to get back in again. Endless hours of fun. Of course, we're just happy to have the work, aren't we, Clifford?" The apprentice nodded. "You know how many Carabians are employed making, installing, and testing these things?"

"So that's why this city has such a low unemployment record," Julius mused.

"Well, one of the reasons. Everyone's busy working on the governor's pet projects."

Still puzzled by the whole door idea, Julius and Sal stumbled out of the workshop and back onto the busy city streets. The carpenter had pointed them east, but they soon got lost again. Whenever Julius and Sal asked pedestrians for directions to the center, they were ignored. The resident dogs and cats may have been used to wayfarers, but for some reason, they shied away from the two newcomers.

The only cats willing to stop and talk to them were other visitors, on their way to the information office or a tourist attraction. They weren't much help, not knowing their way around town either. Julius started to get frustrated, pawing at pedestrians who deigned to ignore him.

"Hey!" he yowled at one townie at a main thoroughfare. "Who do we have to lick around here to get some directions?"

"Keep it down, doofus," the offended cat said. "You wanna get me in trouble?"

Indignant at the slight, Julius followed the cat down Hoff Street. He expected such rude behavior from a dog, but a cat who lacked manners was one who needed to be taken down a peg.

"See here," Julius called out, raising his voice as loud as he could so that everyone within earshot could catch it. "That's no way to treat a visitor."

The cat pretended not to hear and kept walking. Julius tried to catch up with him, but he was stopped by a long-legged serval.

"What's all this going on 'ere, then?" The serval flashed a badge at Julius; he was an undercover prowler, policing Hoff. "We can't have anybody causing a disturbance, now."

"What disturbance?" Julius spluttered. Sal tried to help by saying, "We're not causing nothing."

"We're just trying to get some directions." Julius looked into the cop's eyes, trying to find some form of compassionate rapport. He couldn't.

"I happened to notice that you were stopping cats as they went about their business. Obstructing their progress."

"Of course! Directions, remember?" Julius was fuming by now.

"The gathering of more than two cats in a public place is prohibited. By stopping someone, you're breaching the peace."

Townsfolk had tried to ignore the exchange, but by now, curiosity had gotten the better of them. They gathered around, listening incredulously—not at the prowler, but at Julius's daring to challenge him.

"You're not even a proper cop. You wouldn't last five minutes in a big city."

"Lower your voice, please." The prowler seemed embarrassed by all the attention they'd drawn. "I've spent years building up my undercover identity in this area."

"Look, everyone! He's a prowler."

"I don't know how they carry on in your native city, Mr. —."

"Kyle. Julius Kyle. Name mean anything to you?"

"Can't say that it does. I don't know how they carry on in Bast, but here we are civil. We are reverent. We respect the law."

"Law, shmaw." Julius enjoyed the look on the cop's face when he said this. "We're looking for a missing Siamese. Maybe you can make yourself useful and assist us." Julius started rooting through his pockets, looking for his letter of travel. As he rummaged, scrumpled salmon wrappers and pieces of thread dropped to the ground.

"Here it is. She's called Moira. Can you help?"

The serval was stony-faced. "Julius Kyle, I arrest you for breach of the peace and littering."

Sal rolled his eyes; this prowler was the opposite of helpful. "We don't know your laws, officer."

"Ignorance is no defense." The prowler looked at the crowd as if he was committing their faces to memory. The rubberneckers quickly dispersed.

"If we have to pay an on-the-spot fine, we'll do it." Julius sighed. "We need to be on our way."

The prowler shook his head slowly. "You're going to have to come with me."

Although Julius was ready to pop his claws out, he clenched his teeth and controlled his animal urges. The cop would take him to a smarter superior who'd drop the charges after one sniff at the letter of travel.

No one in their right mind would risk incurring the displeasure of Mayor Otto.

As they left Hoff Street, the prowler's radio crackled to life. *Major disturbance at the Baki Souq. All available officers required to assist.*

"I guess that means we'll be on our way then," said Sal with a well-practiced sidle.

"Not so fast." The serval swiped a spotted paw at them, forcing them to walk in front of him. "Down this alley. Move it."

Such was the authority in his voice that Julius and Sal complied. At the end of the alley, they witnessed a messy kerfuffle between two prowlers and a brown-coated, big-footed friend of theirs.

Sergeant Barr snarled at the cops, shaggy jowls bristling as he lunged at them. One prowler fell back into a stall, knocking over a crockery display. Barr's tufty ears vibrated as the plates smashed to pieces; taking their chance, the policecats—the serval included—pounced on him and subdued him.

Julius and Sal turned to run, but other prowlers had received the radio message. As they leaped over the debris of the messed-up *souq*, the serval singled Julius out. Barr stood up, noticing Julius for the first time.

"What are you doing here, Sergeant?" asked Julius.

"Tryin' to get out of trouble. I was supposed to deliver my goods here—the goods that you fed to those ferals."

"I'm sorry, Sergeant," said Julius.

Barr and Julius were surrounded by the prowlers, noses wrinkled into unsavory snarls. Sal had already ducked behind a box by this time, hoping that the thugs wouldn't be interested in a pipsqueak like him. He was right. They closed in on Julius and the sergeant.

"You got me into this predicament," Barr hissed. "Any ideas to get us out?"

"Oh, Bastet in a basket. So what if he lost your black-market bundle?" Julius said to the cops, shaking his head in disbelief.

"Don't say that word." For the first time, Barr sounded scared.

"C'mon, everybody knows the army marches on its black market profits. I wrote an exposé..."

"Not *that* word," one of the cops growled. "You can't use Her name around here."

"Oh, because I might get in trouble? How can I get into any more than I am already?"

Barr tried to shush the tabby, but Julius had lost all patience. "I'll use Bastet's name if I want to. I use it all the time. Bastet in the local bar. Bastet in a coop. Bastet in the bathroom when I'm taking a—."

The cops cuffed Julius and the sarge, pinning them down through force of numbers. But to Sal's surprise, the prowlers didn't scratch them half-dead and leave them in a crumpled heap. Instead, they dragged them off to the Old Exchange building, Sal huddling tight behind his box, eyes shut, waiting for his friends to signal the all-clear.

This structure was the oldest in Carabas, a white-painted wonder where travelers had conducted their business affairs since the dawn of the domestic age. Ionic columns supported the edifice, an anachronism in the company of the wooden prefabs that filled the rest of Main Street. Julius couldn't help but crane his neck to gaze up at the place, wondering what kind of ego could fill it.

He soon got his answer. The prowlers left him with Barr in a locked room, dark and soundproofed with thick walls and doors. With a reporter's curiosity, he noted that the picture rails were gilt with gold. He was surprised that none of the errant travelers who passed through had nicked it. Perhaps they knew something he didn't.

"The governor will see you now," said one of the MPs, not bothering to knock.

"Oh, goody. Lead the way." With Barr following sullenly behind, Julius was taken through to the governor's office. It was quite a contrast from the room they'd waited in, spacious with large windows and a high ceiling. Julius suppressed a gasp as he entered, but not because of the architecture. "What an unpleasant surprise," he scowled. "This explains a lot."

Tarquin Quintroche, the Abyssinian Governor of Carabas, looked spiffy in a gold waistcoat and tailored black jacket, but his slight build didn't help him to fit in with his surroundings—two large mahogany tables lit by an impressive chandelier, with chairs carved specifically to fit the feline form in repose. The whole room was dominated by Otto's family crest on the wall. Hundreds of miles from Bast, the mayor's presence was still felt; he made sure of that.

"I'm sorry, have we...?"

"You don't remember me? I know you, Sinner. Otto's aide-de-camp who made a sneaky deal with the dogs. Offered them a quarter of our city in exchange for peace. How'd you end up in this backwater? City life too tough for you?"

"The very idea! My hard work for the mayor was rewarded with this post. He needed someone dedicated, meticulous—."

"He obviously didn't need a guy he could trust!"

"He knows that I went behind his back with the best of intentions. My treaty with the dogs was more of an administrative slip-up than a deception. It wasn't my fault that the dogs misunderstood the treaty."

Julius shook his head sadly. "I don't think they were the ones doing the misunderstanding."

"The mayor still has faith in me."

"That proud poltroon has faith in no one since his mom disappeared. You wouldn't happen to know anything about that by the way, would you?"

"I found the news upsetting," said Tarquin, eyes wide with innocence.

"I find your presence here upsetting."

"Steady on, chum." Sergeant Barr placed a paw on Julius's shoulder in an attempt to restrain him. "You might have another eight lives to lose, but I've gone through all of mine," the soldier whispered to him. "Besides, my head is very fond of being attached to my body."

"Can he..?" Julius asked.

"He certainly can," Barr replied. "Say you're sorry."

Julius gave Tarquin a nod, the closest he could get to an apologetic bow. "You got a raw deal, Sinner, I'm sure. It looks like you've got it made now though, with your rules and your prowlers and your doors."

Tarquin wasn't oblivious to Julius's caustic tone. "This is progress, Mr..."

"Julius Kyle. Representing *The Scratching Post*."

Tarquin didn't look impressed. "This is progress, Mr. Kyle. The future. We're a model for the entire land. Someday—hopefully within our lifetimes—all cat cities will be this way."

"I don't think Mayor Otto would approve of that future."

"No, he wouldn't, would he? He likes things the way they are. He set me up here, expecting me to fail. He must be very surprised."

"Who knows? When I left Bast, he'd been missing for days."

Tarquin looked genuinely shocked. "I wonder why I haven't heard about that?" The governor relied on Otto's underlings to provide him with up-to-date information from Bast.

"Maybe someone doesn't want you to know. Looks like being out in the wastes has its benefits and its drawbacks," Julius purred. "Maybe you've got a kink in your tinpot telegraph wires."

Tarquin gave the tabby a wry smile. "You have violated a municipal law, my friend. I appreciate your press credentials, no matter how tenuous. But if I bend the rules for you, that won't set a good example for my citizens, now will it? You're going to have to be punished."

"If you liked me better, would you bend the rules, then?"

"Not for anybody," said Tarquin with plain irritation.

"Not even yourself?"

"I never break the law."

"I don't think he likes himself very much," Julius said to Barr, sounding smug. Turning to the Abyssinian, he used his best diplomatic tone. "You don't need to hurt us. We're passing through is all. You don't want troublemakers like us sticking around—we might curse at a kitten or something. Before we go, though, we need your help."

"What with?" Tarquin sighed, sitting down and shuffling through some papers.

"He's lost his missus," Barr explained. "She's been abducted. We think she's in this town. Can I go back to my regiment now?"

"It's a terrible thing to lose a mate. I'll do everything I can." Tarquin scribbled down Moira's details, then took a small bottle of scent and squirted a few drops on the document—his official seal. Then he handed the document to an aide and told Julius, "You'll still have to be punished, of course."

"What do cats usually get for this sorta crime? Bearing in mind that I didn't know you had this silly rule to break?"

"Unawareness cannot vindicate you in the eyes of the law," said Tarquin.

"I thought justice was blind. How can it have eyes if it can't see?"

"Law and justice are two entirely different things."

"And only one of 'em gets disability benefits, eh? That's a shame." Julius ran a paw along the edge of Tarquin's desk, marveling at its clean, smooth surface. "This place is nuts, you know. You must feel like you're in charge of a big, fat asylum."

"This is my dream come true," said Tarquin, amazed by his own self-control. "Dogs coexisting with cats as equals, or as damn near it. They have their own beliefs and we must respect them."

"But they're ... dogs."

"Yes," Tarquin said proudly.

"You really think they're a good influence? Don't get me wrong, some of my best friends are dog lovers. But this isn't right. It won't end well. I'm cool with the idea ... get everyone to love each other and forget their differences. But you can't repress their urges, Tarquin. Dogs will never get on with cats, not in the long run."

"Your punishment is incarceration—."

"Great." Julius rolled his eyes. "You forbid your citizens from doing anything and if they do anything, you lock them up so they can't do nothing."

"Followed by participation in our monthly Well Day celebration."

"I love a party." Julius tried to sound calm, but there was a wicked edge to Tarquin's voice that gave him cause for concern.

"Sergeant Barr," Tarquin addressed the soldier, "Carabas has only one penalty for a satyr such as yourself. Take them away."

As Julius and Barr were dragged out of the office, Tarquin got on with his paperwork. There was a lot of preparation to be done for Well Day; it was his favorite day of the year.

Cheryl Carina had sore paws, no surprise there. She'd been standing all day, taking care of whining tourist customers while she wore her sunniest disposition. It was in her contract—all employees of the Wayfarer Boutique had to have a beaming smile on their faces whenever they took care of a customer. This was hard work for Cheryl; she should have known better than to work for a Cheshire, not that the boss was ever there— he kept disappearing, usually when the boutique got busy. But she stayed on because of her perk. Once a month, she got to be pampered by her colleagues.

They'd take turns dressing each other, arranging and dyeing their fur, adding ribbons and bows. The Wayfarer was the place for every fancy cat in Carabas to visit when they wanted to catch up on the latest Bast fashions, and it was one of the main reasons why travelers visited the Longhair Quarter.

Today, Cheryl had spent her lunch hour at the store, asking her workmates to fix her fur. They'd done a plum job with an orange-tinged permanent that would make her stand out anywhere.

Cheryl felt excited as she headed for home, her eyes glittering in the evening darkness. She took a shortcut down a back alley, taking care not to step in any mud puddles; this fur was too good to muss.

Usually, she'd stick to the main roads and bright streetlights, for her own peace of mind as much as safety's sake. Tonight, she was desperate to get home and change into a dress that matched her new do. Then she had friends to visit, errands to run, and in the morning—oh! In the morning, before work, she'd be able to make it to the execution. She was looking forward to that; she loved a good drowning.

The last one she'd seen had been a doozy. Some poor schmo had made a chance remark in a down-market sports bar, something along the lines of, "Longhairs suck as servers 'cause they shed in yer booze." The barmaid—scratch that thought, the bar*feline*—had taken offence, being as longhaired as she could get. She'd reported the barfly to the authorities and wup! His petty wisecrack had been blown out of all safe proportions. Despite a heart-breaking last-minute plea for clemency, the schmo had got dunked in the central square. To the rubbernecked crowd's surprise and delight, he hadn't come out alive.

Cheryl kept track of the time, checking her claws to make sure they were clean and free of loose sheaths, planning a decent night's sleep. She would be too excited to sleep for long, though. She always tossed and turned before an execution. Cheryl would feel safer, knowing an irredeemable criminal was off the streets for good. She found the elation of the crowd was intoxicating, and she got a strange thrill from being so close to something so horribly violent. In real life, Cheryl got queasy when she bit the head off a mouse. Too much blood. In the crowd, she was brave and stronger than one cat could ever be.

In lieu of sleep, Cheryl Carina was ready to party.

Two sour-faced guards took Julius and Barr into the City Detention Center, a septic building a block away from the Old Exchange. They were shoved down a long passageway into a white room full of three-tiered steel cages with mesh on the front to help hold the inmates.

Small, dry noses poked through the mesh, although most of the occupants lay at the back of their cages, sleeping or anxiously scrubbing themselves. Some had small, coffin-shaped cardboard litter boxes barely larger than themselves. The luckiest ones had small dishes of stale food or brackish water; the sorriest-looking ones begged for scraps. They'd all displeased Tarquin or broken his politically correct rules.

Julius's cage seemed smaller than all the rest. In the cell above him, a long brown cat was trying to stretch out, dangling one paw through the mesh. In the tier below, four itinerant kittens were packed tight together, mewing for their mother. *No chance of a good sleep tonight then,* Julius thought ruefully. He sat still, already planning his escape as Barr was placed in the cage to his left.

"What are you in for?" he asked the lounging brown cat.

"Some idiot dog pushed past me in the street. I called him a mutt. They sent me here."

"I'm Julius and this is my ... acquaintance, Sergeant Barr."

"Call me Lugs, okay?" Barr told the tabby. The soldier's ears waggled, and Julius stifled a laugh.

"Why would I call you that?" he asked, straight-faced.

"We're in a sticky situation together," said the gruff sergeant. "Which makes us friends, whether I like it or not. And Lugs is what my friends call me."

"Er, thanks. But why would I call you...?"

"Because of my ears, okay?" Barr took a hasty swipe at the tabby. "Muh big, tufty lobes. Lugs has always been my nickname. When I was born, none of muh brothers or sisters had ears as big as mine. I mean, they were tufty, aye, but none of them could compare to my massive lobes. Me maw started calling me Lugs. So did muh dad. Everyone teased me."

That explains why he's such a tough nut, thought Julius.

"At school, they sang a song about me. Wanna hear it?"

"I don't need to..."

Barr burst into song anyway.

"Lugsy, Lugsy,
"The sun shines east.
"The sun shines west.
"It shines on your ears and puts a shadow on
your chest.
"I'd brave a million bugs for a look at your lugs,
"Oh, Lu—ugsy!"

Julius nodded sympathetically. "You must've had a horrendous time."

"Yeah," Barr grunted. "Teachers can be so cruel."

"Lugs it is, then." Julius agreed, trying not to look at Barr's ears. It was impossible; they were huge.

Getting into Carabas had been easy for the puma. With Moira still unconscious, he'd explained to the border patrol that she didn't travel well, was suffering from exhaustion, and was in desperate need of medical attention. The checkpoint Charlies had fallen for his sob story, letting him through without even asking for ID. That had probably saved their lives; the puma was in no mood to let any obstructive jugheads live that day.

Now Moira was awake, struggling even as her captor offered her a saucer of water. She batted the crockery aside, a stubborn look on her face.

"Where are we now?" she asked, not expecting him to answer. She seemed to be in a small cabin, the roof and windows covered with canvas.

"The marketplace. Can't you smell the spices as they waft into your nostrils? Can't you hear the hawkers selling their trinkets? It's so noisy here, no one will hear you cry out."

"Must be your favorite hangout," said Moira. "Why haven't you killed me yet?"

"I like a lady who gets straight to the point. You're too important to some bigwig to die right now. But nobody lives forever."

"I've noticed they don't live much at all if they bump into you."

"Chalk it down to the circle of life. My career ladder's caked in blood, and I'm proud of every ruddy rung. Sure you're not thirsty?" The puma lapped some fresh water from the cracked saucer.

"Got a name?"

"Not for you, no."

"Be like that then. Oh, I get the picture—if I knew your name, you'd have to silence me for good."

"You know it," said the puma.

"I'm not afraid of death. Bastet is preparing a better place for me when this world's done with me."

"Don't mention Her name here. It's not appropriate."

"I meant no disrespect," Moira said quickly. "I'm serious."

"I don't have to kill you to silence you. It would be a shame, though. Your tongue looks so soft and pink. I would miss it."

"Me too," said Moira, then shut her mouth quick.

Not far away in the *souq*, Sal was feigning interest in the goods on display. He had been expecting Julius to return for hours. Whenever he saw a prowler, he would duck behind a butter churn merchant's stall. The merchant was getting mighty sick of it.

"If you're not going to buy anything, move on," the stall owner snapped.

"Er, do you only sell butter churns?" Sal asked, watching a serval pass by. "Do you have any milk churns?"

"I sell butter churns. If you want milk churns ... you're in the wrong place." The merchant pointed to a sign on the adjacent stall: MILK CHURNS.

"So, that's the right place?"

"Not for me," the merchant grumbled.

"Thanks. I think I'll browse a bit longer." Sal waited until the serval was out of sight. "Okay, thanks!"

While Sal had been watching the prowler, someone had been watching him. As Sal approached the milk churn stall, a longhair sidled up to him.

"Looking for a bargain, eh?" the longhair asked. "Can't decide how to spend your money wisely?" Sal turned to face him. With his glasses and spit-slicked fur, the stranger looked professorial.

"Yeah," Sal told him hesitantly.

"Thought so." The longhair offered him a gentle smile. "Follow me."

Taking one last glance around the *souq*, Sal allowed the longhair to lead him away. He wondered when Julius would be back to look for him.

For a time, Bridget had tried to ignore the real world. The toll of keeping tabs on everything that went on in Bast (and trying to control it) had been heavy; in an attempt to relax and recharge her wits, she'd abjured all contact with television, radio, or carrier pigeon. The media didn't know where she was, and she didn't know what the political situation was back home. Most of the time, she didn't care; she was busy enjoying her vacation.

Nevertheless, her morning lope took her past the radio room. The crew had been ordered to turn the radio off as she passed, but she'd still catch the occasional squawk. Today, the crackling chatter was louder than usual; some swab had turned into Bast Radio.

Bridget recognized the soothing voice of DJ Scratch, his tones as smooth as slow-trickling cream. But the personality's laid-back style didn't lessen the seriousness of his news.

"It's been weeks since our Regal Badness Mayor Otto went missing and there's still no sign of the lion leader. After a whole lotta speculation, the City Council has announced that there'll be a new mayor in town—and we get the chance to elect him.

"That's right! You heard it here first, and don't you forget it. We vote for an interim mayor who may become permanent if Otto never returns to roar his head in these parts. Primary candidates to be announced."

The radio operator realized that Bridget was peeking through a porthole and switched off his apparatus. Bridget said nothing, deep in thought.

So her son had vanished—and there was no way a big-mouthed egotist like him would lie low. Something bad had happened; Bridget suspected a coup. Rather than fret for Otto, she worried about herself. If there was any putsching to be done, she should be the instigator.

Bast had been under her family's control for generations. Even when she'd relinquished her role as mayoress, a small part of her had been satisfied that a lion still ruled.

Now it was her turn again; she could taste it. With a full head of steam, she could rush back to Bast and revive her power base, leading her subjects to a new golden age of liondom. There would be other mates and other, longer-lasting progeny. As for the nonsense about voting? One mighty roar would smash any notions of democracy.

Moira walked alongside Toxic, realizing that their relationship had changed. He still had the edge—he was bigger, stronger, and he knew where they were going. But she had shown endurance, cunning, and determination over the past few days. She knew Toxic respected her for that, even if he never said so. After all, he never said much of anything.

They'd lain low for days, waiting for a summons from Toxic's boss, and finding a hiding place hadn't been that tough. The ideal of New Carabas hadn't reached every part of the city. Toxic found a flophouse on the East side where he and Moira could stay for a song. All the beds in the flophouse were raised high off the floor and placed against one of the walls. There were no cushions or blankets, and space was tight. All the guests were on their guard, but they felt secure— they were away from ground level, lying at a vantage point where they could see everyone coming and going.

Toxic slept, but this time Moira stayed put next to him. The flophouse beat a crate or a grassy hidey hole, and she wanted to know where Toxic was going to take her. Who had gone to all the trouble of ordering the puma to bring her to Carabas? What kind of mighty cat could command Toxic? She had to know.

She cursed her weakness—that need to know what was around the next corner, who was pulling the strings, even if it led to more danger. She couldn't help it. Curiosity was the bane of her entire species.

The flophouse smelled of old, sweaty cats who'd given up bothering to wash. Smart. If anyone came sniffing around looking for them, their scent would be hidden by the staleness.

Every now and again, a roach would scuttle past Moira's pallet. Eyes popping open wide with fascination, she'd watch it for a bit, then slam a paw down on the greasy brown body, letting go and then catching it again. As she played with the plentiful bed bugs, she momentarily forgot about her predicament. Moira had reverted to kittenhood, immersed in the experience.

By the wee hours, she was too tired to play anymore. She fell asleep listening to the scuttling insects and the hoary sound of Toxic breathing. Despite the games, she hoped that the next day would bring some news. Then perhaps she'd get to meet Toxic's boss at last.

The longhair was a kindly chap named Milo. He led Sal to a tall tenement block that looked rough around the edges, reminding the snowshoe of his days growing up in a similar building. Milo had an apartment on the top floor that he jokingly referred to as his "penthouse suite." They took an elevator that was rimmed with mold and urine.

"It must be awful, having all that money burning a hole in your pocket," said Milo as they reached his floor.

"Well, I wasn't really after a milk churn. Or a butter churn, come to mention it."

"I knew it as soon as I saw you. The bloodshot eyes. The wiry limbs. You're on the nip, aren't you?" Milo opened his front door and motioned for Sal to enter.

"I'm a retired addict." Sal stopped on the threshold. "I'm not looking to score, if that's what you're thinking."

Milo had disappeared into his apartment. For a moment, there was silence. Sal peered into the gloom, but Milo didn't turn any lights on.

"I'm not a rich tourist either." Sal bowed his head. "Sorry." He was about to return to the elevator when a longhaired paw appeared in the doorway. It was holding a bag of green herbs with tiny tooth-like leaves and crushed off-white flowers.

"First sniff's free." As the paw waggled, the herbs seemed to dance in the bag. Sal couldn't resist.

Otto glared through the bars of his cage, his eyes attracted by the moonlight that bounced off Chico's bunch of keys. The jailer looked lonely.

"Your family must really miss you," Otto purred.

"Does yours?" Chico asked.

Otto fumed at the little cat's insolence. "I may be your prisoner, but it wouldn't hurt to show some respect, Chico. I won't be in here forever."

"You have a point." Chico looked Otto in the eyes, steadily, carefully, as if deciding whether Otto cared about him. All he saw were two cold, coal pupils in their blood-cracked white eyeballs. "Yes, they miss me. But you know what? After hours stuck in this black hole with someone like you for company, I get frustrated and take it out on them. So even though I look forward to going home more than anything else I can think of, they don't stay pleased to see me for very long."

"A pity. I imagine they're a fine bunch. How many did you say you had in your litter?"

"Six," Chico said with pride. "Three males, three females. No cast-offs."

"That's good. Good that you've kept count. I lose track of all my brood. I have staff to take care of their upbringing. Coddle 'em too much, if you ask me."

"Yeah, the missus dotes on my lot. Spoils them too. Her excuse always is, 'They're not with us for long, so we should make the most of them. Give them plenty of affection. They might not find so much in the big wide world.'"

"Mowbray's my eldest, I know that much. That impatient tyke has a lot to learn before he becomes a lion king." The moonlight faded, presumably obscured by a passing cloud. Otto tore his eyes away from the keys on Chico's belt.

"So who would you like to replace you when you, uh, step down?"

"I will never do that," said Otto with a low growl. "Not voluntarily." The change in tone reminded Chico of his instructions to be tough with his prisoner. "Some things you can't volunteer for," he said sadly.

"I love my long lies as much as the next cat," Cheryl told her friends at the Pussy Foot Club. "But I get up extra early for a drownin'. So I can get a place up front."

"I don't know how you can stand to watch," said her best buddy Colline. "I think the whole idea's disgusting."

"Yeah," said Bea, an overweight Persian with a gentle lisp. "Getting up that early. My sleep is sacred."

"No!" Colline tried to look extra serious to combat her girlfriends' giggles. "I mean such a harsh punishment for petty indiscretions."

The friends faced each other as they danced, three cats out for a good time, tails wagging to a hypnotic beat.

"Better watch what you're sayin'," Bea lowered her voice despite the raucous music. "Or you'll be the next kitty in the well."

"So you're not going tomorrow?" Cheryl asked innocently. Bea and Colline shook their heads; they didn't fancy the drowning.

The dark stripes on Cheryl's back rippled as she stood up. "Time to lick my paws. Don't wreck the place while I'm gone."

Colline looked embarrassed. She'd ripped half the stuffing from her seat. "I'll come with ya."

They left Bea sitting alone, looking lost, bedazzled by the strobing lights. She'd be okay; she was used to getting left behind.

The Pussy Foot Club was divided into three cube-shaped levels, each staggered so that patrons had to climb to reach the rooftop bar. The first level was dedicated to live performances; it had hosted big-time acts like Kitty Perry down to a country bumpkin novelty act called The Furzels.

The second level piped in popular tunes while offering ramps, ropes, and hidey-holes for all-night clambering fun.

The third level appealed to more refined clubbers, with a DJ spinning electronic hits, a vast dancefloor, and VIP booths. The real VIPs were on the rooftop, shmoozing under the moon.

Cheryl, Bea, and Colline had chosen level three that night where the restroom was decorated in splendid sickening magenta, with plenty of mirrors and scratch pads perfect for rapid claw-clean. A row of cubicle doors led to trays full of dainty gray granules, chemically treated to clump when it came into contact with excreta. But Cheryl and Colline weren't there to go potty.

"She makes us look bad," Cheryl spat. "She's the reason why we never get picked up in this place."

"Ever wonder if this place is the real reason?" Colline indicated the garish surroundings. Cheryl scowled; this was the only nightspot in Carabas, and everyone knew it.

"The Pussy Foot is cool. Too cool, in fact. I'm surprised they don't shut the whole thing down for being too funky."

"So Bea's the problem. We should ditch her." Colline's voice moved up a register and her biscuit-arsed expression transformed as the restroom door opened. "Hi Bea!" she mewled. "Any luck out there?"

"Yeah." Bea sounded suspicious. "None of it good. I wanted to let you know I'm going home."

With a frown, Bea's companions followed her out of the club. Despite the catty remarks and backbiting, the trio had stuck together for years. Curfew was upon them, and the musicians were winding down, anyway. Out in the street, the girls could hear a slow dance number echoing from the building.

"I should be jigging to that tune with some hot tom," Cheryl sighed, slinking through the shadows. "Did you see the way that Singapura was looking at me?"

"I thought it was me he was looking at," Colline giggled, mentally conjuring a muscular cat with large hazel eyes. "He's there most nights. He's interested, I can tell."

They crossed the Dell, the cobblestones pale blue in the clear moonlight. They had to hurry to beat the curfew. Cheryl barely had time to glance at the well. The whole area would be crowded in the morning.

Colline's house was closest to the club, so she said goodnight to them on her stoop and gave Bea a hearty hug. Cheryl figured that Colline felt guilty for the things she'd said in the restroom; she was peculiar that way.

As her friends mewed a soft goodbye, Colline scratched at the door until her housemate let her in. The two remaining cats headed for Bea's apartment, their irises widening as the moon slipped behind a cloud.

"I found this sweet shortcut this evening," Cheryl said gleefully, leading Bea into the alley. Any sense of unease that Cheryl still felt was overwhelmed by excitement. Bea didn't share her enthusiasm but followed dutifully, listening out for the clock tower's midnight chimes.

"If they find us out here past curfew—."

"What are they gonna do? Make us drink tap water? This shortcut will save our skins, you'll see."

Cheryl stopped suddenly. Bea almost collided with her, crying, "What's up?"

"Am I mistaken," Cheryl replied, "or is that a freshly dead pigeon I see over there?"

Bea could see a shape in the dinge. It could have been a clumped gray cloth or a lump of plastic; it was hard to tell. She crouched down to sniff at the object and Cheryl commenced her prank. Using her head to shift the loose crate from the bottom of the pile, she sent the whole lot crashing down around her friend. Bea let out a yelp of fright or pain—Cheryl wasn't sure which—as a particularly heavy wooden crate landed on her shoulder.

"Serves you right, you fat tart!" Cheryl's laughter cut short when she saw Bea lying, unmoving, on the ground. She'd expected Bea to hear the crates, sense their movement, and get out of the way with typical feline agility.

"Come on, hen. Get up," said Cheryl, slowly circling her friend. "It was a joke!"

A deep growling sound made her turn to look behind her. Several pairs of grimy yellow eyes stared back.

"Bea, get up. We've got to move," Cheryl implored. Bea began to stir, moaning, groggy. A group of matt-furred feral cats, annoyed at having their sleep interrupted and their makeshift shelter wrecked, put their weight on their hind legs, ready to attack. Cheryl tried to back away but stumbled against the fallen crates.

"Get up, you thick slob! We have to leave." Bea got onto all fours, emitting a pitiful mew as she saw the ferals. As they tried to leave, they found themselves surrounded, with more ferals appearing from the shadows at both ends of the alley. As the clock chimed twelve, Cheryl and Bea looked at each other, sharing a silent farewell.

Cheryl picked up the pieces of a shattered crate and threw them at the nearest feral. It lunged, aiming not for her but for Bea, who was too dazed to defend herself. The Persian was torn to shreds.

That's my fault, Cheryl thought, throwing more crates and debris and anything else she could get her paws on. She found a long sliver of wood with a jagged, pointed end, noticing with satisfaction that the sliver was studded with rusty nails. Then she ran down the alley through a hairy, biting gauntlet, swinging her weapon wildly, hissing and spitting her way past the ferals onto open ground.

She realized that she'd instinctively made her fur stand up to make herself look bigger. *Funny. I look fatter than Bea now.*

She needed sanctuary and found it in the Detention Center. "They're after me," she told the guard. "You're next! You're next!" Still brandished her wooden weapon, she prodded it in the guard's face.

That got his attention. He straightened his limbs, had a quick stretch, and stifled a yawn as he checked his monitors. Cheryl focused long enough to read the name "Stout" on his ID badge.

"You can put your stick down, ma'am," he purred. "You're not a dog."

Cheryl placed her makeshift mace on the reception desk.

"There's no one outside," said Stout, trying to soothe the troubled visitor. "The cameras would pick them up. This building's bristling with CCTVs. What did they look like, these guys who are after you?"

"They ripped Bea to pieces," Cheryl sobbed. "They were wild. Ugly. Looked like they'd never washed themselves. I don't know what they were."

"I told ya. There's nobody here but us mon—." The guard stopped mid-sarcasm, hearing a nasty scratching sound on the windowpanes. He glanced at his monitors again and thought he saw a flash of hairy movement on Camera Six. He shakily picked up a bunch of keys and locked the main entrance. "You shouldn't be out this late, doll," he said, returning to his desk. "It's past curfew."

"My best friend was murdered by those things," Cheryl cried. "I know I missed curfew. I—we heard the bells."

The scratching continued, growing louder, with more paws battering against the windows. The guard stared out into the inky blue darkness.

"This ain't right," he muttered, pressing his face up against the glass. "Things like this don't happen here."

"Be careful," Cheryl said quietly.

"Don't fuss, puss," said Stout. "I protect this place all night, and I have done all my lives. I've never needed any help and I ain't gonna start now."

"Can't you call someone?" Cheryl begged, noticing a cracked seam across the window. "You're going to need help this time. There's so many of them."

"So many of what?"

The glass smashed inward, forcing Stout back as a horde of ferals burst in, more than Cheryl had seen before, so many that they filled the overwhelmed guard shack in seconds. Cheryl popped out her claws and scratched at the ferals, buying Stout enough time to free himself and take her deeper into the center. Behind them, they heard glass smash and crunch under paw.

"Is there another way out of here?" asked Cheryl, checking herself for wounds. She was uninjured, for now.

"Nope." Stout shook his head.

"How can you stay so calm? Oh, if only I'd kept my stick..."

"Don't expect me to fetch it for you. This is the safest building in Carabas, ma'am."

"Cheryl. Cheryl Carina."

"Cheryl, there's no safer place to be. You're in the city jail."

Sal lay in a melted heap on a bright red and green rug in Milo's apartment. The rug looked far too colorful to match the bland gray décor of the place. The snowshoe's legs felt like jelly with his brain as the topping. "What is this stuff?" he asked in a slow drawl.

"Valerian root," Milo answered, equally supine. "Strongest in the marketplace. You like?"

"I love," Sal purred. "Can I have some more?"

"How much you got?"

Sal dug into his pockets and found part of the rat's paw that Julius had given him days before. "Is this worth anything?"

Milo sniffed suspiciously at the morsel of meat. "Since you're a friend and you've got an honest face, I tell you what I'll do. This can be a down payment, and you can owe me the rest."

"Cool." Sal took more valerian from Milo, breathed deep, and fell backward in a contented heap.

***

After the fleas and grub of the flophouse, the mansion was a dazzling contrast. Toxic led a recalcitrant Moira to the most magnificent home in Carabas, with white colonnades, a sun-dappled porch area, and fake pink flamingos planted in the flowerbeds.

Inside, a wide staircase wound up to a landing decorated with paintings of distinguished-looking cats. Moira noticed the thick red carpet beneath her paws, begging to be scratched.

"Don't even think about it," said Toxic, grabbing her by the scruff of her neck.

"What is this place?" she asked. Toxic didn't reply. He drew her attention to the Abyssinian descending the stairs, done up in a splendid new waistcoat.

"Governor Tarquin!" Moira struggled to escape Toxic's grip. "Only you could be so bold. You ordered this lunkhead to drag me here?"

"I'm afraid so, my dear. Though it pained me to give the command."

"You could have just asked me." Moira broke free with a jolt, stumbling to a stop in front of Tarquin.

"You would have said no. Besides, this suits my purpose better. By whisking you away to be my betrothed, I've taken you out of harm's reach and befuddled my enemies in Bast."

"What harm?"

"There's a coup being planned back home, Moira. Didn't you realize?"

This was a lot for her to take in. She paused for a moment. "Wait ... did I hear right? Did you say 'betrothed'?"

"It's for your own safety, Moira." Tarquin rubbed up against her legs, making her shudder.

"Getting here wasn't safe. We encountered some ferals along the way."

"There are no ferals in this region," said Tarquin. "Not that we can't handle, anyway."

"I'm not marrying you for my protection or any other reason, you furry freak."

"You could learn to love me." Tarquin gave Moira another rub.

"Nothing could make me stay in this house a moment longer." Moira pulled herself away from Tarquin.

"Not even the identity of the cat who ordered Ambassador Frenkel's death?"

"Okay, that could make me stay. For as long as it takes for you to give me a name."

"Later," Tarquin cajoled. "First, let me show you around."

Stout led Cheryl through the white room where Julius and Lugs were cooped in their cells.

"You're not leaving me in here with them?" Cheryl protested, feeling less safe than ever. Ignoring her complaints, Stout pointed at a treat dispenser and said, "Help yourself."

The kittens cried out, awoken by the new arrival. The brown cat looked down from his cage, dreaming of a slinky assignation with Cheryl. Julius and Lugs sat on their haunches, silent, staring at the guard.

"You'll be safe in here," said Stout, reassuring his guest. "I'll come back for you when I've taken care of … our problem."

"Problem?" said Julius. "More like unmitigated trouble. How many mistakes are you going to make tonight?"

Stout ignored Julius and hissed at the kittens. "Keep it down there!" he said, his voice trembling. The little ones piped down.

Julius didn't think the guard was scared of a few fluffy orphans. The danger outside had disconcerted this tough nut. Once Stout had left the room, Julius scratched frantically at the floor of his cage.

"What're you doing?" Lugs grumbled. "You do know there's another cage underneath yours, don't you?"

Julius looked in Lugs's direction for a moment, then started scraping the back of his cell instead.

"You're not going to dig your way out of here, wherever you dig. That's metal, not kitty litter."

Julius was too busy scratching to reply.

"Is this some kind of nervous disorder? Any other uncontrollable urges I should know about?"

"I'm nearly done." Julius kept flexing his right forepaw and scrabbling his claws until he declared, "Aha! Got it!" and triumphantly held up a sheath. He used it to pick his lock and pop his cage open, holding a paw up to his lips to shush Cheryl.

"Stay away from me, you criminal," she said, brandishing a pack of bisque-flavored Lickables.

"Not much of a weapon," said Julius, introducing himself. He was a journalist, he explained. A stranger in town, looking for Moira. Wrong place, wrong time, big mouth.

"I shouldn't be here," said Julius.

"That makes all of us," the brown cat drawled.

"That doesn't make any sense," said Cheryl. "If you were innocent, you wouldn't be in cages."

"I'm not in a cage," Julius pointed out. "You can trust me."

Cheryl was not convinced of Julius's good intentions. She threw the sachet at him and ran out of the room.

She noticed the meowls first; they were wrong. A mass of cats howling, grinding their teeth, not sounding like cats at all. Next, she saw shadows on the white walls, too long, too jagged, extremely unfeline.

"Run!" Stout pelted down a corridor toward her, eyes wide, strange pieces of meat on his fur. Cheryl realized that the meat had belonged to other animals, the ferals who had broken in.

Stout sped past Cheryl, and she followed him back into the white room, catching their breath.

Stout noticed Julius was free and growled at him. Julius gave him a shrug and left the room, turning right back around. It was too late for him to escape.

The ferals had torn their way through the Detention Center and were hauling themselves into view. While Julius tipped over the treat dispenser to make a barricade, Stout led Cheryl across the white room, shoving her into one of the cubbies.

"You'll be safe in here," he explained, locking her in. "Nothing can get in or out of these suckers."

Cheryl looked at him as if he was crazy, then told him, "Go help that tabby." She watched Stout for as long as she could, the cage constricting her view.

She could smell stale urine and moldy food. A small, empty dish was attached to her cell door, presumably for food or water. There was barely room for her to turn around, not that she wanted to turn her back on the ferals.

Tarquin was giving Moira the grand tour of his mansion. He'd dismissed Toxic, assuring the puma that he could handle the captive.

"She's feisty," Toxic had warned.

"I know," Tarquin had giggled in response.

Moira was cooperating for now, listening to the Abyssinian's uninteresting tour talk. He'd had the mansion built from scratch, a sumptuous home fit for the ruler of an up-and-coming city. He pointed out the music conservatory, the state-of-the-art domotics, the infinity pool, and the library. He saved his favorite room for last.

He led Moira up the broad staircase onto a landing. She grimaced at some of the faces in the portraits.

"Previous governors," Tarquin explained, indicating a bare frame-sized patch on the wall. "Mine is still wet. I'm the first Abyssinian to govern a city and its surrounding region, you know."

The cats turned a corner, Moira making sure she was slightly behind Tarquin. She was still wary of him. At the end of a long corridor was a cluttered room that looked to her like a cross between a nursery and a museum. She saw a dead mouse, a squeaky toy, and a glass case full of fabulous jewelry with tinkly bells on it.

"This is where I keep my most prized objects," said Tarquin proudly. "From kittenhood through my ascent to power, I have kept all these things. To remind me where I came from ... and what I have yet to accomplish."

"What a load of junk," Moira thought out loud. "I knew you were nuts before, Tarquin. Now I double know it."

"How can it be junk when you are going to be associated with it? Your presence raises the importance, the value of everything else in this room."

Moira wasn't sure how to respond. "Thank you."

"So you will stay, then."

"No."

"It was not a question." Tarquin smiled in a way that Moira didn't like. "You will stay here and add some luster to my sad, old trinkets. Look around. Take your time. I will be back tomorrow morning."

"Tomorrow morning?"

Tarquin stepped out of the peculiar room and swiftly pulled a metal shutter down over the entrance, locking it and sealing Moira in. As the governor disappeared with a fey waggle of his paw, she was left with nothing to do but wander around the room and try to find a tool that she could use to break out.

Some of Tarquin's objects were common as much. A fishing rod leaned in one corner, with a ragged piece of cloth tied to its line instead of a hook or a fly. Something else from his kittenhood, Moira supposed, that used to be dangled for the blighter to play with. She blanked out the thought of the infuriating cat's formative years. On a plinth sat a chewed-up length of twine, tied in a loop and covered with fur. *Why do boys never grow out of their toys?* Moira wondered, batting the twine off its plinth and across the room.

Other exhibits she found were less plain. A scroll marked a pact between dogs and cats, signed by His Honor, Mayor Otto. The pact, engineered by Tarquin while he was still in Bast, had allowed a mendacious faction of dogs to enter the city, almost causing its ruin. Yet the Abyssinian was obviously proud of the societal seeds he'd planted. If different species didn't want to live together, then government policy could force them into close quarters so they could get to know each other and find out they weren't so bad after all.

The glorious centerpiece of the exhibition gleamed in the moonlight that now pierced the room. On a higher pedestal than any other object was a solid gold litter tray, thankfully empty and clean, with a plaque set beneath it:

AWARDED TO TARQUIN BY THE
GRATEFUL CITIZENS OF CARABAS
FOR HIS UNPRECEDENTED SERVICES
TO THE COMMUNITY.

Not bad for a guy kicked out of his hometown.

The plaque failed to note that the tray had actually been commissioned by Tarquin's executive secretary, under threat of imprisonment if she didn't have it made. It was the thought that counted, though, and Moira was sure somebody somewhere was impressed with Tarquin's achievements. Maybe his stringent means would be justified by the end of the eons-long dog-cat conflict, and maybe not.

Moira laughed at the tray despite her predicament, letting herself relax some. She felt more trapped than she had in the crate. She was in shtuck for the long haul, so there was no point staying mad. Instead, she curled herself up into a ball and closed her eyes, glad at least to be free from Toxic's ugly stench.

Julius arched his back, doing his best to block the way into the white room. The ferals raced down the corridor toward him, and they seemed to have grown in number since he'd encountered them on the train.

"Come and get me, you fusty ferals!" Julius cried. His last skirmish with them had fueled him with bravado, but he didn't expect to leave this fight unscathed. Even if he survived this attack, he'd have Tarquin to contend with. He smiled grimly as he imagined how disappointed Tarquin would be, denied his blasphemous prize.

As the ferals came within snapping distance of Julius, a yowl from above made them skid to a halt and look up. There was Stout, clinging to a duct pipe, mouth wide open to show a clean, white set of teeth. The courageous guard let himself drop onto the menacing mongrel cats, flailing with his claws as he descended. Julius tried to drive the ferals back toward an elevator shaft with his own claws extended.

Lugs battered at his cell door in vain. It was ridiculous that he wasn't out there fighting, doing what he'd been trained for and helping his fellow felines.

"Stop that banging," pleaded Cheryl. "They'll hear you."

"I—can't just—sit here," Lugs told her between rams. "Those poor guys need my help."

Once Julius had been forced back into the white room, Cheryl could see him valiantly defending his fellow prisoners. The ferals scratched and nipped at him, but he kept them away with his nimble paws. Stout wasn't doing so well; Cheryl could only see his ears surfacing from a sea of matted fur.

"Get back in your cell," Stout told Julius. "Now."

"I don't think so." Julius shook his head. Stout broke free of the mob and shoved the tabby into a cubicle, locking him in and breaking the key in the lock, tossing his keychain in a dark corner. Julius would not be able to break out again. Julius watched, horrified, as the ferals overwhelmed Stout with victorious howls of delight, then tried to get into the cells.

The kittens cowered in fright; the brown cat was petrified. Cheryl hunched herself as small as she could at the back of her cubby as ugly faces spat at her through the bars and tried to chew the metal. She hoped that they'd get to Julius and Lugs first, sate themselves on those out-of-towners, and leave her alone.

More ferals battered at her cell door, throwing themselves at the bars, leaving dents, and bending the metal inward. One tried to squeeze its nose in to get at her; she sliced at it with a manicured claw.

After a terrible hour or more, the howling and battering stopped. Perhaps the ferals were tired after their long pursuit; Cheryl felt exhausted too. Perhaps they realized the bars were unbreakable. Whatever the case, the room grew quiet. Cheryl could hear the sounds of padding paws receding into the distance and a strange whimper—she realized the sound was coming from her.

"How do we get out of here?" Julius asked. He'd been so close to freedom.

"We wait until dawn," said Lugs. "When it's time for us to be punished."

20

The Rat Pack

In which the rats reach Bast.

The rats stayed close the whole way along the track, moving with great purpose: scuffling, sniffing, following their noses. With their snouts still pressed close to the cold steel, they reached the Bast train station, excited by the scents of the vendors who sold hot food there.

The lead rat raised its head and took a look around with his beady eyes. There was a chugging, metallic sound in the distance, and he stood up straight to get a better look. The 10:45 to Bubastis was heading straight for the small pack of rats, its lights bouncing off the power lines above as it moved closer. To the rat, the flashing light shadows looked like low-level shooting stars.

On the platform, a group of pilgrims waited patiently for their train. A pilgrimage to the mecca of Bubastis was common, especially for young cats looking for spiritual guidance and elderly ones seeking absolution for a lifetime of sins.

Unlike the cosmopolitan cats around them, they were dressed simply—gowns draped over their bodies, no fancy colors, no jewelry or other accessories. Their luggage was minimal, and they refused help from the porters, carrying all their worldly possessions in small bundles. The priests of the Church of Bastet had convinced them to hand over all the ostentatious clothes and objects that they owned to Bishop Kafel; only by losing their material possessions would they be free to do their soul-searching. The bishop exchanged the belongings for capital that paid for more churches, where more priests urged their congregations to empty their pockets in an unending circle of guilt and charity.

These pilgrims were skinny, rangy even. With all their wealth away to the Church of Bastet, they hadn't had a good meal in days. The smells from the vendors' stalls were making them antsy. But they tried their best to stay calm and ignore the temptations around them—mainly the urge to leap on the nearest sushi seller—and only a rare nostril twitch gave away their true feelings.

Until they saw the rats.

With the train grinding into the station and passengers ready to board, the rats became agitated, looking for a way to get from the tracks up onto the platform. With a strength surprising for their size, they leaped toward the pilgrims, landing with a rolling stumble at the paws of the hungry cats. A burst of steam loosed from the engine as it came to rest, distracting the cats and giving the rodents enough time to right themselves. One particularly thin pilgrim snatched a rat between his teeth and bit the morsel in two. This sparked a free-for-all, with all the passengers on the platform—hungry or no—dropping their luggage and chasing the rats around the station.

Some of the rodents headed for the vendors' stalls, knocking over wares and disappearing into tiny crannies. The pilgrims who followed them couldn't resist taking a bite of the food on display, upsetting the vendors. Within minutes, the whole place was in an uproar, with rats biting back, vendors scratching at acolytes, and staff struggling to diffuse the situation.

The skinniest cat found the chief rat trying to board the train. He picked up the pesky rodent and squeezed tight, enjoying a vindictive moment that rated high on the sin-ometer. Losing lung power, the chief rat faced the cat and squeaked, "No."

The cat ignored him, squeezing even tighter, opening his jaws wide to bite the wee guy's head off. The rat squeaked again.

"No ... more!" He twisted his body sideways, sank his teeth into the cat's paw, and chomped down with energy drawn from years of persecution and domination. The cat let out a high-pitched yowl, dropped the rat, and watched enraged as it fled from the station. The surviving rats followed, leaving a heap of vexed felines piled up on the platform.

A few blocks away, the rats stopped and counted their losses. Their small pack had dwindled to an unhappy few. But the chief was determined to restock his numbers with back alley rats and go on the offensive. It was time to teach the merciless moggies a lesson.

Toxic's Night Off

Toxic had been itching to get out of the flophouse for days, desperate to stretch his legs and get some fresh air. He never felt content to be in one place for too long, stay still, or waste time. He needed to keep moving as much as possible. It was what his muscles and sinews always ached for—to run, to leap, to hunt.

With Moira stuck in Tarquin's barmy museum, Toxic was free to roam Carabas for the night. He was drawn, like all visitors, to the large structures in the center of town: City Hall, the Kindness Tavern, and the mighty Tolerance Tower block. A long, wide thoroughfare led all the way from the docks to the Friendship Center, which was heaving with nocturnal tourists now that the sun had set. Toxic wasn't the tourism type.

He kept walking past the massive architectural triumph, enjoying the feel of asphalt under his paws. It was very different from the wild lands where he had learned to fight and kill as a wean. There he'd been encouraged by his father not just to catch a mouse but to appreciate its terror, toy with it a while, then drag his claws slowly down its belly and enjoy its excruciating death.

It was the way of all pumas, but his proud parents had noticed the particular pleasure he'd gained from his kills. Instead of presenting his captured prey to the elders of his clowder as a gift, he'd keep the mice and terrorize them for as long as was painfully possible.

His assertive mother, a slim charcoal beauty with the easy grace of a huntress, had sat down with him one day and asked him why he liked to intimidate his victims.

"I love to see their eyes grow wide, to feel their heartbeats quicken beneath my paws. To watch their blood seep slowly from their fur. These things make me happy."

That was the right answer; no mother could refuse her son happiness. Encouraged to continue his wicked ways, the youngster had tracked larger creatures as he grew: squirrels, hares, raccoons, deer ... and domestic cats. Since his touch was as deadly as poison, he earned the name Toxic. Even his parents were endangered when they displeased him, threatening to call for help when they found a kitten in Toxic's cooking pot. He'd slain his mother and father, burying them in shopping bags in their backyard. The bushes he'd planted to cover their graves had withered and failed to flower.

Without his family to support him, Toxic had sought other sources of income. His questionable skills had led him to work for questionable cats in the city of Bast, killing for them, hunting down their enemies, and occasionally abducting she-cats.

Toxic continued his walk through Carabas, scowling at the vacuous inhabitants. Near the North Gate was a mighty tree, towering into the sky and scraping the clouds. Toxic was impressed. Its wide, solid branches cast cooling shadows all across the uppermost part of the city. A couple of cats were in the branches, meowling their heads off. The Great Tree was the one place in Carabas where they were allowed to vent their frustrations and clean their claws with abandon. The scratch marks in the trunk had whittled the wood away considerably.

A mother cat stood near the trunk, a worried expression on her face. She was staring with her neck craned upward, watching a small kitten in the uppermost branches.

"Please help me," she implored, dragging her eyes from the heights to meet the puma's.

"What's up?" asked Toxic, barely interested.

"My son is," the mother replied, "he's got himself stuck up there. Would you help get him down?"

Nothing to it, Toxic thought, scaling the tree with his powerful paws. The kitten was mewing, looking balefully at the ground. How pathetic.

It took mere seconds for Toxic to reach the cub. The puma looked deep into the little kitten's eyes and saw something of himself as a youngster within them. Then Toxic shook his head and approached the cub, who backed off, fur bristling.

Toxic decided that this spit of fur was nothing like him. He'd never been this cowardly or weak or helpless.

He kept moving forward, the branch sagging under his weight until the cub had nowhere to retreat but thin air, tumbling to the ground beside his hysterical mother.

Toxic calmly climbed down and began to wash himself.

"You monster," the mother cried; Toxic took it as a compliment.

"I got him down out of the tree, just like you asked me to," he said in an emotionless tone. "You should be careful what you wish for."

Toxic returned to the flophouse where an urgent note had been left for him. His night-off was over, apparently; Tarquin the Great needed him.

Sal woke from a stupor into a mild state of befuddlement. He screwed up his eyes, trying to focus on getting another fix of valerian.

He had been lying on Milo's rug all night. He could tell from the patch of kitty drool beside his head. Sal could see Milo's bag lying on a table. He was sure his new friend wouldn't notice if he sneaked a whiff or two, so he snuck over to the table and raised his head, nostrils wide with anticipation.

"Oh no," he moaned. "It's empty."

"You snarfed the whole bag," Milo chuckled. "You owe me quite a lot of coin."

"My best pal's got a job," Sal said, his spirits rising. "He'll pay the bill."

"You hope."

"I'm surprised this stuff's allowed in Carabas." Sal suddenly felt very thirsty. "It's too good to be legal."

"It's not strictly legit," Milo admitted, throwing the empty bag in a trash bin. "But so many Carabians use it, it's tolerated." He hauled Sal upright. "Let's get to work."

"Excuse me?" Sal was gaining a real aversion to the w-word.

"Time for you to pay off that debt. You're my new employee."

22

Well Day

It was still dark as Milo led Sal into the smart west side of Carabas. Gazing up at the moon high in the sky, Sal estimated that the witching hour had just begun, but he couldn't be sure. He didn't even know where he was going.

"How long will it take me to pay off my debt?" he asked Milo, who had been silent since they'd left the apartment. "I have a couple of cats to look for."

"One little job, that's all," Milo smiled. "Help me out tonight, then you're free to do as you wish."

Sal wished he had more valerian. "Hey, I know this place!" he said as they entered the Friendship Center. Animated chatter came from one of a cluster of conference rooms at the far end of the building. Milo went straight there—he was obviously used to taking the trip.

"Go on in and see if anyone would like to buy these," Milo told Sal just outside the room. He passed a pawful of small bags packed with catnip and valerian.

"I'm no peddler." Sal's eyes watered.

"Don't worry, I think you'll find these an easy sell. Bring the cash straight back to me, mind." Milo shoved Sal into the room, where he saw a score of middle-aged cats and dogs chatting and making notes on small scraps of paper.

"What we need is a common language," one distinguished-looking dachshund was saying. "There's too much room for miscommunication with all these meows. If we all barked, life would be much easier."

"What's wrong with everybody mewing?" suggested a chartreux.

"I don't think so," the dachshund growled.

"How about coming up with some new words altogether?" Sal suggested. "Um, like, 'upita' for open, 'capito' for close."

"A new vocabulary?" A dalmatian nodded to his secretary. "Make a note of this, please."

"Dogs could be popples and cats could be..." Sal noticed that the entire crowd was hanging on his every word. "Wimbos?"

"Splendid!" the chartreux clapped his paws together. "And what section of the city do you represent?"

"I'm from Bast, actually. What's going on?"

"Why, we're Tarquin's think-tank, personally chosen by the governor himself. We try to augment the lives of his citizens by anticipating anything that might injure or offend them. Then we suggest that a law is passed to prevent that injury or offense from occurring."

"A law?" Putting his paws in his pockets, Sal clutched the bags that he'd stuffed there and tried not to look guilty.

"Yeah." The chartreux bowed slightly. "I'm Judge Pumpkin. This is Sherriff Bismarck." He pointed to the dalmatian. "And that agitated dachshund over there's Seth Curcio, head of our Chamber of Commerce."

"Hey, Milo." Sal poked his head out of the room to look for his friend. "Come and meet these nice gents." Milo had scarpered. Although he regularly sold his herbs to the high and mighty of the city, tonight's greater-than-usual police presence was obviously too much for him.

"Tell us what you think of this." Bismarck gently pulled Sal back into the conference room. "We've received a complaint from a little, old poodle in the east district about cats being referred to as 'mouse catchers.' Don't you think that's terrible?"

"I've been called worse," Sal muttered.

"I feel that it's too function-oriented," said Pumpkin. "It suggests that we only exist to perform one function."

"Well, that's not true." Curcio pursed his lips. "We'll have to ban the use of the word. All in favor?" The room erupted with mews and yips of agreement.

"We have a similar situation." Bismarck nodded. "There have been reports of dogs being referred to as 'ball chasers.' It just isn't dignified enough."

"It's downright disrespectful." Pumpkin looked around the room. "No more references to dogs as ball chasers." The ayes had it again.

"This is cool," Sal giggled. "Y'know, back home, nobody cares about anyone else. They're so busy, so hung up with their own lives. We even went to the Stray

Cats Bureau looking for a friend of ours and ... well, we didn't get much cooperation. But here it's different. You obviously care enough about others to get involved in their affairs. It's kind of refreshing. What happens once you've agreed on these ... recommendations?"

"We convey our decisions to Tarquin, and he passes them as law." Curcio wagged his tail. "Popples and wimbos, eh? If only we had more cats like you in Carabas. Any more questions?"

"Yes," said Sal eagerly. "Do you have a litter room?"

The morning light didn't usually wake Julius. If anything, it was a sleep aid, as he was well-versed in napping in patches of sunshine. Just like those dumb stroodles at home, stopping in the middle of the street for a break, Julius loved to soak up some rays. But the city seemed far away to him, even in his dreams.

Lugs liked to wake up early; as a military cat, he insisted on it. At sunrise, he opened his eyes and stretched, gave himself a quick bath, and started to turn around in his cell, as much as the tiny space would allow. In his mind, it was a pint-sized parade ground, and he was marching as he'd always done back at base. It was a simple, tough, familiar place that didn't encourage sentiment.

"I never thought I'd say this, but you impressed me," Lugs told Julius.

"How so?" the tabby yawned.

"Yer fighting. It was pretty good for a wee Jessie like you. You got moves."

"I get plenty of practice."

Cheryl opened her eyes and peered out the cell door to see the white walls dirty with fur and blood. Stout lay alone on the floor, badly injured but still breathing. *Bastet be praised!* she thought, wincing at the bite taken out of his left forepaw. *He deserves a medal after what he did.*

But what did I do?

She started to worry that she'd be dragged away with Julius and Lugs. Guilt by association. After all, she was locked in a cell in the Central Detention Center. Only hardened criminals got locked up in here, right?

Even if her fellow inmates vouched for her, they were hardly credible witnesses. She could see her fate unfolding in her mind's eye. *Oh no, Your Honor, I had nothing to do with this guard's injuries. It's not my fault if he was left for dead. What am I doing locked in this cubicle? Uh, the guard put me in here. For my own safety. No, I'm not a danger to myself or others! I was in danger! And yes, I'll admit it, I put others in danger, too. That was foolish. That doesn't mean I'm not good, Your Honor. I don't belong here. I belong in my salon, giving pedicures to Persians.*

"What's going to happen to us?" Julius asked, breaking the anxious silence as he stretched himself awake. He could hear a group of cats approaching. "What are they going to do to us?"

"First, they'll drag you into the main square past rows of onlookers, jabbing you with claws and aiming for maximum humiliation," said Cheryl, sounding morose. "Then..." she winced. "You do know what day it is, don't you?"

Julius shook his head; he could barely remember his own address at that moment.

"Maybe it's best that you don't know."

"I can take it," Julius urged.

"They'll string us up by our weary, little tails. After that, if we're lucky, they'll burn us quick."

"Bet you're glad you asked," Lugs chipped in.

"I'll be okay though, won't I?" replied Cheryl, all sweet and innocent.

"We'll put in a good word for you. Explain everything," Lugs assured her.

"That's what I was scared of." Cheryl scrabbled at her cell door; it still didn't budge.

She was somewhat relieved when Tarquin flounced into the detention area and ignored her completely. "It's high time you were dealt with," he declared. "All set, gentlecats?" The Abyssinian led a group of guards that brought no extra sunshine into the white room. Chief Rusty Maxwell was there, an Anatolian shepherd dog who Tarquin had placed in charge of the prowlers. Maxwell had a tan-colored coat, a black muzzle and ears, and brown eyes that shone with loyalty. With him was an impressive-looking Airedale priest.

"Looks like you had a disturbing night." Tarquin put his face up close to Julius's cell door. "You're a liability to the cat kingdom, Kyle. We'll try to make this as slow and painful as possible."

"That makes me feel, ooh, about one percent better," the tabby replied with a sneer. Nevertheless, he detected a faint sympathetic taint to Tarquin's officious tone.

"You're a complicated cove, aren't you?" Lugs grimaced.

"Let them out," Tarquin told a prowler. "Carefully. We've got some tricky types here."

Maxwell was busy ordering a stretcher for the comatose Stout. The chief prowler rolled his eyes, wondering why Tarquin was present. It was bad enough having the priest tagging along.

"Oh, Goddess forgive the blasphemers, the ignorant, the heathens and the disbelievers: they tread in darkness, too blind to see your light. May their sight return when you embrace them in the afterlife."

"We going to be preached to death?" Julius asked. "What are you really going to do to us?"

"Something your mother should have done as soon as you were born. You were the runt of the litter, weren't you?"

"Don't confuse my kittenhood with your own, chum. Lead on; I've got an itinerary to keep." As they were escorted from the building, Julius ran through his schedule so far. "Fight with large, fearsome tom? Check. Lose mate in bizarre abduction? Check. Risk life to save trainload of ungrateful travelers from feral beasts? Check. Get roughed up by an overzealous police force? Check." He turned to look at Lugs. "Am I missing anything?"

"Losing your friend's cargo," Lugs added, "so he's forced to seek out more goods, misses a briefing session with his superior, and risks a likely court-martial."

"Oh yeah, I forgot that one."

"I don't think we'll have to worry about a court-martial," said Tarquin smoothly.

"Gonna fix it for me, are ye?" Lugs perked up.

"You're the one who's going to be fixed. Permanently." They'd reached the main foyer of the Old Exchange. "Take Sergeant Barr to The Vet," Tarquin told a guard. "He'll end this lynx's lusty ways. Mr. Kyle—your public awaits."

Outside, the streets were lined with Carabians of different breeds and backgrounds. As Julius was led down the street, the cats and dogs jeered and hissed at him. Any remaining wisps of bravado vanished when he saw their faces; they were excited, anticipating an entertaining spectacle. He was the main event. For all he knew, he was the main course.

"This must be the biggest turnout we have ever had." Tarquin marveled at the cats and kittens waving flags and yowling at the passing prisoners. "Haven't they got jobs to go to? Schools?"

"It's still early, sir," said the chief prowler. "And a lot of these guys are transients. They don't plan on stayin' here long. I guess they're looking for something fun to spice up their travel stories."

"A tale to tell the family back home around the dinner dish," Julius mused bitterly.

"It'll all be over soon," the priest told him.

"Seems to me you're dragging this out as long as you can!" Julius told Tarquin. "This is crazy! We haven't done anything wrong. The only thing I've ever been guilty of is padding out a cheap novel or two. But being a hack author never warranted this sort of treatment, not where I come from."

"You truly believe that you do not deserve this punishment?" the Airedale asked Julius.

"I sure do."

The pup-faced priest bowed his head solemnly. "Then you are damned."

"If we let you go," Tarquin explained, "then other transients won't take our laws seriously, either. I've already explained this." Tarquin's tone remained gentle and persuasive. "I can understand you're upset."

"You've lost what few marbles you ever had, you bargain basement tyrant."

Julius's attempts to rile Tarquin had no effect. "We're almost there," the ruler said. "You can hear the drums now."

Sure enough, at the end of the street, a band played. Fiddlers, harpists, and old toms on strum-scarred washboards ushered the prisoners into the main square.

"It's a very popular tradition." Tarquin had to raise his voice to be heard over the din. "We look forward to it all year."

"Everyone loves a parade," Julius said charily.

"I don't think you're going to love this one." Tarquin shoved the tabby forward and joined the crowd of cats and dogs along with his guards. Cheryl and Julius were left in the middle of the street, spinning around, trying to find a face that expressed reason or friendliness. They couldn't find one.

"And there was me thinking this was a progressive place," Julius said, but no one could hear him. They were too busy making catcalls.

Julius and Cheryl moved down the street—a big mistake. The assembly closed its ranks behind them, forcing them to walk in one direction. The Carabians crowded in on either side, their jeers getting louder. Julius's walk became a fast trot. He was being corralled and didn't know where.

Lugs was led to a dark brown building with no windows. He took a ramp up into the structure, cool and foreboding as a mausoleum. Behind a small counter, a female cat waited. The room reminded Lugs of a dentist's waiting area, except the posters on the walls showed colorful pictures of skeletons and organs instead of teeth. He could hear faint howls and moans coming from the back of the building.

"Hi, doll." Lugs wiggled his whiskers at the female.

She was a beautiful Persian, but her eyes were cold and unwelcoming.

"This way," she said without emotion. With the lady in the lead and the two guards at the rear, Lugs was taken to a smaller room with a steel table in the center.

"Hop up on there, please." At least the Persian was polite, even if she couldn't manage friendly. With a charming smile, he complied, effortlessly scaling the table.

"Hold him down," the Persian told the guards. As they forced Lugs down onto his side, they each grabbed two of his limbs and pinned him against the metal surface.

Now the lynx was worried. He looked around the room, looking for something that he could use to aid his escape or distract his guards. The Persian approached with a tray of surgical instruments, which she laid close to his head. He could smell her saliva on the newly sterilized tools.

"What's a nice cat like you doing in a torture chamber like this?" he asked, pouring on the charm despite his predicament.

"They call me The Vet," the Persian purred as she picked up a scalpel, twirling it between her pads. "I understand that you've been bothering the female citizens of Carabas."

"Well, not all of them. Not yet."

"There's a procedure that I perform on toms with an overactive libido; it puts paid to any future harassment."

As The Vet approached Lugs's nether regions with the scalpel, he tried to squirm his way out of the guards' grip. They averted their eyes, but they had to listen to the screams as The Vet set to work.

Julius had no choice. He had to follow the path left open by the crowd and walked to the beat of the drummers, flattening his ears when the crowd booed him. Cheryl was shocked, speechless, wondering how she'd gotten associated with someone so despised—and how they could be treated so badly after helping to fight the ferals. If this was the fair legal process, then Lady Justice definitely needed her eyes checked.

When she realized where they were headed, Cheryl finally found the wherewithal to talk again.

"The Dell," she told her fellow prisoner. "They're taking us to Ding Dong Dell."

"You live here," Julius said. "What's really going on? What's this all about?"

"It's a tradition," said Cheryl sadly. "I didn't think they'd make us a part of it." Usually, she'd been part of the crowd, not the source of its entertainment. "Every first Tuesday of the month, a lawbreaker is taken through the streets and—."

"I don't want to know."

Julius found out soon enough. The Carabians began to close in on him and Cheryl, swiping at them with their claws popped out. Scratched and shoved around, Julius looked pleadingly at Cheryl.

"Sorry I got you into this," he said. "I know I said I didn't want to know, but I need to."

"It represents the—," Cheryl winced as her shoulder was nicked. "Threshing of the harvest. In order that it should grow again, returning stronger than ever next spring."

"What's next?"

"Depends on the mood of the crowd—and the executioner, Johnny Thin. Drowning or burning. Nothing fun."

"You call anything remotely related to this 'fun'?"

"I always thought so." Cheryl had tears in her eyes. "Until today."

The crowd had left room in the Dell for two methods of execution. A cat-size basket sat next to a large bundle of firewood; nearby, an old brick well waited to swallow up its next victim.

Cheryl was crammed into the basket, which was winched up above the firewood. Johnny Thin, a squat, brutish cougar with a hood over his face, held a blazing torch against the wood and started it smoking. Once that was done—Cheryl yowling protests all along—Thin picked up Julius and held him over his head, making the crowd cry out with delight. Julius sank his claws into Thin's hood, ripping it from his face, but this didn't stop the executioner from throwing his prisoner into the deep, echoing well.

At the sound of a mighty splash, the crowd cheered again. Trapped in her basket, Cheryl spluttered as smoke rose around her.

"That's what I like to hear," Tarquin told the long-suffering Maxwell. "Happy townsfolk and a very unhappy criminal."

Flames reached greedily for the basket. Cheryl wanted to jump out, but the bundle of firewood was too large for her to avoid. She was still tired from the feral attack, and the hot smoke was smothering her.

A small cat pushed his way through the crowd, ducking under tails, slipping between legs until he reached the clearing. It was Stout, heavily bandaged but fully conscious. He was joined by Sal, looking more focused than usual, and a horde of ferals. Thin was preoccupied with fixing his hood, so he didn't have time to stop the ferals from scratching him into a belly-up, submissive position. The crowd scattered, panicking at the sight of ferocious beasts in their civilized town. The lead feral snuffed at the air, following Julius's scent.

Splash! Julius had fallen hard into the well, righting himself mid-descent to land in a pool of water, all fours instantly treading to keep himself afloat. Under the surface, he could feel bones jutting from the bottom of the well; if he'd fallen with any more force, he would have been impaled. Obviously, some of his predecessors had been injured in the fall, probably drowning in a short space of time.

Julius paddled furiously, stretching his neck to keep his head up. He hated water; he didn't much like the dark, but top of his loathe list at that moment was Tarquin, that jumped-up barmy bureaucat. Julius had unraveled the Abyssian's previous scheme—the one that had brought a menacing pack of dogs into Bast. Now Tarquin had a whole city at his command. Julius had to bring him down to size and save Cheryl before she burned to a crisp.

Far above, he could hear the crowd cheering on his death. Thanks to the governor, this was their one chance to let off some steam, but to Julius that hardly excused their bloodthirsty behavior. Popping his claws out, he tried to find purchase on the mossy walls of the well. Far above, he could see a circle of blue sky, beckoning with its warmth and light. Up ahead, he could hear the faint sounds of the drums and fiddles, more frenzied, more insistent, as if they were underscoring his fight for survival.

Finally, he found a couple of pockmarks in the wall, dug his forepaws deep, and started to hoist himself up. The going was arduous, but as he smelled wisps of smoke drifting down from the Dell, he doubled his efforts. His ascent was half complete when a large toothsome form blotted out the blue and hurtled toward him. A feral, mean and slavering, landed on top of him and knocked him back down into the water. This time, the bones nicked Julius's ear as the water murked around him. The blood made the feral crazier, flailing around in the dark, trying to rip its prey to pieces.

Backed up against the slimy wall, Julius ducked into the water. The feral ignored his misgivings and lunged, missing Julius as he swam to the other side of the well. The tabby tried to climb up again, his fur matted flat against his body; as the feral leaped, he landed on a shinbone splinter that Julius held in front of him.

Dismayed, the feral tried to grab at the makeshift weapon sticking from his brisket. He fell back into the water with a large, undignified splash.

With the rest of the ferals busy chasing the flummoxed townsfolk and Stout finishing off the executioner, Sal went unchallenged as he grabbed the rope that suspended Cheryl's basket over the fire. He lowered her slightly, making her protest, then swinging her clear of the rising flames.

"Can I borrow this?" asked Stout as Cheryl climbed out of the basket.

"Sure," she batted her eyelids at him, noticing Thin lying prone on the ground. Stout lowered the bucket down the well, then used the rope to hoist it back out. To Sal's relief, the retrieved basket was occupied by Julius.

His matted fur made him look like a skinny, wee thing. A v-shaped tear had appeared in his left ear. But the tabby hardly took a breath before he started running as far as possible from the Dell.

"You okay?" he asked Cheryl and Sal, tagging along behind him.

"Still ticking," Cheryl said. "But what happened to Lugs?"

"That's what we're going to find out," said Julius. "Can't be as bad as getting thrown down a well." Cheryl looked back at her half-cooked tail but said nothing.

"Who put me in?" Julius continued.

"Big Johnny Thin," said Cheryl.

"And who pulled me out?"

"Little Tommy Stout."

The small cat nodded a greeting to Julius. "Least I could do after last night's swedge," said Stout. "Looks like I got you right in time. Not frightened, were you, pussycat?"

"Nah." Julius shook his head, slowing drying off. "Same old, same old." He turned to Sal, pleased to see the snowshoe. "Where have you been, Sal?"

"I made some friends."

"Like Tommy?"

"Oh, I met him in the hospital," said Sal.

"He OD'd on some bad valerian," Stout explained. "Said he knew you. I was taking him to you when the ferals made their move."

Julius halted, forcing Sal to stop as well. "Who gave you this bad herb?"

"From one of my new friends." Sal frowned. "I had to get rid of it so I wouldn't get into trouble. I got *myself* into trouble instead."

"Must have been a novelty for you."

"Huh?"

Julius sighed, then started walking again, following Cheryl's lead. "I'm glad you're okay, Sal," he said.

"Bright-tailed and bushy-eyed," Sal chirped.

"But where did you get to when I was arrested?"

"You were?"

"You were right there in the market with me, Sal."

"I didn't know you'd been *arrested*," said Sal, his whiskers twitching.

"You didn't get an inkling when the prowlers put cuffs on me and dragged me away?"

"I thought they just wanted a chat."

"I would have thought them reading me my rights and telling me I was 'under arrest' would have been a giveaway. Sometimes I worry about you ... You've been on the nip again?"

"No. yes. Like I said, I made some new friends. I couldn't say no to them. That would have been rude."

"So you're a *social* addict. Now I understand perfectly. You sure know how to fall in with the wrong kind of people."

"What do you mean? I'm with you, aren't I?"

At least he was safe. "C'mon. Let's go find Lugs."

"Lugs?"

"I mean Sergeant Barr. Calls himself Lugs."

"Why?" asked Sal.

"Never mind."

"Will he arrest me?"

Julius stuffed his paws in his pockets. The gesture reassured Sal.

"I think he has more important things to worry about right now," said Julius.

"If you want to find Lugs, then I think I might know where he is," said Cheryl.

"That's great!" said Sal. "I still don't get the Lugs thing." He tugged at Julius's coat sleeve. "You were worried about me."

"A bit. Okay, a lot. I've lost enough friends. Don't want to lose anymore."

"We're friends?"

Julius nodded, glancing at Stout, Cheryl, and Sal. Carabas seemed to create strange alliances.

Tarquin hadn't run for his life for a long time; the pain in his lungs was proof enough. He didn't look back as he ran from the Dell, didn't stop to help the cats who fell or were caught by raging ferals. Chief Maxwell herded him back to the Old Exchange, where he scurried to his office and tried to collect his senses.

"How could this possibly have happened?" he asked the chief once his breath had returned. "No warning. A meaningless attack. Who were they?"

"Outsiders, sir." The chief maintained his constant air of professional courtesy despite the emergency. "Not a group of dutiful citizens. Obviously not residents. That's all I know." Truth was, the chief hadn't looked back to observe the ferals once the commotion had started. He'd been focused on his main tasks in life—keeping Tarquin safe and as happy as possible so that he could keep his job.

"Double the guard around this place. Clear the streets. Issue a curfew." Tarquin sank onto his haunches, exhausted by his flight. "And get me a nice big bowl of milk."

Tad Tybalt woke with a flinch. He'd been curled up on his office chair after a late night examining the quarterly reports. Since the factory had clunked to a halt, creditors were calling in their dues, and he was struggling to keep his business afloat. The strain was getting to him. It wasn't like him to fall asleep at his desk; as far as he was concerned, sleep was for wimps.

"I must be getting old," he said to himself in the dawn light.

"Could be," said a small voice, squeaked from a dim-lit corner of the room.

"How did you get in here?" asked Tad, licking his lips.

"I scurried."

Tad hunkered down and opened his eyes wide, taking a good, close look at the intruder. "You've got some nerve coming in here."

"In a building like this," said the visitor, indicating the large window that looked out onto a factory floor, "you'll find lots of my kind. Plenty of warm, dark nooks for us to breed in. Factories and allotments."

Tad decided that he was being tricked. His VP, a prankster of the highest rank, had left this little guest for him as a snackable joke, a gag he could gorge on. He moved closer to the corner, jaws open wide and dripping with saliva.

"Don't corner me. You wouldn't like me when I'm cornered." The rat's beady eyes glimmered in the shadows. Despite all Tad's great power and greater appetite, he backed off a little.

"Give me a good reason not to make you my lunch," Tad snarled.

"One's all I have and all you'll need. I have a proposition for you."

It was hard to gauge the speed of the Leo, but Bridget noticed the wake was smaller than usual as she took her daily walk to the bow of the ship. There was no wind in the air and no land in sight, just the immobile sun blazing down on the deck, scorching the wood so that her pads stung as she strolled. *I'll find some lackeys to carry me,* she smirked to herself. Let them deal with the pain of a burning deck. She was too important to put up with such trifles.

She padded farther down the deck, crusts of sleep still in her eyes from her noontime nap. She'd have to ask Pollet to lick the rheum from her eyelids when she saw him; she always enjoyed watching his face when she made the command.

Bridget left the deck and headed for the ballroom, glad to escape the sunlight for a moment. There were bound to be servers preparing the room for her nightly entertainment; she'd order them to drop everything and give her a lift. They'd quake at her roar and rush to raise her; she'd seen it happen a hundred times before.

This time, there was no one to lift her. The ballroom was empty, as was the adjacent galley and dining area. *Those shiftless nuisances are no doubt hiding in some filthy cabin, playing cards and laughing about me,* Bridget fumed. *Well, I'll take the laughter off their faces.*

She checked other parts of the ship—sleeping quarters, cargo hold, the swimming pool on the upper deck—but the Leo had become a ghost ship.

Bridget didn't feel unsettled very often, but this was one of those times. Someone must be driving this heap, she realized, so she stalked toward the bridge.

On her way, she encountered the first mate in a hurry, running to the area where the lifeboats were kept.

"Why aren't you doing your work?" she asked. "I want this tub headed for home, now."

"C-Captain's orders, ma'am," the sailor stammered, pointing a paw toward the bridge.

With a roar, Bridget barged past the first mate and ran toward the bow, her belly swaying from side to side, her tail flicking with rage. By the time she reached the bridge, she was ready to bite the captain's head off, but he wasn't at the wheel. In fact, the Cheshire was nowhere to be seen.

"Fine," Bridget yelled, "I'll change course myself." She gripped the wheel and tried to turn it to the left. It wouldn't budge.

Bridget pawed at the wheel, turning it sharply. The boat maintained its course. Furious, she slammed all the controls she could reach. She felt claustrophobic in the small control station, hot and bothered, harried with desperation. She saw a lit-up panel that read, "AUTOPILOT" and didn't know how to override it. She left the cabin and continued her search of the ship; when she found a crewmember, she'd force him to get her home.

In his office in Bast, Tad Tybalt sat on a comfortable leather cushion, leaning on his desk and listening intently. The rat sat on top of the desk, gnawing on a penholder.

"Your job would be to oversee packaging and sell the whole concept to your fellow cats," the rat told him, concluding his pitch.

"I don't think the public would need much convincing." Tad sounded doubtful.

"That's my point exactly!" The rat's voice reached an even higher pitch than usual. "All you really have to do is collect the proceeds and (the really hard part) count your profits. You'll have our complete cooperation. What do you say?"

"I've certainly got the distribution capabilities..." Tad doodled on a notepad, his trademark quirk that helped him to muse. "Okay. First off, my 'fellows' probably got their fill of you when you invaded our city last year. I understand a fair few of you were eaten..."

"And the rest were chased away by the army. So your people got a taste for us, and with your help, we can be back on the menu."

"What's to stop me rounding your lot up anyway, without any of this negotiation?"

"With respect, you don't know us very well, Mr. Tybalt. We can hide in the darkest corners of your world and are happy wading through the deepest sewers. We have acid-sharp teeth and instincts that have allowed us to survive countless wars, wipeouts, and heartbreaks. We've carried plagues blacker than you would want to imagine. Our families and lives intertwine in a network of incredible proportions, writhing through the underbelly of this city you love so much. We're rats, Mr. Tybalt, and we're on your side."

"I still don't understand why you would offer your-selves up to me like this," said Tad suspiciously.

"Self-preservation is my specialty, Mr. Tybalt. I have joined forces with a cadre of elite rats who have a great amount of control over their packs. By offering those run-of-the-mill rats to you, the leaders want an assurance that they will be left alone. That would be an essential part of the deal."

"So you're serving up your underlings to keep your own skins safe?" This was something that Tad could understand. He took the rat's tiny paw in his and shook it carefully. "I'll have someone draw up the contract this afternoon," he promised.

"Glad to hear it." The rat jumped off the table and zigzagged for the door. "My people will be in touch with your people."

"Uh—what shall I call you?"

"Call me Alejandro."

"How about Al? I like short names, makes them easy to remember." Tad was talking to thin air; his new business partner had left the room.

The executive allowed himself a smile. A deal like this would bail him out of debt and give him the chance to regain the power he missed so much. He began to plan the best way to spend his latest fortune.

As soon as news of the feral attack reached Bast, the city's administrators launched into a full-blown, multi-stage panic.

Woodrow ran through various scenarios with his staff, poring over maps of Carabas and the sur-rounding area.

"What should we do?" asked Woodrow.

"I know what Mayor Otto would do," said the self-assured official, Joey Hondo. The lean, charismatic cat had taken an increasingly important role at City Hall since the disappearance of Otto and Moira. "He'd let the ferals devour the Carabians until Tarquin Quintroche was stooped down on his immaculate Abyssinian belly, begging for help. Then he'd move in and take advantage of Carabas's weakened state."

"That's brilliant," Woodrow replied in as calm a voice as he could muster. Although he was excitable, he was also an opportunist, and he saw a chance to make a good impression on his citizenry if he acted quickly and decisively. "But we won't be doing that."

"Why not?" Hondo asked, incredulous.

"Because I'm not Otto. I can't let innocent cats be killed in exchange for territorial gain." It seemed like the right thing to say and judging by the reaction of the rest of his staff, Woodrow was right. "We send the sentinels to help them now."

Lugs had never fainted before, not in the battle of Ringtail Ridge or the tense impasse with the dogs preceding the Bast riots. This time, though, the pain in his private parts had been unbearable, making his whole body shut down, his military mind unable to cope with what was happening to him. Now he was in a back room with a collection of sorry-looking cats, no guards, no Vet, and no painkillers.

Beside him was an attractive female, all doe eyes and silken fur. But he was in too much discomfort to tell her so. Besides, there was something aloof about her, as with all the Carabian ladies he'd met.

He sat up gingerly, his ears catching cries of alarm and smashing glass coming from the street outside. More trouble. Where there was trouble, Julius wouldn't be far behind.

"How do you get out of this place?" he asked Doe Eyes. She didn't even bother to shrug.

"Dunno," she said after much prompting. Her voice didn't sound female or male, something in between instead. As Lugs asked her how long she'd been at the clinic, he realized that his voice was different, too. Drying, rasping. Higher maybe. He didn't sound like himself, Mr. Butch Warrior Hero. The Vet had done something serious to him, and he didn't really want to know what it was.

He hobbled out of the clinic, surprised to find that he wasn't locked in or guarded. The only cats in the building were the sorry-looking patients, making no attempt to leave. It was as if they didn't care about what happened to them anymore.

Lugs left them doing nothing. By moving, taking actions, he evaded the necessity to think or worry about The Vet's procedure. As he searched for his friends, he understood for the first time why Julius was so determined to look for Moira.

23

Trouble in Paradise

*In which the Governor receives a visitor,
and Lugs reaches nirvana.*

Although she'd never been there and never wanted to, Cheryl knew The Vet's location.

"You don't want to go in there," she told Julius.

"If that's where they've taken Lugs, then we should go and help him." Julius was resolute.

"If he's in there, then he's beyond help."

"We go anyway."

With an unhappy nod, Cheryl led him toward the clinic. It was within sight when they crossed the Talking Fields, an expanse of long green grass and cool stone benches where Carabians were encouraged to sit and discuss their problems. The fields had been declared neutral territory so that no dog or cat would fight for a personal scrap of land there. Julius saw relaxed-looking cats sitting on porch swings suspended from the trees, and he realized that there was a good side to Tarquin's madness. As a stiff breeze twisted its way through the fields, the sound had an extra calming effect on him.

As Julius looked down, he saw two mighty triangular shadows cast on the rustling grass. "There's Lugs! There he is!" Julius ran over to the sergeant, who was deep in conversation with a geeky-looking wirehair.

"Of course I did *want* to join the army," Lugs was saying in a soft voice. "Although when I was younger, I wanted to be a ballet dancer."

The wirehair looked unconvinced.

"Get all the ladies that way, y'see," Lugs explained. "But my father wouldn't have it. He was determined that I follow in his bootsteps, become a warrior. Sometimes I wonder how I would have turned out if I'd rebelled. Run away and joined the *Corps de Dance*."

"Lugs!" Julius beamed at his friend. "You're okay!"

"I feel serene."

Julius observed that Lugs looked smaller than usual. His slack posture was to blame. His shoulders were relaxed, not rigid. His spine curved and his head drooped.

"We have to go." Julius tried to haul Lugs off the bench, but the soldier was just as heavy, no matter how he looked. "There are ferals in the city. We need you in killing mode."

Lugs looked at him with pity.

"All that bluster you've given us, all the bravado, the tales of battle and cat-eat-dog bile?" Julius continued, trying to drag the lynx away. "It's time to back up your claims, Lugs. Follow up the talk with the walk."

"Don't feel like it," Lugs mumbled.

"Since when?" asked Julius.

"Since I went to The Vet."

"He's been done," Cheryl explained. "They cut into his scrotal sac, cut and tied up his spermatic cord, removed his testicles..."

"Don't tell me anymore." Julius could feel bile rising in his throat. "I know they do that kind of thing in medical emergencies, but as a punishment for being randy?"

"It's a bit harsh," said Lugs, still serene.

Julius and Sal looked at Lugs, their faces agape. This new, castrated cat would take some getting used to.

With a mighty roar, Otto threw the full force of his body against the cage bars. They shook with the impact but did not buckle.

"Don't make me get the chair," Chico told him, voice quavering.

Otto sank back on his haunches, catching his breath. "Don't you have a conscience?" he asked.

"Yes. I feel bad for you all cooped up like that. I don't sleep so much as I should since we locked you up." Chico moved closer to the cage. "You're asking me that just to mess with my head, aren't you?"

"Not at all. I'm concerned about you. If you set me free, then you could ease your troubled, little mind. Sleep better."

"Oh yeah. I could get to sleep—permanently. You know what my boss would do to me if I opened your cage?"

Nothing compared to what I'd do to you, Otto thought, licking his lips.

"Even if he was in a very, very good mood," the guard continued. "I'd never get a job around here again. I'd be the laughingstock of the underworld … I'd never hench in this city again."

"It contents you, being someone's lackey?"

"Staying alive keeps me content. I don't take any pleasure from following these orders, though. I want you to know that in case—."

Otto approached the bars so that he was close enough to see the wrinkles on Chico's nose. He looked at the guard and urged him to go on.

"In case the boss decides to put *you* to sleep." Chico jumped back as Otto slammed himself against the bars again. This go-around, they seemed to bend slightly. Time was running out for both of them.

When Julius's group reached the Old Exchange, it was swarming with prowlers, security guards, and harried officials. They looked like furry tumbleweeds skittering up and down the street, moving in a blur, never stopping to plan a strategy. Julius surmised that they were almost as concerned about looking busy as they were about another feral attack; the governor's temper could be almost as unpredictable, and just as deadly.

Julius raised his forepaws in surrender and was led to Tarquin's office. It was a complete mess, the papers now spread across the floor, cushions upset, snacks spilled everywhere. Tarquin's trademark waistcoat was creased, and a button had gone astray. He was too caught up in his own panic to ask how Julius and Cheryl had survived the Well Day ceremony. But their arrival did give him someone to blame his misfortunes on.

"Julius Kyle," he muttered to himself. "The bane of my lives. You're responsible for this chaos, just like in Bast. You led those beasts here. On purpose."

"Who, me?" Julius was the picture of innocence. "I don't think so. Even if I did, you should thank me for the wake-up call. They would have gotten into Carabas, eventually. Your security's so lax."

"C'mon, credit where it's due," added Sal.

"Oh yes. Thank you so much for wrecking my town, frightening the populace, and making me look like an ineffectual idiot." Tarquin moved around the desk, getting nose to nose with Julius. "Hold still while I shower you with praise and riches." Tarquin prepared to pounce.

"I think he's being sarcastic," said Sal.

As Tarquin glowered at the snowshoe, Chief Maxwell entered the office. His usual glossy coat was all mussed up.

"Sir, the townsfolk need guidance," the chief gushed. "They're afraid for their lives."

Instead of responding, Tarquin hissed at Julius. The Abyssinian didn't like to let petty problems bother him, but he couldn't help it. Some worry always had to occupy his brain, some unfinished business, usually in the form of a regret. "I should have had you drowned there and then," said the governor, raising his high-pitched voice. "In front of me, in my own suite. You rapscallion. You nuisance. You knave-come-lately. You—."

"Aw, you poor thing." Julius peered out the window at a flock of terrified Carabians. "How does it feel to be powerless, Tarquin?"

"Not completely." While Tarquin had Moira, he had the upper paw.

"What are you actually doing to get rid of these beasts?" Julius asked the chief.

"Doubtless your city will send its sentinels to help us soon," Maxwell replied with eager anticipation. "We're trying to keep everyone safe until then. We're telling all Carabians to stay in their homes."

"What if the ferals are in their homes? Has the Friendship Center been cleared yet?"

"No. Why? You think we should all hide in there?"

"I understand you're pressured, Maxwell, but there has to be a better way to deal with the ferals. You must have defense plans."

"Our city's geared toward openness and forgiveness," said Tarquin from behind his desk.

"The governor thought that considering—let alone condoning—violence against visitors would be bad for his program and his image, not to mention hell on the tourist trade." The chief's tone was lemon sour. "Presumably the governor is having second thoughts now."

"We were voted 'most civilized city' at the end of last year," Tarquin said wistfully.

"I think you're going to lose that title." Sal jumped at the sound of smashing glass coming from the street below. Tarquin looked out the window and saw a dozen ferals shambling past his building, snarling at a scattering of citizens in flight. He realized that some of the ferals might end up at the mansion.

"If you take Dalton Street, you can probably beat them there, sir," the chief told Tarquin.

"You're coming with me?"

"Sorry sir." Maxwell slowly shook his head. "I have to stay here to coordinate operations."

"So it's true what they say. When chaos reigns, you find out what your friends are really made of." Tarquin jumped up from behind the desk. "Watch these indigents for me until I return. Don't let them out of your sight. I have to go."

"Too much fiber?" Sal frowned as Tarquin ran out of the office.

"Definitely not the moral kind." Julius asked the chief, "Why do you stick by that spineless nerp?"

"He's the governor." That seemed to be all the reason the chief needed.

"What's he got at his mansion that's so special?"

"His most precious possession."

"What do we do?" Sal wondered.

"Wait for the sentinels," Lugs shrugged.

Julius didn't agree. "We get down there, help whoever we can, and find what's left of your police force. Chief, it's time to reclaim your city."

No one was safe from the ferals: prowlers, tour guides, big bad toms, the highest and the lowest all became their prey.

The beasts scattered into the farthest corners of Carabas, lurking in alcoves and passageways, waiting for easy pickings—a single passerby with a slower step or lesser strength than others. Any sign of weakness, and they'd be feral food.

Their prey soon took to staying indoors. That made lunch more of a challenge for the visiting savages, but they made sure they didn't go hungry. They climbed through windows, down chimneys, or simply waited for their prey to open the front door and retrieve their morning milk. Then the ferals would strike, too ferocious to resist.

The Friendship Center became an impromptu sanctuary for locals. Emergency teams nurtured orphaned cubs there and old cats rested in the auditoria, too scared to go home alone. The prowlers ceased enforcing Tarquin's law of non-assembly; with the city in peril, there was safety in numbers.

By the afternoon, the center stopped communicating with the rest of Carabas. Its lights went dim. Instead of laughing, talking, and singing, the only sound coming from the building was a feral growl.

As the last of Bridget's many ex-lovers, Tarquin was still concerned about her strange disappearance. She had such a strong, unremitting personality—it wasn't like her to become reclusive or die without a fight. Some feared that her son had ordered her secret execution. Tarquin preferred to believe that she was still alive somewhere. If this was true, then the lioness would not sleep for long.

The stress of running a safe, pristine city was taking its toll on Tarquin. Gray hair flecked his ears and back; his nose was often damp. Whenever he was asked to make an announcement to his citizens, he would get a sore stomach. His tummy troubles weren't the result of some worry that the public would disagree with his decrees—no chewing lawn grass, no (excessive) scratching in the street. He was worried about making a fool of himself, messing up his speeches, becoming an embarrassment. He didn't trust himself since the run-in with the mayor that had led to his backwater banishment. Despite this loss of confidence, he'd been raised to do the best job possible wherever he was stuck. To him, that meant turning a grotty outpost into a secure haven for the travelers and inhabitants that brought Carabas to life.

Tarquin was proud of all that he'd achieved in less than a year. Sometimes, when he took one of his official naps, he would dream of the future; a return to his home city and the implementation there of the regulations he'd set up here. A ticker-tape parade would herald his arrival, Abyssinian cubs looking up to him, adults purring with adulation. And in his embrace, appearing as if by some miracle, would be Bridget.

Then he'd wake up to face a pile of paperwork, requests, suggestions, complaints, advice. Toms were running too fast when they went hunting—what if a small kitten happened by, was knocked over, and injured? In an effort to prevent this from ever happening, speed limits had been posted in all backyards. But what about the small, defenseless creatures who were hunted? They had lives, families—maybe they had souls. A growing number of Carabians were protesting against mousing, with Tarquin as their figurehead.

He dealt with what-ifs and consequences, anticipating the concerns of his people. And now the ferals presented a new issue. They had no consideration for the paradise he'd built. They didn't follow rules. They ate peacekeepers for breakfast. He didn't want Moira to become their lunch. He had to brave the potentially dangerous journey to his mansion. If he was going to die in the claws of some willful monstrosity, he wanted his fiancée to die with him. Then the last thing he would ever see would be perfection.

Plan B

In which Tarquin takes a nap.

INJUSTICE IN PARADISE

As a reporter, I like to get involved in my stories. I'm not afraid to get my paws dirty. If I'm critiquing visual arts, I'll have a go at painting a picture. If I'm reviewing a cat's chorus, I'll get up there on that wall and wail a song or two myself. That way, I get to truly appreciate the hard work and sweat that goes into any endeavor.

Occasionally, I don't get to choose what I'm roped into. Now I've personally experienced a Carabian detention center, and I can tell you without a shade of a doubt that the conditions there are disgusting.

Too many cats crammed into tiny cages, underfed, unexercised, and, worst of all, uncoddled.

With so many rules to abide by, it's inevitable that many citizens will screw up and land some jail time. Carabas's Governor Tarquin Quintroche has a solution to the center's overcrowding—excess criminals are put down.

I was lucky. I got out of the center. But there are thousands of cats and dogs still incarcerated who really don't deserve to be there. Yes, they've broken the law, but no amount of law-breaking merits being kept in such a miserable state. I say relax the rules, close the center, and bring on the coddling.

Special to *The Scratching Post*
By Julius Kyle

Moira wasn't happy. Stuck in the trophy room for hours, she'd knocked over three pedestals and torn the drapes to shreds. She'd grabbed the fishing rod, using it to try to lever the shutter open, but it was locked tight. So she'd moped in a corner for a too-long period. She perked up when Tarquin returned.

"You better be here to let me out."

Tarquin looked at her through the impenetrable shutter. "There's been a, uh, an upset. It's better for you to stay in here where you're safe."

"What kind of upset?" asked Moira petulantly, brandishing the fishing rod. "If you want to see upset, then I've got a fragile possession or two in here that'll get busted if you don't open that shutter right now."

"My dear, you're worth more to me than anything else in that room. You are welcome to break everything—except my heart. Go on, have a field day. I'll still have you."

"If you're trying to butter me up..."

"I'm just speaking my foolish mind."

"If you're not going to raise that shutter, then go boil your head. I'm sick of your lovey-dovery nonsense."

Tarquin couldn't help himself. He slumped against the shutter with a sigh. "You know, the first time I saw you, I hated you?"

"The feeling's mutual. Now."

"Sounds funny, doesn't it? But you have to look at the situation from my point of view. There was I, a refined Abyssinian with years of experience as the mayor's elite aide, demoted for overstepping my mark."

"Slightly."

"The temptation was too great, I'm afraid," Tarquin admitted. "Mayor Otto never so much as sniffed any official documents before he signed them. Whereas I ... I wanted to improve Bast."

"Your treaty was misguided. I know dogs aren't as bad as folks might think, but—."

"So I was down in the dumps and then you come along, eager as you please, a coarse, little wretch who rockets to the top of the administrative staff before I could say 'reverse discrimination suit.' Abyssinians have long been a mistrusted and despised breed."

"I wonder why?"

"I seethed as you got hotter and more essential to the mayor's regime, until I could not take it anymore. I stomped into his office and told him I'd had an affair with his mother. Otto was not impressed. Practically exiled me here. But I have been busy in the eleven months and two weeks since he did that. I showed him."

"That you're a nincompoop. I'd be a lot more impressed if I was on the other side of this shutter, Tarquin."

"The hardest part of leaving Bast was having to say goodbye to you. I have missed you like a Manx misses his tail. Pretty soon, though, we will be together forever. I cannot wait, can you?"

"Are you totally oblivious to my feelings," Moira snarled, "or are you planning to give me a slow death by steadily raising my blood pressure?"

Tarquin smiled a sickly smile.

"Quit looking at me, Tarquin. Makes your eyes look like a puppy dog's."

"And you don't like that?"

"I don't mean—."

"I know about your Pa, remember. How you never really knew your biological father. How a dog raised you as his own, living amongst cats so that he could be close to you."

"And help other young cats like me. He was a good dog."

"Maybe it is time for you to follow his lead. Help me with my work here."

Amazingly, the Abyssinian was winning Moira over. "Our conversation would be a lot more pleasant if you opened your shutter," she purred. "We can discuss your work. I might even let you rub my forehead."

Tarquin couldn't resist the speculative offer. With another smile, he took a key from his waistcoat pocket, with Moira walking in small, impatient circles as she waited for him to let her out. He slid the shutter upward, but as soon as he stepped into the trophy room, Moira pawed past him into the corridor, smacking him on the head with the fishing rod. Didn't get far. She halted on the landing, a strange sound catching her attention.

Tarquin saw her ears swivel toward the stairs. "What is it?" he asked.

"I thought I heard something," said Moira. "Might be one of your little difficulties."

The ruler of Carabas looked dazed, as if he couldn't envisage anything going wrong in his utopia. He couldn't see Moira as she reached the top of the stairs, but he could hear a maddened growl. *There's no way that little Siamese could make a sound like that*, he decided, locking himself in the trophy room. That made him feel safer. Nothing could get through the shutter.

"Tarquin?" Moira heard the shutter slam down and raced back to the corridor. "You've gotta let me in," she meowed, scrabbling at the shutter. She saw a massive shadow shift across the corridor wall. Tarquin was an idiot, a power-tripper who'd made her life a misery for days. Yet surely he wouldn't let her perish. Together, they might be able to face the shadowy beast.

A horrible whine filled the air—Tarquin's voice. Peering through the shutter slats, Moira saw a huddled, waistcoated cat slumped against a plinth. Tarquin had fainted with fear.

"Wake up, needlehead!" Moira scratched harder at the shutter and noticed that he hadn't pulled his key all the way out of its lock. She banged against it, knocking the key to the ground. But there was no way she could fit a paw through the slats.

I should turn and face whatever that thing is, she told herself. *I'll survive. Unless that creature pins me against this shutter. At least in the corridor, I'll have a chance of escape.*

She didn't really have running in mind. After being cooped up for so long, she was quite prepared for a fight. A second loud growl soon quelled her appetite for destruction, though, and she was also concerned about the unconscious Tarquin. As the growling grew closer, she raised the fishing rod and dangled some of the line through the shutter, trying to ignore the string's mesmeric movement. She snagged the key and brought it closer to the shutter. Not close enough. She could just barely reach a claw underneath the barrier, but the key was still too far away.

Moira glanced over her shoulder and immediately regretted doing so. A large, salivating feral appeared at the far end of the corridor, sniffing the air, wondering why Moira was so still. She calmly threaded the line back through the shutter, dangled it again, and used it to bring the key right up to the lowest slat. She retrieved it, opening the shutter enough to slip inside. The feral tried to follow, but he was too big, ramming the shutter instead as Moira closed it and locked it tight.

"Looking for this?" she flashed the key in front of the feral, who started to chew through the barrier. Moira was forced to switch to Plan B, grabbing a pedestal to use as a weapon. At least now she knew what she was up against—a savage, slavering killing machine.

He's not as big as a puma. I can take him. Moira had fought all her life—with her brothers, with street gangs, with canine haters who'd picked on her for having a dog as an adoptive father. She looked down at Tarquin, looking so innocent in his curled-up position. He'd tried to change the world with his talk and his rules and his doors.

Sometimes, however, doors weren't enough to keep evil away.

25

Die Pretty

In which Tarquin sleeps through a tussle.

Hear that rumblin'? That's the A-train, "A" as in Action-Packed. The Northern railroad's rarin' to take our troops to Carabas where there's battlin' to be done.

Some cats say it ain't our fight. Others say those conservative Carabians should be left to their just desserts. Well, I say chill. The generals will sit down and have a nice talk with the feral moggies. Speak some sense into them. And nothing's more persuasive than a battalion of sentinels at your back. Let freedom reign, baby!

The DJ Scratch Laid-back Listenin' Hour
With DJ Scratch

"C'mon, Tarquin." Moira tried to stir the Abyssinian with a lick, gagging on his pomade. He seemed to have recovered from his faint, but he didn't move, staying curled up in his fetal pose. He was too heavy for her to move, so she shoved a pedestal on its side and rolled it next to him, creating a shelter for him as best she could.

The feral burst into the room. It had half-chewed, half-smashed its way through the door, and the effort had maddened it. Moira backed into the shadows at the far end of the room, glancing around for an object to use as a weapon. Everything looked too fragile or soft or chewed up.

"If I'm going to die," Moira decided, "I'm going to die pretty." She licked a paw and dragged it over her head, smoothing her white fur down and checking her reflection in a glass display case.

This action surprised the feral; it had been expecting an attack. Instead, this cocky female was grooming herself. The moment of confusion passed quickly, and the feral lunged at her. Moira sidestepped smartly, so her attacker crashed into the wall behind her.

She ran for the exit, but Tarquin chose that moment to stand up, and Moira bumped straight into him. Seeing the abject fear in his face, she pitied him. "Time to leave," she said, shoving him out into the corridor. The feral was right behind them, ramming into Moira and knocking her to the floor. Tarquin kept going, running downstairs in a blind panic as the feral drooled over Moira.

This is where you arrive in the nick of time, Julius, Moira wished. *This is your chance to save me and win my heart back. Take me home.* But her mate was far away. *At least he's safe.* She contented herself with this final thought.

Chico missed his family. He missed his TV, his daily paper, and all his other home comforts. Above all, he missed sleep. He'd been stuck on duty guarding Otto for what seemed like days, and whenever he began to snooze, the lion would roar, disturbing his rest.

"Who are you working for?" Otto asked with a bone-shaking bellow that made Chico want to run into a corner and hide. Bravely, he stood and faced his captive instead.

"You wouldn't believe me if I told you," he said to the mayor. "Now hush up or you'll get me in trouble. I'm supposed to be keeping you quiet!"

"Is that so?" Otto replied.

"Yes, Your Honor."

"This is actually quite good for me," the mayor said slyly. "Like a vacation. I don't have to worry about civic duties, paperwork, public forums, or PR. I can put all that aside and focus all my attention on escaping from this cage and biting your ears off!"

Chico didn't like the sound of that. "Please don't do that, Your Wiseness. Remember, I have a wife and six cubs to support. The tuna bills alone are enormous."

"I'd be quite happy to leave your ears on. I'm prepared to leave you alone completely if you tell me the name of your employer." Otto placed a paw on his chest, his head inclined toward the guard. "It will be our little secret."

"You know I can't do that."

"Then I'll grant you this: I'll be quiet on one condition."

"What's that?" Chico cringed.

Otto smiled one of his cunning smiles. "That you stay awake."

—————

The feral smelled of rank meat and river silt. It had never bothered to clean itself. As it got closer to Moira, she closed her eyes, blanching at the stench. She swung a paw at the creature, hoping to fend it off. Instead, the move provoked the feral to make its final move for Moira's throat.

With a yowl, the feral was knocked aside and sent rolling across the floor. Moira blinked her eyes open, barely believing that she was still alive. Her rescuer killed the feral with several swift slashes of his razor-sharp claws, caught his breath and then padded over to Moira.

"You okay?" Toxic asked, his brisket patched with blood.

"What do you care?" Moira picked herself up off the floor.

"I'm protecting my investment."

"Any sign of the governor?" Moira asked.

"He passed me on my way in," Toxic told her. "I don't know if he's any safer out there than he was in here."

"Then we're going to be indoor cats for a while."

"Whatever it takes to keep you alive." For a moment, Moira thought she saw some sympathy in Toxic's eyes. It vanished, replaced by his trademark cold stare. "Like I said, I'm protecting my investment."

"You've done your job. You delivered me to my nutty suitor. You don't need to keep me captive anymore."

"No. I don't *have* to." Toxic kept staring at Moira, making her feel uncomfortable. "It's your choice. Stay here with me or go out there and face a rampaging mass of ferals."

Moira stood near the front entrance, considering how much trouble one feral had given her. Then she made up her mind.

"Anything's better than being here with you."

Toxic let her go. He had a fair idea of where she would head, and he was hungry. He went to raid Tarquin's larder.

26

Claws

*In which the ferals extend
their teeth in friendship.*

Instead of tall grass and mudded riverbanks, the ferals used fences to hide behind and ditches to lurk in. Any prowler or civilian unlucky enough to pass by their boltholes would be attacked. Tarquin's townsfolk dreaded walking the streets and life ground to a halt until the sentinels arrived.

Salvation came on a northbound train with squealing brakes and grubby steam pumping from its smokestack. If the Carabians hadn't been so scared, they would have run to the station to greet the soldiers; a few bold souls poked their heads out of their windows to see the train packed with tough toms, roofs loaded with kit bags and sharp weapons, and a carriage full of pigeons to help feed the hundreds of new arrivals. Behind that was another carriage full of brown, meaty stew, ready to drink or season the birds. Riding full-pelt on their gravy train, the sentinels were self-sufficient, well-organized, and ready to lay down their own brand of martial justice.

The Carabians had never seen so many cats in one clump. Even in the town's state of emergency, with prowlers blocking streets and cordoning strip malls, it was unusual to see more than four or five cats together. Just because the ferals were running loose, that didn't mean the citizens should start breaking the law—they were conditioned to abide. Besides, a gathering risked provoking another feral attack, as on Well Day.

The sentinels' vanguard, the Soldiers of the Paw, didn't fear an attack; they wanted one. Bring it on! With their claws unsheathed and game faces on, the slick-furred warriors swept through Carabas, billeting at the Unity Hotel. After a brief respite, they were split into patrols, distributed in sectors throughout the city. All cats with shaggy hair, snaggly teeth, or a hungry expression were stopped in the street, ID'd, and occasionally detained or more permanently dealt with.

As soon as news spread of the sentinels' arrival, Carabas began to return to normal as best it could, safe in the assumption that the soldiers would protect the city. The *souq* stall owners set up their wares again, the schools reopened, and Julius was able to wire a report home. While the ferals continued to pick victims off whenever they got the chance, their attacks became less frequent.

There couldn't have been that many ferals in the Friendship Center. Twenty at the most, as far as Julius could figure. So why did he feel overwhelmed?

The center had been cleared of guides, tourists, and any personnel who couldn't handle themselves in a fight. The prowlers had cordoned the area off, covering all entrances and exits. Julius had been deputized along with Stout, Lugs, and other able-bodied cats; no mention was made of his attack on the executioner. For once, Chief Maxwell had disobeyed Tarquin and was practically giving Julius free rein. Being a pragmatic soul, Maxwell had already sent some deputy dogs into the building before the prowlers. None of them had returned.

The Carabians knew that there were ferals in the center. They could hear the growls, snuffles, and sounds of rending meat through the arched windows. They didn't know how many.

"Twenty," Julius said loudly. "No more than that, I'm sure."

"Sure, are you?" the chief replied.

Yeah, Julius felt like saying, *because I saw about two score grubbing around my train, we picked off a few last night, and they've spread themselves across town.* "At the most." He sounded more confident than he felt.

"Why don't you go confirm your theory?"

Julius couldn't say no without losing face in front of the cops, and he'd already convinced them that hitting the ferals in the Friendship Center would be a great way to destroy a whole bunch in one go. Leaving Sal and Stout to help with the cordon, Julius entered the center via the East Portal with two fellow deputies and a prowler fresh from the academy. As soon as they stepped inside, the growling and crunching stopped.

It was strange to find it so quiet and empty, no guided tours or mewing school parties, no pageants or cat-dog bonding seminars. The only movement came from a few banners fluttering in the air conditioning, all lively colors and positive slogans. The ferals could be anywhere.

"Let's check the Fountain of Understanding." The rookie was doing everything by the book, track an animal by going to its water source. The ferals were bound to get thirsty and make for the running water. The deputies didn't question the fact that a cat half their age was leading them. They respected his uniform and his training.

At the academy, the rookie had been taught to be observant at all times. "Weren't there three of you when we came in here?" he asked as they passed through the auditorium.

He was right. One of the deputies had disappeared, lost in the bowels of the cavernous center. Picked off.

"Stay close." The rookie popped his claws. "Watch my back." The second deputy was so busy doing this that he didn't notice a feral slavering behind him until it was too late. A hairy paw clamped over his nose, and he was dragged into a dark corner of the auditorium.

Away with following the rulebook. Julius slipped into the shadows as well, relying on his keen vision and sense of smell to follow the action.

"I said to watch my back!" the rookie hissed, looking in vain for Julius. Claws outstretched, he crossed the auditorium, following the sound of trickling water coming from the fountain.

He blinked in the bright light shining from a pyramidal glass ceiling. The sun made the water shimmer, cool, and inviting in the stifling building. What feral could possibly resist stopping for a slurp?

The rookie couldn't. Ears peeled, he moved on his hunkers toward the fountain. No sign of the enemy. He placed his forepaws on the sculpted marble rim and took a big, long drink, tongue scooping up as much as he could. Feral-hunting was thirsty work. The water tasted grand, so he kept slurping it up. Guard down, he was oblivious to the feral sneaking around the fountain. Like his dead deputy, he wasn't attuned to the footfalls of a stealthy savage.

He heard a grunt beside him and spun around, water dribbling from his chops. With the feral about to strike, Julius sprang from the shadows and knocked the wild cat into the fountain. The feral was so used to dry land that it splashed about, crazy. With a professional detachment drilled into him as a cadet, the rookie held the feral under the water, claws still out, until it stopped thrashing.

Between them, Julius and the rookie carried the feral out of the center. Emboldened by this sign of victory, the prowlers moved in and searched the building thoroughly. There were no more of the creatures within; the loner had kept the police force at bay for hours.

"Good work, son," the chief told the rookie as he grabbed a haddock from a makeshift mess table. "Keep this up, and you'll make lieutenant by lunchtime."

Julius fumed. If one feral could cause this much death and disruption, what could twenty or thirty do? To beat them, the prowlers would need more than due procedure and old-fashioned tactics. They needed to get street tough.

To share his discoveries and get faster results, Julius needed the cooperation of the sentinels.

27

Tooth and Claw

Sentinels! Grizzled veterans of the Canine Contra wars, their claws sharpened to needle tips, their bodies battlescarred. Sentinels! Grim-faced militia from the Great Mouse Massacre, teeth missing from feasting on too many rotten rodents, unrelated yet connected with each other by blood, ready at the drop of a dewclaw to shed plenty more.

Sentinels! Would-be combatants in the standoff with the dogs a year ago, when they almost fought a war with Alsatian centurions from the North. With a truce called at the last minute, the sentinels had been itching for conflict ever since. Now that they were stationed in

Carabas, it was all their commanders could do to keep them from scrapping with the local pups.

The prowlers felt powerless. They couldn't exactly stick the soldiers in jail if they broke the city's interminable rules, and the well-armed scamps seemed determined to break them all. Name-calling (scruffmutts, fleahounds, curs, snot-nosed whelps): check. Soiling of public property (regurgitation grass on the Talking Fields, peeing on flower beds, failing to cover up feces in litter trays): check. Invasion of citizens' personal space (chatting up fishwives, congregating in great, rowdy numbers, disturbing curfews with late-night carousing): check.

"The sooner those sentinels wipe out the ferals and go home, the better," said a disgruntled golden retriever in the Kindness Tavern. He intentionally raised his voice so that he could be heard by the soldiers who quaffed in a far corner.

"We'll leave when we're good and ready, butt sniffer," a sentinel told him.

"Yeah," grunted a cat with an eyepatch. "We like it here. We might stay."

"We can handle the ferals ourselves," said the retriever, hackles raised.

"Sure. You're doing a real good job." There were about ten sentinels in the tavern and dozens of civilians. Unfortunately for the locals, the soldiers were well-trained and eager for an opportunity to brawl.

The retriever showed his fangs but wasn't quite sure what to do after that. Before he could make up his mind, two infantry cats had their claws in his spine and his tail drooped between his legs. The tavern owner yelped, ducking behind the bar with a miserable whine. A Carabian calico's ears flattened as he surrendered his belly to a towering halberdier. Smart regulars fled the tavern or ducked under tables. Foolhardy ones were flung around like stuffed toys, shortly to lose their innards.

The halberdiers slammed two hound dog heads together. The retriever collapsed unconscious, his tongue lolling from his slack mouth. The tavern was a mess of breaking bones and flying fur.

When the soldiers were done, no Carabian dared to complain about their presence again.

If Otto had been present in Bast, then Tarquin might have feared some rebellion or plot; Otto always had a plot. When he'd sent Tarquin away, the lion hadn't thought much of Carabas—to him, it was a backwater burg that had lucked onto a main trade route. Since, Tarquin had built it into an important microcosmic destination for curious cats everywhere. Although all of the racier clubs had been closed down, the city remained a source of fascination for merchants and others visiting on business.

The ferals were methodically driven from the streets; their ferocity was no match for military efficiency. If a few chumps got caught in the crossfire that was unfortunate, but the citizens were prepared to suffer anything to be rid of the ferals.

As much as it could under martial law, life went on. Tarquin's concern for his personal safety overrode his concerns about the soldiers' impact on his community. He no longer feared the shadows; knew that if a monster leaped out at him from a dark corner, a sentinel would rush to protect him. He knew that he'd shortly have to ask the troops to leave, but right now, it was his own skin that mattered. If he fell, who would take care of his populace?

It wasn't his fight.

Toxic had been sent to Carabas to do a job—drop Moira off, take care of her if necessary, go home.

There had been no mention of attacks from savage weirdies whenever he ventured out. He found the whole business tiresome. It wasn't that he had to throw his attackers off when they sprang on him; they were smaller than him, and he always got rid of them. It was their determination that got on his wick and wore him down. He could never relax or marshal his thoughts. Another feral always came along and tried to sink its teeth into him.

A regular cat would have cut his losses and slunk away after an encounter with Toxic. The ferals weren't so easy to deter; they kept coming back. Either they didn't think of the consequences of their actions, or their will to destroy was simply indomitable. All Toxic knew was that it wasn't his fight to begin with.

It took three ferals to stop Toxic in his tracks as he left the governor's mansion. Even then, not for long. On a narrow street that led to the train station, he was jumped by a trio who didn't know better. One ran straight for his legs, trying to bring him down with a claw to his hamstrings. He cuffed it away dismissively. Sure enough, it picked itself up with a hiss and returned to the fray. The other two attacked his flanks, biting down on his tough hide. One of them must have hit a nerve because he fell with a twitch, crashing to one side and knocking the breath out of one of the ferals. The one he'd thrown off ran straight for his face. He allowed it to get dangerously close before opening his jaws wide and clamping them down on the feral's chin, biting so hard that he rendered the creature unconscious. *That'll teach you,* he thought bitterly, killing the last feral with a nasty hind-pawed strike.

Toxic got up and shook blood and fur from his body; most of it belonged to the ferals. He couldn't ignore these pests any longer; it was time to seek some out and take direct action. This would require more effort than he would have liked, but peace and quiet wasn't an option until he'd put the message across: Don't mess with a pissed-off puma.

The things he had to do for a slice of tranquility. And it wasn't even his fight.

28

Homework

The light hurt Vil's eyes. The sun was rising, gobbling up the shadows in his side street hideaway. He'd gone to the ground beside a bin, sniffing scraps thrown out by a gourmet restaurant, ducking in doorways if someone passed by. It was a quiet street. His plaintive grunts were the loudest sounds it had suffered that day.

Vil was smart for a feral. Smart enough to know that if he attacked one of those passers-by and caused a commotion, the sentinels would come running.

He'd seen them assail his brothers, who'd sunk their teeth into a couple of troops before collapsing under the weight of the clean-clawed, regimented cats. Instead of helping his brethren, Vil had found the side street and made it his hideout. Now his belly rumbled, and he craved something fresher than the restaurant's garbage. He missed Dalen, the feral who'd led him to this stuffed larder of a town, but the fearless leader had been driven into hiding elsewhere.

Vil would have to make a move. Wait any longer and he'd lose whatever cover the pre-dawn shadows gave him. He left the side street, head low, his matted fur sticking up in spikes, his face wrinkled and grizzened, a slight hunch to his shoulders. He moved in a straight line, hoping that no one would see him and call a patrol. Vil'd been a strong link in his feral family chain; now he was a drab, disconnected creature badly in need of a meal.

He recognized nothing. The urban canyons around him bore no resemblance to the hinterlands of home. Without major landmarks or waterways to track, he could only follow his nose.

After several long minutes of loping, he found the perfect scent to pursue: warm blood and feathers, massed together like a feast ripe for eating. It was the smell of troops' food. The waft led him to the train yard, his first sight on entering the city.

There were no trains running; no civilized cat was awake at this uncouth hour. A few carriages perched patiently on side tracks, waiting to be emptied and hauled away. One of them fluttered and chittered to life—the source of the scent. Nostrils wide with anticipation, Vil closed in on a massive birdcage on wheels, its circumference lined with thin, close-set metal bars.

A sound caused him to look up sharply to see a white blur rise above the yard. A small pigeon reached the sky, fluttering at a wayward angle, full of panic and obviously not sure where to go, but it righted itself, leveling out, then rising with the wind. Vil dribbled as he watched, then grew forlorn as the bird vanished from view. It was free in its favored environment. He was still disoriented, feeling trapped.

The pigeon had somehow escaped from the carriage full of birds. Perhaps its small size had enabled it to squeeze through the bars. Vil moved closer to the carriage and as he reached the tracks, he scrabbled up and reached a paw through the bars, scooping out half a bird with his merciless claws.

This caused a cacophony so great that Vil shrank back, his food dangling from his mouth. This was bad news. Within moments, a pair of station guards ran toward the carriage, followed by a sentinel, who wanted to know who was bold enough to disturb the army's food stock.

Vil ran and hid under an engine, waiting for the guards to give up their search. He would fight them if he had to. He wished his brethren were around to help him and embolden him.

Julius gave the guards a respectful nod as he passed them near the tracks. He stared up at the gravy train, thinking. Leaving Sal, Stout, Cheryl, and Lugs to hand out emergency aid to wounded Carabians, Julius had hooked up with the Soldiers of the Paw, trying to figure out the best way to help them defeat the ferals. He wondered if the creatures' point of access—the depot— could be the key.

It was broad daylight by now; all of Carabas was awake and the station was starting to fill up with commuters. The sentinels cordoned off the bird carriage and its silent neighbors just in case a feral had caused the commotion.

"There's nothing here," Vil heard one of the soldiers tell Julius. "The birds got spooked for no reason."

With a befuddled drop of his shoulders, Julius turned to leave the yard. He saw something on the ground that changed his mind. It was a trail of fresh blood leading under the engine.

Peeking underneath, he was thrown back by the desperate Vil. The feral's pupils shrank in the bright sunlight, his teeth aimed at Julius's hind paws. Julius dragged himself upright, and Vil ate dirt instead.

Backing up, Julius was pinned against the cage by his desperate attacker. The birds went crazy, flinging themselves against the bars in a bid to escape. Julius managed to slip aside and Vil fell face-first against the cage; the frenzied birds pecked at him until he collapsed, in shock with the pain. The sentinels moved in and finished him off.

Funny, thought Julius. *The birds helped us, yet the sentinels will be dining on them tonight. You never know where your next ally will come from.*

As he left the depot, he snagged a small pigeon that he found fluttering aimlessly. As he snacked on the bird, he wondered if Carabas would ever return to normal—and whether that would be such a good thing.

Since her arrival in Carabas, Moira had only caught glimpses of the city. Running from the mansion, she'd got her first real chance to take in her environment. As she wandered the streets, she admired the ornate architecture of the west side, turrets spiraling into the sky like giant, multicolored screws. She appreciated the way that cats and dogs shared the streets without scratching and biting at one another. Many of them helped their neighbors to collect their belongings as they prepared to leave the city. Above all, however, she noticed their apprehension. As far as Moira could tell, a fearful mood had descended over the entire area.

Like scared rabbits, the residents popped out of their houses, hurriedly looking all around before they led their families into the open. They were obviously wary of being attacked at any moment. Moira hoped her confidence was catching; these locals needed all the boldness they could muster to survive. If they froze or ran, the ferals would be on them, their appetites as insatiable as any cat.

Moira did what she could to help, reuniting a lost kitten with its father or giving a wounded dachshund a sympathetic lick. The dog accepted her aid with a thankful whimper.

What an incredible place this is, Moira thought. *Two completely different species sharing the same territory.* How could Tarquin be so twisted and selfish, yet so adept at social engineering?

Slowly, the streets cleared and Moira was left alone to find her bearings. She had no funds to cover her passage back to Bast, but the chaos caused by the ferals might provide a chance to freight-hop her way home. Any official would be too busy dealing with the threat and panicked passengers to worry about a young Siamese stowaway.

"Get off the street, you crazy broad!" A voice hissed from a shop doorway. Moira's whiskers twitched. Ferals couldn't talk and the dogs she'd met here weren't so rude. This had to be a city cat.

"Why?" she slinked into the shadows cast by a broad green awning.

"Too dangerous to be out there." The longhair's fur was scruffed up and his glasses were broken. Milo had outrun the ferals, resting in the doorway, when Moira had happened along. "Those ferals eat their own. I've seen it. A tasty bite like you would suit their gullets down to a tee."

"What are you talking about?" asked Moira. "Where are they?"

"I don't know," said Milo. "Close. There are so many of them, gathered to attack us. They decimated the Waystation, devoured all the food in the *souq*, and used the market stalls as toothpicks. They move so fast, too."

"I know."

"Those monsters were in the city before anyone realized. They say the leader's as big as a boerboel with a brain to match, smart and truculent." Milo took a breath in an attempt to calm himself down. "I had everything figured out. Everything was copacetic until those locusts turned up."

Moira looked down the empty street. "I need to get to the train station," she said.

"You and half the city," Milo laughed. "Better to lay low."

It was getting darker. Moira shook her head. "I didn't choose to be here. I choose to go home, to Bast."

"Last guy I met from Bast didn't give me much hope for that place. You close all the schools there or something?"

"What do you mean?" asked Moira, checking the street again.

"I gave him a sweet opportunity to make some serious bank and what does he do? Gets high on my supply."

"I'm ... sorry to hear that." A thought occurred to Moira. "Why stick your neck out for me, then, if everyone from my hometown skipped school for life?"

"I didn't say *everyone*. Here's how it works, toots. I save your life. You're in debt to me."

Moira arched an eyebrow.

"Don't worry," said Milo. He raised his paws, pads foremost. "I don't need no help right away. My entrepreneurial activities are on hiatus."

"How uneducated was this cat from Bast?"

"Dumber than an Afghan with amnesia. Who has the munchies *before* they've inhaled?"

"His name wasn't Sal Finney, by any chance?"

Milo nodded vigorously. "By a short chalk. He was a trip, until he overdid his excesses. I shoulda known; he was too chipper to be true."

A thrill ran through Moira's abdomen. There was no way Sal could have made it all this way without Julius. They'd come looking for her. All she had to do was find them in a city that was falling apart, threatened by remorseless beasts, with danger on every street corner.

Just another typical day for Moira, Julius, and Sal.

The sentinels moved from house to house, trying to root out the ferals, but it was tough. The wild creatures had gone to ground, and their hunters kept getting distracted, helping themselves to any food or females they found. Leaving smashed windows, broken furniture, and the bruised pride of locals in their wake, they seemed more intent on looting than rooting.

Only a few ferals were unearthed. To the soldiers' delight, the miscreants didn't like being cornered. They put up a hardy fight. No feral life was taken easily.

There was no sign of the feral leader, although somehow his disparate group continued to receive communications from him. Go to ground. Kill to survive. The ferals hardly needed telling.

The communications were simple but effective; any Carabian unlucky enough to find a feral in his basement was doomed.

***

Dalen had made himself at home in the old sector, surrounded by loyal followers in an abandoned factory not far from the flophouse. When necessary, he sent out a messenger who would use back alleys and broken windows to get to the ferals he had placed throughout Carabas.

His right eye, ruined by Julius's lucky scratch, still bothered him occasionally. Not because of the pain; it wept translucent puss first thing in the morning and last thing at night, and he could not allow his followers to see him weep. He cursed his tabby adversary for making him look weak. Out of his normal territory, he risked losing his dominant status. Dalen had already been challenged by a couple of the stronger males in his group. He had seen them off with sharp words and sharper teeth.

Aside from those upstarts (now deceased), his feral tribe would continue to turn Carabas upside down until they found his immolator. In the meantime, they were having the time of their nine lives terrorizing and chowing down on everyone in sight.

29

Cats Reunited

In which Tarquin plays his trump card.

IMBEDDED WITH THE SENTINELS

Q. What has 4000 limbs, 2000 eyes, and a mean disposition? A. The sentinels, who have vowed to rid Carabas of its unwelcome guests.

If any place is in need of a shake-up, it's Carabas, with its moribund laws and patronizing government. But no one would wish for feral invaders to fall on a cat city. To the rescue come the sentinels, felines in shining armor, crushing all resistance, and teaching the Carabians a few lessons along the way.

Lesson One: Self-defense. If it growls at you, attack it, a simple yet effective method of personal preservation that's certainly worked for the soldiers so far.

Lesson Two: Improvise. The ferals don't work as one; they split up and fight guerilla-style. The sentinels know to break ranks when necessary to crush an enemy combatant. They don't just blindly follow orders. Are you listening Carabas?

Lesson Three: Effective leadership. Commander Jonas Conway: "We're here to complete a simple mission. Get rid of the bad guys. That's all."

Conway is no stranger to feral tactics; he was stationed in the grasslands for three years prior to commanding his current crop of cats. The highly decorated officer is wise to their wiles.

"They're interested in one thing: meat. Cat meat. Dog meat. Any kind of meat; it doesn't matter to them as long as it's meat. Like any animal, we can defeat them by cutting them off from their food source, denying them what they want, and wiping them out while they're in a weakened state."

A confident, square-jawed sand cat, Conway was raised in the desert plains of the Southeast. He has a plain-speaking manner and a sense of humor as dry as his birthland. According to his inferiors, he eats his enemies' bones for breakfast (presumably in a stew). If any military leader can deal with the feral menace, it's Conway.

Only one lesson remains to be taught; how to cope with a pigheaded administration that's bound to get in your way.

Special to *The Scratching Post*
By Julius Kyle

As soon as they entered Carabas's Happiness Hospital, Cheryl, Sal, and Stout were put to work. They didn't have time to appreciate the irony of the hospital's name in comparison to its drab gray exterior and exhausted staff. They didn't have time to take a break as they were sent from one ward to another, helping overworked doctors with bloody patients. But they did take time to notice that they were surrounded by feral victims, some heavily wounded, many dying. Since the first sign of the ferals on Well Day, the hospital had become one giant emergency room.

At first, Cheryl and her friends weren't trusted with much. Changing linen. Emptying litter trays. But as patients continued to arrive, Cheryl found herself in a feline ward tending to a badly bleeding bobtail. With no nurses in sight, she did what she could to staunch the nasty gash on its chest.

"Sal," she said, voice trembling. "Go fetch some nepetalactone from the medicine room."

"There's a medicine room?"

"Quickly!"

Cheryl was so intent on binding the wound that she didn't notice Stout leave her side until he'd almost left the ward.

"You're not staying?" she mewed.

"No. No, I can't." Stout's nostrils twitched.

"I could really do with your help here." She watched her paws redden as she clutched the bobtail's chest.

Stout hesitated at the door. "I have something ... there's something I should tell you about me."

"What?"

"I can't. Not here. Someday. It's better if I don't stay, that's all." He stared at the blood oozing from the bobtail.

"Go if you have to. But remember, this isn't me either. I'm out of my depth, too."

With a deep breath, Stout joined Cheryl by the gurney. "In that case," he said, "we may as well flounder together."

While Cheryl licked the lesion clean, Stout found a tray full of sterile catgut. Together, they used it to stitch up the gash. The results weren't neat, but the bleeding stopped and the bobtail slept peacefully.

"Sal's been gone a long time," Cheryl said, trying to wash her paws clean. The salty taste of the patient lingered on her fur.

"Where did you send him exactly?"

"The medicine room..." Cheryl stopped her scrubbing. "Oh no."

They found him lying in a stupor on the floor of the medicine room, a big, fat smile on his face.

"At least we got to him before he snorted all our supplies," Cheryl sighed.

Sal groaned and blinked awake. Looking at Cheryl and Stout, he asked, "Got a spare bed?"

Chief Rusty Maxwell ran through his reports, his dark muzzle snuffling at the sheets of paper in front of him. He was about to deliver it to Tarquin, and he wanted to make it as palatable as he could for the governor.

It didn't make for pretty reading. The civilians had calmed down and commerce was picking up, but the heavy-booted sentinels were making a real mess. As they moved from house to house, they demolished walls, invaded schools, and despoiled outhouses. As far as he was concerned, bringing them into the city was like using a mastiff to crush a flea. But then, this flea had a deadly bite.

He pored through the report one more time. Citizens killed by ferals: 96 at a rough estimate. Citizens killed in disagreements, bar brawls, and accidents caused by the sentinels: 23.

Maxwell had always been average, the middle sibling of a six-strong litter, with so-so grades at obedience school with an unremarkable build and IQ. When Tarquin had picked him out to head the prowlers, many cats had complained, arguing that a dog's job was to follow, not to lead. Maxwell had worked hard to prove them wrong.

At first, he'd agreed wholeheartedly with Tarquin's policies, all geared toward safety, tolerance, and consideration for the community. Over time, however, the Well Day executions had increased, growing grander every month. The regulations had piled up, becoming increasingly ridiculous. Dog parks were closed because they smacked of segregation. Cat's eyes were removed from roads in case they gave someone the bright idea of running over a real cat's eyes. Maxwell found himself spending so much time enforcing petty rules that actual bad guys slipped from his grasp. Now the sentinels and ferals were decimating the entire city. All the while, Tarquin was spoiling Maxwell's burning urge to excel for the first time in his life.

Tarquin had to be put on a short leash and shown the madness of his ways. But the chief was too subservient to do it, and he didn't want to lose his 401K9. He needed an outsider—someone who didn't hang on Tarquin's every charismatic word.

"I heard something."

"Good for you." Moira was out of patience. Her tail switched from side to side as she perched on the back of Milo's couch, looking out his apartment window at the city skyline. "I hope it was a milk delivery because I can't live on sunfish soda forever."

"We're good up here, frisky whiskers," said Milo. His hair was slickly fixed and his second pair of glasses, while nerdy, sat straight on his nose. "Nothing can reach us on the top floor."

"Except any animal that can climb stairs."

"I got plenty of food, beverages, and valerian."

"So, why are you so agitated?" Moira hopped down from the couch.

"Because I heard something." Milo twitched an ear to the door. "All the neighbors have gone plus, I hate to break it to you but there's zero milk deliveries right now. If it's prowlers out there, then I've got some prizes to hide in my litter tray."

"I'll check, you wait, and I'll give you a signal if it's the prowlers." Moira had grown up the hard way, and she knew plenty of cats like Milo. In Bast, valerian was a legal substance, but she didn't condone any root that impaired the faculties; feline life was too precarious for such dissolution.

Moira poked her head outside the apartment, drew it back in, and yelled to Milo, "Fire escape!"

"I just gotta finish burying my evidence," Milo replied from the bathroom.

"There's no time! The ferals have found their way up here."

The noises Milo had heard were made by Dalen and his flock, ripping the apartment block to pieces, floor by floor. Moira opened a window and jumped lithely onto the balcony, beckoning to the longhair.

"You go," said Milo. "I'll be right behind you."

Moira thought her friend was making a bold attempt to hold off the ferals until she saw him scoop up several packages to bring with him. Dropping one, he reached down to pick it up, giving Moira a wink.

"Look out!" Moira cried as Dalen attacked Milo, scattering bags of valerian everywhere, the ferals crushing the life out of the longhair. There was nothing Moira could do but fly down the fire escape, tears in her eyes. She would have to find somewhere else to hide.

As the army continued its sweep through the city and enemy sightings lessened, an emboldened Tarquin returned to his office, swiftly tidied up by his staff.

"Now that life's returning to normal, we have to get the sentinels out of here," he told Maxwell as the dog brought his report, clutched in his mouth.

"They're still tracking down the ferals," the chief pointed out, mouth still full.

"You can do that, can't you?"

Maxwell dropped the soggy report on Tarquin's desk. "Not in an effective manner like they're doing, sir." This was obviously hard for the chief to say. "We should give them a few days, at least."

"A few days? They're an occupation force, not a panacea. If I didn't know better, I'd say this is a ploy by Mayor Otto and his minions to take over my city."

For once, the chief disagreed with Tarquin. "They didn't let the ferals into Carabas, sir. I take full responsibility for that." He paused, choosing his words carefully. "Is the city really yours to lose?"

"We all have areas of responsibility, Maxwell. Mine just happens to be the size of Carabas."

Everyone in the command center snapped to attention as Commander Conway strode into the room. His uniform shone with medals and the fur on his head was done up like a magnificent plume. He looked majestic, and he knew it.

It had only taken a few hours for the sentinels to erect a large metal box-shaped structure to act as their HQ. The box looked ugly next to the mighty tree that had been a tourist attraction only the day before.

"Who's this civilian who wants to see me?" Conway asked, his voice clear and deep with a mere hint of a rural accent.

"He's been deputized by the prowlers, sir," a lieutenant told him. "But he's new in town, and he's a member of the press."

"I don't like him already."

"Chief Rusty Maxwell speaks very highly of him, sir."

"That's different. Maxwell knows his business." Conway tugged at the hem of his tunic, yanking out the creases. "Five minutes only, Lieutenant. We'll be purging the northwest quadrant at 0600."

Julius introduced himself to Conway with a confident meow. Conway looked Julius up and down; this skinny tabby looked harmless. Conway blinked a hello and led Julius through the command center.

The center was a lively hive of activity except for one section, filled with plump cats who continually ate food rich in protein and taurine.

"I hope you don't mind me saying this," Julius said, "but they don't look like crack-killing machines."

"They're the zoomers," Conway replied proudly. "Wait until you see them in action!"

"I think I can do that."

Conway found a quiet corner to sit with Julius. The tabby looked ruffled but his eyes were keen, and the sandcat decided that Maxwell was right to vouch for him.

"I'm told you're a journalist," Conway said amiably. "Here to interview me?"

"Not quite, no. Don't think of me as a reporter. Think of me as a writer. There's a difference."

"Really?" Conway replied, uninterested.

"All my life I've had ideas, Commander," Julius told him. "I've thrived on concepts. For novels, for newspaper articles, for characters. Now I want to offer my talent to you."

"We have crack military intelligence types to plan our battles for us, Mr..."

"Kyle. That's just it, Commander. This isn't a battle. Not the regular kind that you're used to. The ferals are crafty, and they don't line up and wait for you to press upon them. You need to think beyond regular military tactics."

Julius noticed with delight that Conway understood what he meant. "Alright," the sandcat blinked. "Tell me your ideas."

"I only have one. It might not work, but it's worth a try."

"You don't sound very certain." Conway gestured for a sentinel to come over and take notes.

"I've never done this sort of thing before." Julius waited until the sentinel was ready to jot his notion down. "Okay, here goes. Instead of feeding your battalion, why don't we feed the ferals?"

Within hours, Julius had a plan coming together. The sentinels' gravy train was moved into the open, just outside the station where it could be seen from multiple high vantage points. A carriage filled with pigeons—the visiting guardians' food source—was left untouched by the troops.

To make the plan work effectively, the train station had to be evacuated and blocked off. In order to clear the area, Conway elected the help of the prowlers, who deferred to Tarquin. Julius made sure that the governor stayed unaware of his involvement by sending him a large, distracting ball of yarn, delivered to his door in crinkly parcel paper—guaranteed to absorb any cat's attention.

Felines squealed and mewed as they were shunted from the station. Canines barked in frustration as all the trains stopped running. They worried that they'd be trapped in the city without a sure way of escaping from the feral menace. Departing under their own steam would be hazardous; the grasslands were too rugged and uninhabitable for domesticated animals. They couldn't go home either, for fear that a toothsome surprise would be waiting for them. The news began to spread; for the first time, Tarquin had failed them.

After lying low for a while in a doggy daycare facility, Moira followed an exodus of townsfolk as they headed for the train station. Her clear-cut plan was to distance herself from Carabas as quickly as possible. The next train home would whisk her far away from Toxic, Tarquin, and all the stupid gewgaws in his mansion.

The crowd of animals got larger as it headed for the station, gathering some citizens wounded in feral attacks, others separated from their kin in the chaos. Their attempt to return to normal life had failed. Although the sentinels were steadily doing their job, they were causing so much destruction in the process that the locals couldn't take it anymore. It was time to leave.

Moira found herself encircled by a mass of fur and whiskers, damp noses snuffling all around her. She was within sight of the station when this curious throng stopped moving. She was shoved up against two wolfhounds in front of her by more Carabians jostling behind. The sounds of confused growling and mewing were cacophonous.

"What's going on?" she asked the wolfhounds. "Why've we stopped? Let me see!"

Ever obedient, the dogs parted the way so she could get a look at the road ahead of them. At the far end was a barricade set up by the prowlers, preventing anyone from going any farther. It was made up of heavy blocks of wood, large bones, metal sheets, and wire curling around the top like a row of murderous claws. It had obviously been put together in a hurry, but it successfully blocked the way of the cats and dogs.

When Moira saw Tarquin, she pushed to the head of the crowd and marched straight over to him, ignoring the prowlers who tried to stop her.

"Let us through right now," she said, her face clouding with rage.

Tarquin signaled the prowlers to give Moira room to fume. "We can't let you by," he said calmly.

"You've spent a year corralling these folks and bossing them about. It's time to let your people go!"

Tarquin crossed one forepaw over the other. "I can't. It's not safe for them."

"Maybe they don't *want* to be safe all the time. Maybe they deserve the right to take some risks for themselves."

"Not this time. I'm responsible for them, and I don't want them ripped to shreds by the ferals."

"Your citizens aren't cats and dogs. They're sheep. When a crisis like this comes along, they have to think for themselves or they'll be devoured, barricade or no barricade. They're helpless."

"I'll take care of them," Tarquin replied.

"I know you'll try." Moira managed to control her temper. Tarquin genuinely wanted to help others, even though he had a strange way of going about it. If she hadn't wanted to leave Carabas so badly, she might even have stuck around and tried to change his mind and his tactics. Right now, though, she sought a clear head and the safe haven of her native city, Bast. She brought herself as close to Tarquin's face as she could stomach. "Tell me. Do you really know who ordered Frenkel's death?"

Tarquin looked around. For a moment, Moira expected him to call a prowler to haul her away. Instead, he sighed. "I know that a paladin was hired to do it."

"I'm aware of that; my mate Julius found him. He was called Carmine, said he was hired anonymously."

"That's what he said. Does your mate trust every word an assassin tells him?"

"He's a journalist. Trust's hard to come by in his profession. Besides, he feels the same way as me about taking life. We don't hang around all that many assassins."

"You keep Toxic's company."

"That's a funny way of putting it. He abducted me from my home, Tarquin. When I got back from work, he was sitting on the couch waiting for me, as patient as you please."

"Was he? How resourceful of him. Good job, good job." Tarquin pushed his face even closer to Moira's. She tried not to breathe in, but she couldn't help it, getting a waft of his tuna breath.

"I was terrified," she admitted.

"You would be dead if not for me. Don't you see? I am protecting you, just like these cats and dogs."

"I'm going to leave this city."

"Are you?" Tarquin smiled. "You know what happened to Carmine? His 'anonymous' contractor wants all witnesses to Frenkel's murder dead. You can't go back to Bast."

"How do you know?"

"It is in my best interest to track the plans of the paladins—even if I do not know all the names of their patrons."

Content that he'd convinced Moira as best he could, Tarquin addressed the crowd. "Go home, everybody!

The train depot is not secure. Please leave this area—it's for your own good."

Moira wondered how many atrocities had been justified throughout history by someone in authority claiming that it was for the populace's "own good." Somehow, Tarquin seemed to have the Carabians mesmerized, and the stubborn Siamese took her chance to slip away. While the governor was busy placating the crowd, she snuck behind him and clambered over the barricade. A tuft of her fur caught on the wire claws, but she kept going, jumping to the pavement on the other side. Some of the crowd saw her and closed in on Tarquin.

"You have trusted me to steer this city in the right direction for some time now," Tarquin told the Carabians as Maxwell forced them back. "Long enough for you to see what I can achieve. I have kept your bellies full, given you roofs over your heads and doors to shelter behind, jobs, diversions, and up until now, at least, peace of mind. I ask only one thing of you: Let me take care of this crisis so that you can get on with the business of taking care of yourselves. Is that not what life is all about?"

The cats nodded, and the dogs shook their heads, but all the citizens relaxed and began to disperse. Tarquin mopped his brow with the side of his paw.

"I am glad that is out of the way," he told Maxwell. "Now to deal with that pest, Julius Kyle."

Julius was too busy preparing his trap to worry about Tarquin. Once the area around the train station was clear, he made sure that Conway kept his troops out of sight. Any sign of military movement would deter the ferals from approaching, and for once, they wanted to encourage the miscreants to enter the vicinity without attacking them.

"They're too quiet," Julius muttered, watching the gravy train from a distant rise.

"What do you mean?" Conway asked.

"The pigeons. They're not making enough noise." Julius tried to lob a rock at the carriage, but it was too far away. "Any ideas?"

The sandcat glanced at a tactical map. "Sergeant Ragnar? Bring in the hurlers. Target reference 024628 by 014869."

"Hurlers?" asked Julius, puzzled.

"A highly trained force specializing in obscuring an enemy's line of sight and placing obstacles in his path," the sandcat told him.

"Oh."

Energetically licking their fur, the hurlers got as close as they could to the carriage without making themselves too visible.

"On my command," Conway shouted. "Hurl!" With a terrible retching sound, the squad lifted their heads back. In unison, they faced the carriage and choked out a volley of massive hairballs that they'd obviously been working on for days. The regurgitated hair and saliva flew over an incredible expanse, slapping against the wire of the carriage in a moist, greasy mess. Some scraped through the wire, hitting the birds and riling them up. As the hurlers backed off to their original hiding places, the birds flapped their wings and squawked for dear life.

Moira heard a frightened cooing from the train depot. She increased her pace, ready for trouble. But to her surprise, the area was empty—only one train was out on the tracks, destination nowhere.

She found the carriage full of pigeons just as they began to calm down. Her appearance started a fresh panic. The Siamese marveled at the clumped hairballs, wondering how they'd got there.

Unluckily for Moira, Julius's gambit had worked. The loud sounds of the birds helped to draw any feral within hearing distance to the train. As she saw the savages approach, she ducked under the carriage, ears flat, trying to make herself look as small and unthreatening as possible. With her white fur, that was difficult, no matter how dirty it had become.

Up on the ridge, Julius saw Moira near the carriages, surrounded by the ferals. If he ran to her rescue, he risked blowing his plans and Carabas's last hope. What would be worse—watching a city die or letting his beloved get scratched to pieces? *Either way, I'm a goner,* he realized, running downhill toward the tracks before he could stop himself.

"Dash it all! Where does he think he's off to?" spluttered Conway. "That tabby's going to ruin everything."

"Julius!" Moira cried. She looked tired and weak, as if she hadn't slept properly for days. Her fur was more sad beige than its usual bright white, dirt-flecked and mussed, more sludge than snow. There was a wild look in her eyes. Instead of the streetwise feline he'd fallen in love with, she'd become what cats more feared to be—the wary prey of other, larger predators.

"Takes a lot to catch you off your guard," said Julius, tucking himself close to Moira to protect her flank. He sounded more assured than he felt, and he hoped that boosted her confidence.

"Where did you come from?" Moira gasped. She wanted to embrace him, but she was too busy hunkering down between two sleepers.

"You're not even going to thank me for tracking you down? Coming to rescue you?"

"I'm still waiting for the rescue part."

"It's coming!" Julius puffed himself up proudly. "I set all this up! The pigeons, getting all the ferals here…"

"You did this?" Now Moira wanted to hit him. "And how exactly did the ferals get to Carabas in the first place?"

Julius shut his mouth. What Moira didn't know wouldn't hurt him. He was busy anyway, beating back a feral who was desperate to bite his tail.

"When's the cavalry arriving?"

"Uh, I'm it." Julius didn't dare give his plan away. The ferals were primitive, but they weren't dumb animals. With the slightest scent of a trap, they'd scatter, fully fed and re-energized, harder than ever to track down and destroy.

With a powerful kick of his right hind paw, Julius sent the tail-biter flying into the sunlight. Above them, the pigeons screeched and flapped their wings furiously. The ferals had broken into the carriage, as Julius had known they would. As they chowed down on the birds, more of their kind were lured to the train. That meant more were nosing under it, spotting Julius and Moira and forcing them farther under the carriage. The ground, untouched by the morning sun, was cold and hard. The brave cats stood back to back, hissing and snapping at any feral that tried to get close.

"I've been thinking," said Julius, short of breath. "We've known each other a long time..."

"A year," said Moira, her heart pounding.

"We like the same things."

"You like sachets of gourmet venison; I like sweet and sour fried mice."

"We both dig the same music." The ferals pressed in, ducking low to scrabble under the carriage.

"You're into opera. I listen to gangsta rap." Moira sounded exasperated, but Julius pressed on.

"We both missed each other, though. Right?"

"Yes, I missed you, Julius."

"Will you marry me?"

"I don't know." Moira swiped her paw at an approaching feral. "I need some space right now."

With a final shriek, the birds' cries stopped.

They've devoured them all, thought Julius sadly. Loose feathers were scattered on both sides of the tracks, coating the gravel with drips of blood.

"Now's our chance," Julius whispered. "Let's go while they're sleeping off their—." A ferocious face appeared under the carriage, drool hanging from its fangs, one eye split. Dalen had found them, and he didn't look tired at all.

Julius wanted to back up, but there was nowhere to go. Moira was right behind him and she was confronting three beasts.

"How can you still be hungry?" Julius asked. "Don't you know it's bad to overeat?"

Dalen crept closer. Julius recognized his pose well. He was coiling up his hind legs, ready to spring.

"You know what you are?" Julius continued. "A glutton. And a messy eater. You've got something on the side of your mouth." It looked like a beak.

Julius didn't dare tear his eyes away from Dalen. "Moira," he said, "remember when we danced together at the City Hall reception?"

"I'll never forget it, my love. But is this really the right time for..?"

"It's the right time for move number four."

"Maybe it is." Moira relaxed a smidgeon, trying to concentrate. Julius hummed a note as a cue for the step. Dalen launched himself at the cats, mirrored by his three cohorts. At the same instant, Julius and Moira leaned and stepped in opposite directions, and the ferals crashed into each other.

Tucking his ears low, Julius used Dalen's head to spring over the ferals, rejoining Moira. Together, they ran to the end of the carriage, looking for a passage to safety. They could see ferals milling about in the light, some sleeping, others drunk on eating.

Julius made the mistake of looking over his shoulder. Dalen jumped on top of him, smashing him against a sleeper. "Keep going!" Julius told Moira, trying to flip around and face Dalen. With satisfaction, he saw Moira go on without him, but then his heart sank. More ferals were slipping under the train farther down the track.

I'll never get to report this, Julius realized as he felt saliva drop onto his shoulders. *I'll never get paid either. Damn! Roy got me writing all those stories for free.* He took one last look at Moira, then closed his eyes and prayed to Bastet as he waited for the killing stroke to fall.

Instead, Dalen's weight slumped down onto his back and stopped moving. Julius opened his eyes and saw the reassuringly massive ears of Lugs, who smiled and meowed hello.

As Julius shrugged the heavy feral off his back, there was a dreadful popping sound. Lugs had sunk a claw deep into Dalen's neck.

"I enjoyed that," said the lynx.

Dalen lay on his back, lifeless. As his forepaws unclasped, a small claw sheath dropped to the ground. Julius recognized it as his and tried to kick it away so his friends wouldn't see it.

"Good to have you back." He returned Lugs's smile, then ran to Moira. Sal had joined her, keeping Dalen's cohorts at bay with her street-fighting moves.

"Thank you," Julius told his friends as they huddled back to back. "Did you bring any company?"

"We're just the tip of the ice cream," Sal purred. Like Lugs, he was enjoying the battle. He actually sounded more lucid than usual. "How many of these beasties are there?"

"I was going to ask you that," Moira told him. "You came looking for me, too, Sal?"

"Beats having a day job." He grunted as a feral attacked him, shoving him to the ground and winding him.

"There's too many of them." Moira scratched Sal's attacker away. It rolled into the daylight and was replaced by two more. "It's as if they have a personal grudge against us."

"We did just kill their leader," Julius acknowledged.

"Or a personal scent." Lugs helped Sal upright.

"What's he talking about?" Moira asked.

"They followed Julius here from the grasslands. This is all his fault."

Moira shook her head. "Oh my love," she said sadly. "My mother always said I'd end up marrying an idiot."

"Does that mean yes?" Julius experienced a rush of pleasure, even though he was surrounded by an increasing number of ferals.

"It's a could be."

"Could be what?" asked Sal.

"We're engaged," Julius said. "Possibly."

"Can I be best cat?" Sal had a nasty wound on his chest. He was losing blood fast. Julius had similar gashes on his back; he felt faint.

Even more ferals had found them, outnumbering them ten to one. Julius slumped against Moira, peering into the bright light. The primal forms without were like tall, thin silhouettes twisting in the haze. Then they vanished. A clarion call signaled the sentinels' arrival, led by the fat cats.

"Zoomers attack!" Conway's voice carried from the rise down to the train tracks. The chonkers moved at incredible speed for their size, running rings around the ferals, then landing on top of several. Within moments, the zoomers had expended all their energy, but they had made an effective dent in the savage horde.

Next came Norwegian forest cats, fur dangling in long, bushy clumps from their chins, thick claws swinging in berserker arcs. They were followed by the regular infantry, marching in a tortoiseshell formation, crushing everything in their path. The Soldiers of the Paw came last, quickly dispatching any surviving ferals.

"You took your time." Julius was dragged out from under the train by Commander Conway, who called for a medic.

"Thought we'd let you have at 'em first." Conway winked. "Seriously, there were still some stragglers arriving here up until a few minutes ago. You understand; it *was* part of your plan to get them all with one strike."

"Moira." Julius saw that his friends were getting medical attention.

"She's quite a cat to survive all that." Conway clapped a paw on Julius's back, making him wince. "If you and your buddies ever get drafted, give me a call. I could use you in the next war."

"What next war?"

"I don't know where it'll be, but I know there'll be one. War's war. Look at this place. Cats and dogs living together in harmony? It's obscene and it won't last. They'll be at each other's throats ere long. It's in our nature to hunt and fight, Mr. Kyle; that's what we're born for."

30

Hide and Seek

*In which Bridget plays
games on a ghost ship.*

"**M**y eldest son, Mowbray ... he's not ready to replace me."

"Really?" Chico had been reading *The Scratching Post*, feigning disinterest until Otto had mentioned his heir. It wasn't like the lion to admit a weakness, even a hereditary one.

"He's young. He needs more training and experience. More preparation."

"He's in the Tower," said Chico, looking up from his newspaper.

"Who put him there?" Otto leaned against the cold metal bars.

"My boss."

That rattled Otto's cage. "Tell me who this boss is or I'll—."

Chico placed his paper on the sawdust ground and looked steadily at Otto. "We've been through this before."

"I miss my son," said Otto. "You have children of your own. You must understand."

"I do."

"We hunt together, Mowbray and I. Used to. Recently, though, he's been rolling with his half-wit friends instead. A rabble of obsequious adherents and thoughtless thugs."

"My eldest is the same." Chico approached the cage. "I always worried that he'd fall in with the wrong crowd. Warned him. He did it anyway. 'Slike a biological imperative with that age group. Inevitable, almost."

Otto pressed himself as close as he could to the bars. Chico thought he could hear the lion's heart beating.

"We're not so different, you and I." Otto stretched a paw through the bars. He could have ripped Chico in two with one short swipe but he didn't. Instead, he placed it gently on his jailer's shoulder.

Chico managed to let out a tiny sigh of relief. "I'll talk to the boss."

Bridget may have been a captive of sorts, stuck on a boat with no crew and no clear destination, but she was still used to being waited on. Even the most wretched of prison inmates were served meat and milk. So, where was her steak?

"Pollet? Where have you got to? I demand you answer." He was playing a trick on her, hiding somewhere. The ship was surprisingly capacious, with plenty of storage space for a tiresome tom to secret himself. Bridget padded down Corridor B, passing through grimy streams of light that poured through portholes and open cabin doors. She opened hatches and cupboard doors at random, ears cocked for the slightest snigger.

"Aha!" she cried, sticking her head in an alcove. It was empty; the shifting light had foxed her. "Come out, little kitty," she said with a low growl. "I don't like to play games."

Although Bridget was fierce and fearless, the empty boat gave her the creeps. She was so used to seeing it busy with deckhands, usually rushing to do her bidding. Now she felt alone and strangely helpless.

She considered taking a lifeboat and looking for land; bad idea. At least the ship had food and drink, heating, and soft furnishings. She wasn't about to give them up for a slim chance of escape.

"Show yourself, Pollet," she growled, louder this time. "I'm getting hungry. You wouldn't like me when I'm hungry."

She continued to stalk the ship's corridors. If she was forced to feed herself, then Pollet was in deep trouble.

31

The Tree of Life

Looks like the race for mayor is on, baby, on. There are three major candidates—don't worry 'bout the rest; you don't know 'em and I don't care. The cat with the most administration experience is Woodrow Cormer, our very own City Hall kitty. His platform: a reliable dose of same old same old.

The great furry hope to rival his popularity is the animal magnate Tad Tybalt. His platform: He ain't Woodrow.

He's certainly rich enough to run a slam-bang campaign, and who knows, he may not crush us like he crushed his striking factory workers many moons ago.

Don't be jealous of ol' Tad. Don't matter how flexible his feline spine may be, he must have a terrible time sleeping at night with all that green stuffed in his mattress. And this election is his idea—he's been pushing for it for days, insisting that Bast should choose its own ruler after decades of leonine leadership.

Last and least, there's Joey Hondo, the working cat's candidate with years of experience in security for the entertainment world and, more recently, the mayor's office. Most people can't tell the difference between the two—it's all one big circus to us. The straight-talking Hondo might appeal to average stiffs, but his City Hall experience extends only as far as checking for bugs under the rugs. He certainly sounds confident about his chances. He told me, "I'll do anything to achieve this position." Is Hondo a hardnose? Maybe, and that's what it'll take to snag the top spot in Bast.

Speaking of which, it's time for a station break. Back in two licks—don't touch that dial, guys.

DJ Scratch's Laid-back Listenin' Hour
With DJ Scratch

Chico bowed his head low to his boss, who was wreathed in smoke as usual. "I tamed him, sir," he said proudly.

"Did you really?" the boss sneered. "I didn't think he'd be so easily managed."

"It took time, but he's quite chatty now. He wants to see his son."

The boss nodded, mirroring Chico's pose. "I'll bring him to Otto myself."

Tarquin announced a meeting at the Great Tree, lifting his restrictions on crowds one last time. Around the trunk flowed a sea of civilian cats and dogs, prowlers, sentinels, and journalists. Julius and Moira stood close together in the front row, trying to piece together the events of the past few days.

"Ruthless. Desperate for power. Now we know who had Frenkel killed," said Moira.

"Carmine, too." Julius nodded. The city was abuzz with news of the Bast elections and Joey Hondo's bold grab for the great brass ring.

"I can hardly believe it. He was so ... fine."

"Hey!" Julius joked. "You're betrothed now."

"Maybe trothed," Moira said playfully.

"We have to get the information back home."

Moira held Julius tighter. "Mayor Otto's gone. He was a tyrant. I can't believe I'm saying this, but we could be better off this way."

"And let Hondo get away with murder? What else will he do to get elected? Bastet forbid that he should ever be mayor."

Moira had to agree. "Better the lion you know than the cat you don't," she said gloomily. "I don't want you to end up like poor Fido."

"I'll be careful. Pick my moment. But if we can help Otto, then we should. It's the right thing to do, and it would make a helluva scoop."

"I thought you were done with journalism?"

"I was. But I don't think it's done with me."

Moira hesitated before she spoke. "In that case, how's this for a story: street cat with minimal education stays in Carabas to help set the city to rights?"

Julius was stunned. "The speech is about to start," he said as Tarquin walked up to the tree. Looking dapper and confident, he was very different from the harried cat they'd seen cowering in his office. Moira and Julius watched his assured performance with eyes wide open.

"The sentinels will be going home soon," the governor announced. This news garnered a great cheer, particularly from the soldiers themselves. "And we have a lot of reconstructing to do. I see this not so much as a disaster but as an opportunity to create a cleaner, better city where the old one once stood.

"In the meantime, we must be vigilant. The group of ferals that invaded Carabas wasn't the only colony beyond our walls. Worse than that, there may still be ferals within. Our curfew will begin one hour earlier to ensure that all good citizens are in their homes before it gets dark. I ask you all to watch your neighbors; glance in their windows as you pass their houses. Report anything suspicious. With your cooperation, everyone will be monitored on a regular basis and will be required to wear tagged collars from now on. Show them, Maxwell."

The chief held up a red collar with a round metal disk hanging from it. The disk was marked with his name, address, and an ID number.

"This is the future!" Tarquin declared, enjoying another cheer from his people. "Put it on, Chief."

"Don't do it, Chief!" Julius yowled from the crowd. "Tarquin wants to control you."

Maxwell looked at the expectant audience, then at Tarquin, who gestured at him to hurry up. Maxwell threw the collar to the ground.

"No." The chief pointed at Julius. "This cat helped us to rid Carabas of the ferals. Listen to him."

Julius stepped up to the tree, glaring at the collar that was stuck between two roots. He stood still for a moment, taking in the eager expressions of the towns-folk. "There's two guaranteed ways to drive a cat to distraction," he bristled. "A: feed him with low-quality canned goods or B: tell him what to do. This place revolves around 'B' and I'm sick of it. For your infor-mation, there's nothing wrong with referring to 'the dog days of summer.' It's a time of year, not a special slur. Calling someone a mutt or a hound is no big deal." He ignored the gasps from the crowd. "If you use the same, boring, old labels all the time—cat, dog, cat, dog—for fear of offense, your brains will go dead and your vocabularies will shrink in parallel."

"Popples and wimbos!" Sal shouted, getting funny looks.

"Dogs are supposed to have gross eating and grooming habits," Julius went on. "And they should be able to revel in that! We all should be able to do what comes naturally to us, no matter how disgusting, and speak our minds. If the pup next to me has fleas, I should be allowed to tell him to back off and take his tail with him. And speaking of tails, I reserve the right to stick mine up in the air and flash my bum at whomever I please. I'm talking about the right of all animals to express themselves and communicate hon-estly with each other without a load of sophisticated crap getting in the way. You can't stifle cat chat!"

Julius was encouraged by some murmurs and woofs of agreement.

"There's nothing to celebrate in being generic," he said. "You know what you've done? You've made this a no-place full of non-entities. By quashing all the things that make our species so different, you've made them extra-ordinary. What a great achievement!"

The Carabians shifted from paw to paw, uncomfortable, wondering why Chief Maxwell was allowing this cat to speak.

"You don't need collars!" Julius snarled. "You need patches of dirt to roll in. Dirty fur to lick. Tails to chase. Yeah, that's what life's all about. Not edicts and stability and being a nosy neighbor. It's about chasing your tail!"

Numerous dogs in the crowd were inspired to do just that, rushing around and around until their heads spun. Other Carabians gave them space to play or joined in. Soon, Tarquin's perfectly ordered gathering was a shambles.

"Julius Kyle," the governor hissed. "When are you going to do us all a favor and stop trying to help?"

Otto kept pacing; it was something to do, a form of exercise. The bars made him constantly aware of his captivity and the sawdust got stuck between his toes. Nevertheless, if he walked enough, it would conjure memories of hunting in the forests south of Bast, guiding his son with a mob of intermediate sycophants and advisors keen to teach his cub the ropes.

Where were all those lackeys? So quick to take a salary from him, so slow to the rescue. Was he really so difficult to work with? Even his trusted Number Two, Woodrow, had been unable to find him.

"I want my son!" Otto bellowed. His roar quaked with pain and loneliness. "Bring him to me!"

Chico was at the tent flap at once, surprised by the emotional outburst. "Here he is," he said hurriedly.

A figure joined Chico at the entrance. The daylight behind him sent a long shadow into the tent. The figure held a large bundle in its mouth.

"Mowbray?"

"You kept asking to meet my boss." Chico sounded sad. "Here he is."

Otto peered across the tent. Was this possible? Had he been so uncaring that his young son had turned against him? His fears stayed unrealized. As the figure approached the cage, Otto saw that it was a cat, not a lion. A cat called Hondo.

Otto felt hopeful. He'd get out of his cage somehow, find his son, and be a better father from then on. Play with the cub more. Guide him personally, without all the intermediaries. He had a second chance.

Hondo dropped the bundle next to the cage. As it unraveled, Otto's hopes were shattered. Out of a velvet sack rolled Mowbray's furry head, surprised eyes staring up at his father.

"Oops," said Hondo. "I've let the cat out of the bag. Sorry, Your Honor." Hondo enjoyed Otto's torment. "Whenever we prepared the security for your self-centered political pow-wows and Machiavellian meetings, you always told me to be ruthless in eliminating any threat. Not just in the present. In the future, too."

What was this rent-a-cop babbling about? Otto couldn't clear his mind. He grasped at a bar to steady himself as Hondo lit a cigar and took a long drag.

"What's up? Can't get your head straight? Here, let me help you." Hondo set Mowbray's bonce upright, the gory stump of its neck collecting sawdust. Otto slumped down in the far corner of the cage.

"Meeting adjourned." Hondo swept out of the tent. "Chico, let His Honor have some alone time with his son." The flap closed behind Hondo and the jailer, leaving Otto weeping in the darkness.

Maxwell's collar lay covered in dirt kicked up by the departing crowd. Tarquin fumed at Julius and Moira.

"That was quite a speech," Moira told her mate.

"I thought you might need some help smoothing things over if you're going to stay here," Julius replied.

"So you think my story's worth running, huh?"

"Front-page headline. How could the art desk resist printing a picture of a beautiful cat like you? It would boost sales for sure." *And staying here gives you time,* Julius thought, *to decide about us.*

Although he was annoyed that she *needed* time, he understood. She'd been through so much over the past week. *Hell, so have I. I need a tall glass of milk and a lamb chop.* Since the best-prepared chops were in a little Bast bistro, Julius resolved to return home as quickly as he could. "Do what you have to do here," he told Moira. "You have my blessing and my byline. We could even be talking syndication."

"Thought you'd see the light."

"I did. The moment I met you."

As Julius and Moira embraced and swayed to music that only they could hear, Tarquin's heart broke. It sounded like Moira was sticking around, but the governor knew who she really loved. Since he wasn't in a sharing mood, he mewled for his champion.

"You're going to have to forgive me," he told Moira. "But I believe someone wants to cut in." Moira gasped as a large puma stepped out of the shadows.

"His name is Toxic," Tarquin introduced the goliath to Julius.

"We've met," the tabby replied. "I owe him one for abducting Moira."

That was what Tarquin hoped he'd say. Moira stayed silent, not daring to tell Julius that Tarquin had ordered her seizure.

Toxic sneered at Julius, who seemed small and insignificant in the puma's shadow. Julius held back a moment, dazed. Then he took a deep breath and ran full pelt toward the puma, landing on the mountain lion's back and digging his claws deep into his hide.

"Stop him, Tarquin!" Moira cried, but it was too late for that. Toxic's blood was up, defending himself and he rolled onto his back, trying to crush the air from Julius's lungs. The smaller cat dragged his claws down Toxic's back as if he were stripping tree bark. When the hurt became too great, Toxic rolled over and Julius immediately righted himself, gasping for breath.

Toxic shook his head to clear the pain, staring at Julius. He couldn't believe that Mr. Insignificant could cause him such agony.

Using his lighter frame to his advantage, Julius scrambled up the trunk of the Great Tree, glancing down just the once to make sure Toxic was following. Anything to draw the bad guy away from his beloved.

Toxic left great grooves in the trunk as he hoisted himself upward, never taking his eyes off Julius. Moira stayed on the ground, tail switching. She was certain that Toxic would decimate Julius as soon as he caught up with him.

Julius dug his hind claws tight into the trunk, then used his forepaws to reach for a lower branch, hoisting himself away from an impending swipe. "There's a weight limit on this thing," he teased, edging along the limb. Toxic's reply was a primal snarl. He tried to reach Julius from the tree trunk but the tabby was too far out, and climbing into the higher branches.

"Come down," Moira pleaded, padding in agitated circles beneath them.

"Don't think I can," Julius called down. "I can do up. Down I'm not so sure about." By now he was on the treetop with Toxic catching up fast. Both cats noticed the sphere dangling from an uppermost branch. Julius jumped into the air, grasping the sphere with his paws and landing on an opposite limb. He could smell the puma's rotten meat breath and shuddered to think that Moira had been in the monster's presence for so long. He blamed himself and realized that he'd never be free of the guilt.

Right now, though, he was trying to stay alive. He spun around to face his opponent, twisting the ball so that sunlight caught it and made it twinkle. Toxic looked up for a second—long enough for Julius to let go of the ball and send it flying in the puma's direction, smacking him square in the face, and knocking him from his perch. With a mighty roar, he toppled from the tree, landing with an ugly crunch on top of Tarquin.

Julius nimbly descended, shocked to see his mate rushing to the injured cats. Back on the ground, he watched her hunch over Toxic's hulking body, her eyes full of concern. Most surprising of all, Tarquin was still breathing.

"How is the big brute?" asked Julius. He vaguely acknowledged Tarquin slinking away, his tail tucked between his legs.

"He'll live," Moira sniffed. Her tone was soft and forbearing. "He'll need medical attention, but he'll live."

"I know just the place," Julius nodded, helping Moira to move Toxic's unconscious form into a more comfortable position. "He can go to The Vet."

32

Leaving Carabas

---

*In which Tommy Stout
reveals his Big Secret.*

DISPATCHES FROM CARABAS

NB: Roy—might be too sentimental for your paper,
but this is what I have to say.

-JK

There are many factors that could keep me in
Carabas. While cats might not be destined to live
with dogs in such close proximity, the experiments
a noble one worth reporting. But it takes nobler
cats than I to stay in the city and try to fix the
experiment's flaws.

Moira Marti, a Siamese born and raised in the Doghouse, is one such decent creature. A former aide to Mayor Otto, she'll stay in Carabas and do her best to make things better. Her job hasn't been made any easier by the recent feral incursion.

"I have to do what I can," she told me shortly after making her decision. "Whether I or the cats who run this madhouse like it or not."

This reporter for one will miss her deeply. I recently proposed to Ms. Marti; I'm still waiting for a definite answer. I'm not taking her new choice of residence as a disaffirmation.

During my career as a journalist, I've asked thousands of questions. It surprised me how hard it was to pop one to Moira. Even tougher were the questions I had to ask myself.

No matter what kind of story I'm working on, I always find myself asking my subjects how they feel. Searching my own feelings wasn't easy. I found that I couldn't give myself the answers merely by observing events around me; I had to experience them.

Moira got caught up in a feral attack on the sentinels' gravy train. I witnessed her predicament and chose to risk my own life and the lives of others to help her. I shook off my own nature as a cynical reporter and a self-centered cat. It made me realize that I loved Moira enough to sacrifice everything for her.

If a skeptic like me can do that, then maybe a true cat-dog détente is possible after all. I'm certain of one thing; It will take strong-willed envoys like Moira to make that happen.

Special to The Scratching Post
By Julius Kyle

With half a city to rebuild, it didn't look like unemployment would be a cause for concern for some time. Cheryl and Stout joined a work team together. They'd grown quite fond of one another since their meeting in the detention center.

"You going to tell me your big secret now?" Cheryl asked Stout as they scooped loose bricks into a wheelbarrow.

"I don't know," said Stout.

"You can trust me."

"You've been wondering why I wasn't killed by the ferals, that first time they attacked?"

"Can't say that I haven't. You shoved us in those cells, and you were surrounded. We thought you'd be eaten for sure."

"They let me live because I'm one of them." Stout studied Cheryl's shocked face. "I'm part feral," he told her. "I was raised in captivity and rehabilitated here. I suppose they recognized that deep-down, bestial part of me."

"Plus, you didn't panic." Cheryl pressed her nose against his forehead, letting him know with one simple nudge that she accepted him for what he was. "So that's your big secret, eh? Part feral."

"One-eighth. On my mother's side."

"And that's why you wanted to leave the hospital. You felt guilty for what your cousins had done."

"No," Stout replied calmly. "I was worried that I'd turn savage myself. All that blood. All those defenseless animals."

"You certainly proved yourself wrong there, didn't you? Stuck with me. Took care of all those patients without breaking a sweat." Cheryl laughed gently. "Do you always keep your cool in a crisis?"

Stout gave her a wink. "Depends on the crisis."

"I admire a cat who can take command of a situation."

"That's me."

"Wanna have lunch?" Cheryl asked.

"That depends whether you're looking for a shoulder to cry on, or a friend to protect you the next time there's a crisis ... or a lover."

Cheryl thought for a moment before she gave her reply. "All three, I think."

"You're on."

With great pomp, Woodrow's private train arrived in Carabas. Flags shining with his family crest waved in the northern breeze. His entourage helped him down from his carriage, and Commander Conway ensured that an honor guard awaited the haughty sealpoint on the platform. He wasn't the mayor of Bast yet, but Conway couldn't take the chance of offending him, just in case.

"You sure this area's secure?" Woodrow quavered.

"Yes sir," confirmed Conway. "You're safe."

"Good. Now where's the governor?"

"In his office, sir. He refuses to come out."

Julius approached Woodrow in full reporter mode, a notepad clutched in his hand. Conway introduced him as one of the cats who had helped save the city, but Woodrow maintained a look of disbelief.

"Is it true?" Julius pestered. "The rumors that you're going to be the next mayor?"

"I don't know what my citizens will decide ... but I can't think of anyone better qualified, either. Can you?" Woodrow's expression of disdain dissolved as Moira approached. "Moira, my dear, I'm so glad you're unharmed."

Julius pocketed his notepad. "No thanks to Tarquin." Moira shut Julius up with a hasty scratch to his hind leg.

"Missed me at the office, did you?" she said to Woodrow. "Paperwork piling up?"

"Nothing that can't be dealt with when you get back. No folders that can't be replaced."

Moira took a deep breath. "I'm not coming back, Woodrow. I'm staying here to help tidy this mess. If you were any kind of real cat, you'd do the same."

"I can't do that. I have a campaign to win—."

"Aha!" Julius retrieved his pad. "So you *do* think you'll be taking over. I knew it!"

"I hear you made quite a speech to the Carabians," Woodrow murmured to the tabby. "Ever considered writing speeches for other cats?"

"Like yourself?" Julius had never considered a career as a speechwriter. He hadn't planned on dairy farming or factory work, either. "I'll try anything, once," he told the candidate.

"Inform Governor Quintroche that I'm here," Woodrow said to Conway. "Also, tell him that I don't like to be kept waiting."

While Woodrow met and greeted a playful group of Carabians, Tarquin slunk over to Julius and Moira.

"Enjoy your moment," Tarquin grumbled. Julius noticed that the governor was limping, his left hind leg bruised from cushioning Toxic's fall.

"Enjoy your city. You can keep it. Moira here will even help you rebuild it."

"Thank goodness."

"You can thank me later," Moira told the governor.

"Are you absolutely sure you want to be within a hundred miles of this guy?" Julius asked her. "I understand the dog-cat thing, but c'mon, it's *Tarquin* here..."

"Sometimes the ends justify the meanies."

Julius squinted hard at Tarquin. "If I hear that you're mistreating her, I'll have words with my friend Woodrow over there, and you'll be sorry."

"I can handle this pussy cat myself," Moira said firmly. She went to tell Conway that Tarquin had arrived.

"I can still have you banished," Tarquin told Julius under his breath.

"You'll be doing me a favor. I wouldn't want to spend another day in this place if you offered me all the salmon in the sovereignty."

Tarquin could see that this wasn't punishment enough. "I can also have your friends banished with you."

This removed the rise from Julius's whiskers. "Now wait, that's not fair. They don't need that kind of grief. They want to help with the reconstruction. They fought for your city, Tarquin! How could you be so rotten?"

"I learned from a master. Sal Finney is an addict. I have seen his hospital records. Sergeant Barr is a deserter..."

"Not through choice!"

"A deserter and a black marketeer. I'll ensure that he is forbidden from any return to his regiment, and he'll be exiled from Carabas to boot." Tarquin allowed himself a wicked, little smile. "It's the least I can do for him."

"Oh, Tarquin. I didn't know you had it in you to be so small-minded." Julius sounded genuinely disappointed. "I'm sorry you're so capable of meeting my low expectations. After all your talk of equality and harmony. Such high hopes, trapped in such a tiny brain."

While Tarquin paid reluctant homage to Woodrow, Julius said his final goodbyes to his mate. "I want us to be together," he admitted.

"You don't belong here," she answered. "You're a Bast cat."

"I know it." Julius didn't want to stop looking at Moira; this would be the last time he'd see her for who knows how long.

"This won't be forever," she assured him.

That seemed to do the trick. Julius dared to look away at last. "Nothing's forever."

Always one for appearance, Tarquin produced a white hankie from his best waistcoat and waved goodbye to Woodrow and the sentinels. They rode their trains out of Carabas, taking their empty bird carriage with them. Once the trains had left and a small cluster of dazed Carabian onlookers had been broken up, his smile vanished.

When he'd finally agreed to see Woodrow, the seal-point had given Tarquin a warning. Carabas would be closely watched, and the sentinels would be stationed at points around the city. Woodrow wasn't concerned about future feral attacks; he wanted to keep Tarquin under control. For now, there was nothing the Abyssinian could do about that. He was prepared to do whatever it took to keep the sentinels out of Carabas.

The army had left Tarquin's town in shambles. The ferals were dead and gone, sure, but so were Carabas's regular food and litter supplies. The troops had used them up, wrecked half the residential district digging out ferals, cavorted with the local ladies, contaminated the minds of Carabian kittens with their uncensored verbiage, and taken the best and strongest with them as new recruits at Bast Academy.

Tarquin wasn't so much worried about the damaged property and lost lives; he was concerned about the morals and manners of the townsfolk that remained. The soldiers had brought a free and easy manner and a compulsion to speak their minds when they weren't in the presence of a superior—the anathema to Tarquin's dream of self-discipline and peaceful, reserved behavior.

It had taken so many months to bring his people around to his way of thinking. He would have to start all over, one cat at a time.

Bridget pricked up her keen ears to hear a muffled thump coming from one of the cupboards. Swiping them open, she found Pollet cowering in a cramped cubby.

"They ordered everyone to leave the ship," the timorous cat told her. "But I hid instead. I couldn't leave you." He looked up at the lioness, eyes wide. "I know where my duty lies."

"Who ordered you? Who's behind this nonsense?"

"Mr. Hondo, ma'am. An official at City Hall. He arranged everything, hired me because he knew I wouldn't rock the boat, so to speak. But he was wrong about me. We'll show him, won't we?"

"I certainly will," said Bridget. "How do we turn this rig around?"

They made their way up to the bridge, swaying as they climbed past the fo'c's'le. The sea looked rougher from out here, waves chopping at the bow. The bridge, like the rest of the vessel, was empty, and the engines had been shut off.

"We're adrift," Pollet said sadly.

"I can see that, you imbecile." Bridget stared out across the water, her eyes flashing with rage. Deliberately, with weeks or months of planning, Joey Hondo had doomed her to drift across the sea until she was overcome by hunger or madness or both. If she ever reached land or found a way to leave the Leo, she would find Hondo and grind his skull to dust.

Tad was sleeping in his own bedroom for a change. Black and white stripes adorned his walls; simple square cushions covered the entire floor. He was sprawled out in the middle, legs splayed, mouth making wide-open snores, eyes clamped shut, and tail twitching in a half-dream.

A tiny figure snuck from a hole in the wainscoting. It was Alejandro, glancing shiftily from side to side as he scampered across the abundant cushions.

Taking care not to wake Tad, he crept up to the cat's left ear and took a breath.

"You are doing well in the polls," he whispered. "But you have a long way to go. You must make some public appearances. TV. Radio interviews. Win the hearts and minds of catkind. You can't play this one by the numbers. You must use a charm offensive." Alejandro backed off sharply as Tad rolled toward him. The cat kept sleeping, so the rat leader returned to his ear.

"You must show the citizens of Bast what a generous soul you are. Announce that you will ship a free box of rat snacks to every home. This is the kind of charity you will show to all if you are voted into office."

Tad murmured in his sleep and Alejandro fled back to his hole, bouncing excitedly over the ductile floor.

When Tad woke up the next morning, he felt refreshed and full of ideas. He would bribe the public with free food. What cat could possibly resist an offer like that?

Tarquin felt more at ease once he was back in his office. Adding to the air of familiarity was Rusty Maxwell, who leaned his forepaws on the governor's desk.

"Obviously you can no longer be chief of the prowlers after the collar incident," Tarquin told him. "However, I am going to need someone to run my detention center."

"Who are you going to put in there?" Maxwell's challenging tone was a surprise after so many months of obedience. "The ferals are all gone. The army's returned to Bast. We're too busy picking up the pieces to commit any crimes—."

"They commit crimes every day!" Tarquin leaned back on his cushion. "Crimes of wrong thinking when they think ill of other species. Crimes of passion when they lust after a member of the opposite gender. Crimes of waste when they throw away broken possessions. Crimes of selfishness when they stay with their families instead of returning to work."

"Then you can lock me up with them," Maxwell growled. "Because I won't do your clean work for you. And when they decide who's mayor back in Bast, I'll be letting them know what a mess you've made of this place."

Tarquin said nothing. He recognized discrimination when he saw it. He let the dog leave, then sat at his big, empty desk, wondering how much he should expand the detention center to make room for all the cats and dogs who'd need correcting.

He would do it, slowly but surely. One cat at a time. Not the dogs. Not right now. His next visitor would be an easier target, he knew.

Cheryl entered the office, curious to know why the governor had summoned her.

"Hello, my dear. I thought a resourceful, eager-to-please young lady like you might be of some help to me as I draft my new plans for Carabas." Tarquin licked his lips as he made eye contact with Cheryl. "I know what you're thinking. Don't worry, I approve. This time."

Though Otto's tears had dried, his throat was still sore from a night of baleful roaring. When he shook his head, dust flew from his mane, scattering across the cage.

Beyond the bars, he could see the velvet bag; Chico had mercifully used it to cover up Mowbray's head, but Otto could still picture the cub's imploring eyes.

Hondo had been so inconsequential, a security guard who he had hardly noticed at City Hall. He couldn't remember ever once thanking the cat or bothering to make small talk with him. He cursed himself for his blindness. How could he not have spotted the cold-blooded psychopath in his midst?

Chico was the key to his escape. He would continue to talk to the jailor, reason with him, manipulate him. Once outside the cage, he had underlings he could count on, allies who would help him get revenge. One call to Woodrow would start the payback rolling. Whatever it took, Otto would get out and make Hondo pay for murdering Mowbray.

Moira watched a small cat and dog snarled at each other, half-playing, half-serious. *They are following the instincts of all young animals*, she told herself. Learning to hunt and survive through chasing and fighting each other.

She had been inspecting the schools and nurseries of Carabas, doing the rounds on Tarquin's behalf. They all seemed well-kept and friendly on the surface, barely affected by the feral incursion. Here at least, Tarquin's insistence on doors, locks, and alarms had been a boon. The little ones were safe behind their fences and walls. So why were they squabbling with each other?

"Aren't you going to break them up?" Moira asked a schoolteacher.

"There aren't enough hours in the day," a prim Persian told her. "Soon as I split one pair of tearaways, another cat and dog go at it. It comes with the territorial disputes, unfortunately. It's what you get when you educate cats and dogs together."

"An' cats are much smarter than mutts," the small cat said confidently.

"Who told you that?" Moira hunched down to ask.

"A sentinel."

As she left the school, Moira propped open the front doors and left them that way. In time, she hoped that she would open some minds as well.

"Do you miss her?"

Back in his own home, Julius was about to snap at Sal for asking a stupid question, but then he realized who was asking it. "I do," he purred, returning to work on his latest story. Writing had always been a lonely pursuit for him; it was strange to be working in a house full of cats—Sal, Lugs and his military buddies, family members, and well-wishers all staying with him, eating his food, laughing at his jokes. He could get used to the strangeness.

"Keep it down, guys," he said good-naturedly. "I'm trying to scratch out a living here."

Julius didn't write for long. The story, a heart-rending examination of factory working conditions, could wait. He was too preoccupied with Moira to concentrate. Too right, he missed her and was determined to get back with her, banishment notwithstanding. He didn't know how, but they would be reunited.

"Hey Sal," he said, standing up and stretching. "What do you say we relax for a change?"

"Now you're talking," Sal replied, giving Lugs a playful bat with his paw. Lugs snarled and shoved the snowshoe away. Julius couldn't help smiling—the sergeant was almost back to his old self again.

"I dunno," Julius said. "Ever tried chasing your tail?"

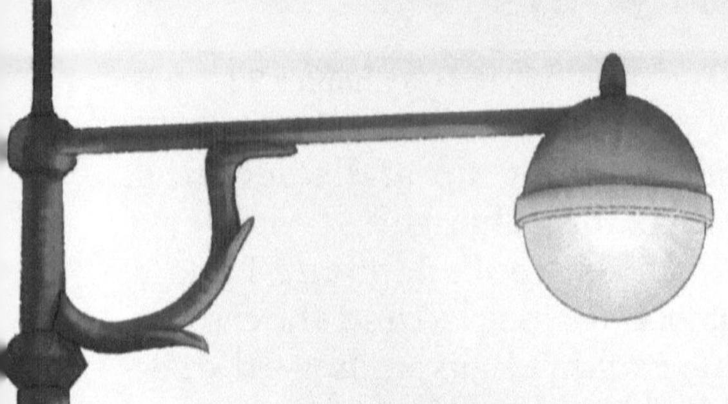

Outro

This is DJ Scratch being real and singing for my next meal. I'll be bringin' you news, tunes, and catty comments all day long. It would take way too much effort to leave the studio on a hot muggy day like this, anyway. And I got my own private sun patch to bathe in right here in the booth.

A little pigeon tells me that the big-britched little city of Carabas has lost a lotta friends. Nobody wants to go there anymore and no one's permitted to leave. To think this increasingly isolated spit o' land was once a nexus point for folks coming and goin'—just goes to show you can never make predictions in the upsy-downsy world of real estate.

Got a call-in from Julius Kyle, The Scratching Post's star reporter. Seems his straight-thinking, personal, caring style blows the cub reporters out of the water. Apparently, you've forgiven him for the riot he caused not so long ago and you're even getting excited about his proposed, self-produced movie project, Whiskers in the Dark. *Seems the best thing he ever did for his reputation was to go away for a while.*

Still no sign of Mayor Otto or his mom Bridget, although the captain of the Leo has been spotted prayin' it up in the religious wonderland of Bubastis. The salty seacat says the ship was lost. Some captain, losing a ship.

More news and gossip soon as it breaks, so stick around, listen awhile, and don't let your sun go down.

DJ Scratch's Laid-back Listenin' Hour
With DJ Scratch

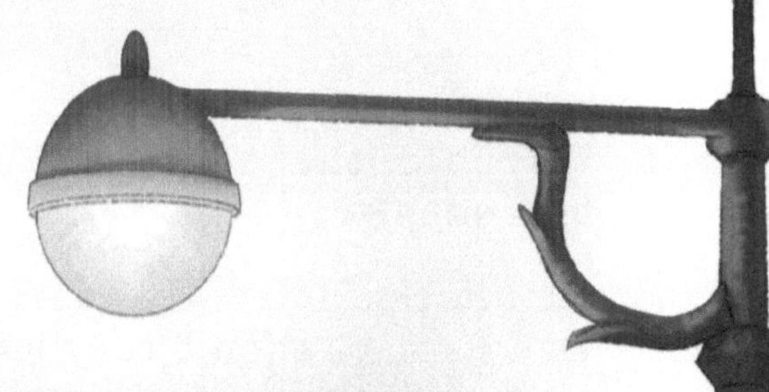

BOOK CLUB QUESTIONS

1. When Bridget needs a break, she takes a cruise. If you were a lion, what kind of vacation would you take?

2. What favor do you think Milo would have asked of Moira?

3. How should Julius help Sal with his addiction, or should he help at all?

4. Tarquin has harsh punishments for cats and dogs who break the rules of Carabas. If you ran the city, what sentence would you mete out to Julius and Lugs?

5. And while you've got this job of running Carabas, what is one edict you would introduce to help cats and dogs get along?

6. What do you think the rats are planning for Bast, as they whisper in Tad's ear at night?

7. The sentinels made a mess of Carabas. Should they have stayed at home?

8. Why did the sentinels bring their own food supply?

9. Should canine ambassadors like Fido Frinkel visit Bast, or should they leave the cat-centric citizens to their own devices?

10.   Julius faced many dangers to find Moira. Should she have returned home with him?

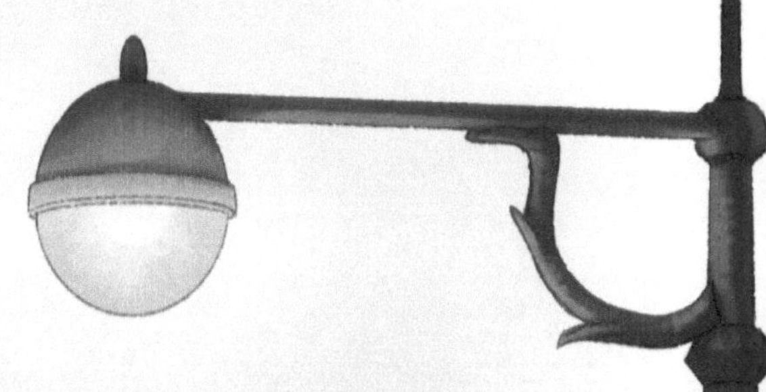

AUTHOR BIO

Nick Smith was born in Bristol, England. His books include *Eat Happy, The Secret Life of Teddy Bears, American Spirit,* and *Cloudwalking.* He is also a feature film director and producer, with 100 movies and TV credits, including the award-winning action movie *Cold Soldiers* and the supernatural adventure *Fears,* which he directed and co-wrote. He lives in New York, where he works as a film professor.

Other works by Nick Smith

Anthologies
Eat Happy
The Secret Life of Teddy Bears

Poetry
American Spirit
Cloudwalking
Songs for Persephone

Non-fiction
Fletcher Crossman: The Age of Endarkenment
Scriptwriting: The Secrets Unleashed

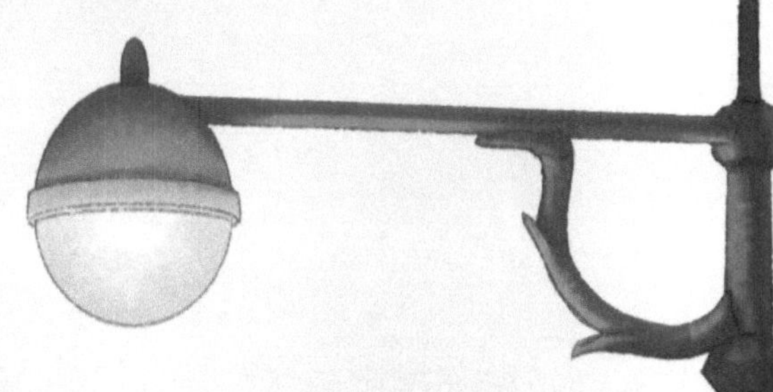

Discover more at
4HorsemenPublications.com

10% off using HORSEMEN10

www.ingramcontent.com/pod-product-compliance
Lightning Source LLC
Chambersburg PA
CBHW030135310726
48970CB00005B/1449